She hoped it was Nathan at the door

Elaine's hands shook as she tried to unfasten the chain lock. Her heart thudded painfully in her chest. *Just open the door*, she told herself as she fumbled with the lock.

She and Nathan stared at each other across the doorsill. Nathan was still wearing the same suit he'd had on the night before. He looked tense.

"I couldn't sleep," he said. "No, actually I didn't try. I just sat on the bed and thought about you. And walked the floor and thought about you. And got slightly drunk thinking about you. And drove around the block out there fifty times thinking about you."

Elaine opened her arms to him.

"I can't make any promises," he said as he engulfed her, agony in his voice.

"I know," she said as she buried her face against his neck. "I know."

ABOUT THE AUTHOR

As the daughter of an army officer, Indiana-born Anne Henry moved frequently during her childhood. Now she makes her home in Oklahoma, where she edits alumni publications at the University of Oklahoma. Anne's enthusiasm for exercise inspired her to write this book.

Books by Anne Henry

These books may be available at your local bookseller.

Don't miss any of our special offers. Write to us at the following address for information on our newest releases.

Harlequin Reader Service
P.O. Box 52040, Phoenix, AZ 85072-2040
Canadian address: P.O. Box 2800, Postal Station A,
5170 Yonge St., Willowdale, Ont. M2N 6J3

A Tough Act to Follow

ANNE HENRY

Harlequin Books

TORONTO • NEW YORK • LONDON
AMSTERDAM • PARIS • SYDNEY • HAMBURG
STOCKHOLM • ATHENS • TOKYO • MILAN

Published January 1986

First printing November 1985

ISBN 0-373-16135-2

Printed in Canada

Chapter One

Court was already in session when Elaine came racing breathlessly into the municipal building. A man dressed in a brown suit and wearing an authoritative air was leaning against the door to the courtroom.

"I'm supposed to be in there," Elaine told the man, who regarded her absently over his crossed arms.

"You on today's docket?" he asked.

"Yes," Elaine answered.

"You're late. What's your name?" he asked, picking up a clipboard from the small desk beside the door.

"Farrell. Elaine Farrell."

"Yeah. Here you are. Pretty far down on the docket. You wouldn't have been called yet. I'll let you in, but next time be on time."

"I hope there won't be a next time," Elaine said, thinking of the work she had left piled up at her office and the monumental traffic snarl she had gone through to get here. A house was being moved across the interstate, and cars were backed up for miles. When she got clear of the mess, she had driven like a bat out of hell, not knowing what happened to traffic offenders who didn't make it to their day in court. And all the time Elaine feared she would get another citation while racing to answer the court summons on her other ones. She really was going to have to start slowing down, Elaine promised herself, or at least she was going to have to space her traffic tickets better. The Heritage, Missouri, city ordinance required drivers who had three moving traffic violations within six months of each other to appear before the municipal judge. This was her second court visit in two years.

Yes, she definitely would have to slow down, Elaine thought as she stuffed her sunglasses into her purse and entered the courtroom. But there just weren't enough hours in the day to get to all the places she needed to get to and take care of all the things she needed to do to establish a new business and keep up with her family commitments. If only they would remove that fifty-five-mile-an-hour speed limit on the highways, she wouldn't have such a problem.

Elaine stared in dismay at the full courtroom. She had hoped to slip unobtrusively into a seat in the back of the room, but the only unoccupied seats were in the front row. Feeling very self-conscious, she made her way up the aisle and took a seat between an overgrown teenage boy and a dozing heavyset woman whose head lolled forward onto her ample bosom.

Elaine's movement apparently awakened the napping woman. Her head jerked up, and her arm moved erratically in Elaine's direction.

Elaine leaned to one side to avoid a flailing hand, but in doing so, managed to dump her open purse onto the floor with a resounding thump, spilling its contents onto the wooden floor—which would have been bad enough in itself.

However, the real coup de grace came when the marbles—the bag of beautiful agates Elaine had picked out for her brother—came pouring out of the small sack she had tucked in her purse. She hadn't bothered to fold over the small bag to keep its contents inside. And she hadn't bothered to fasten her purse.

Because of careless oversight, there were marbles rolling throughout the courtroom. The sound was reminiscent of grade-school days when dropped marbles rolling across the classroom floor brought a furious response from a teacher. But surely schoolteachers come to expect such occurrences. Judges in courtrooms would have no occasion to.

All other sounds ceased. No one spoke. Chairs stopped creaking. Feet stopped shuffling. Coughs became momentarily cured. There was only the noise of dozens of marbles rolling over the wooden floor. It was amazing how loud the sound was. In spite of the number of people in the room, the sound seemed to echo from the high ceiling and off the unadorned walls of the stern-looking room.

Elaine was mortified—totally. She sat immobile in the small space left over between the two oversized people on either side of her and tried to make herself as small as possible. She dared not look at the judge. Along with everyone else in the room, she sat and listened, mesmerized, until the last marble found an obstacle to arrest its progress and the room grew silent.

Still no one moved. Elaine knew some action was demanded on her part, but she wasn't quite sure what. The hulking youngster next to her was the first to move.

He dropped to his knees and began scooping the contents—including some nearby marbles—back into Elaine's large bag. With a whispered thank you, Elaine slid off her seat and joined him. Then, the contents retrieved, she crept back into her seat and bowed her head.

She took a deep breath and tried to calm herself. Talk about embarrassing!

With the excitement over, the heavy woman on Elaine's left slumped down in her seat and resumed her nap, and Elaine dared to take a look around her, still not casting her gaze in the direction of the judge, who unnecessarily cleared his throat and began to address the young woman standing before his bench. Elaine didn't want accidentally to make eye contact with the man. She could well imagine the irritation that would be apparent in a look from the judge after the way she had disrupted his courtroom.

But being in the front row, she couldn't study the other inhabitants of the courtroom without turning in her seat, and that would seem rude. She stole a glance or two at her immediate neighbors whose bulk cut off her view of other front-row occupants.

Elaine tried to content herself with watching the court recorder busily tapping away on his court recording machine and staring at the defendants who marched to the bench after the bailiff called their names. But this was not like the courtrooms she had seen on television and in the movies. There was no high drama. No attorneys. No jury. Only a roomful of accused. And she doubted if there was a hardened criminal in the bunch, although she thought she heard the judge use the word "shoplifting" in his remarks to a teenage boy with stringy blond hair. Elaine decided that most were probably here on charges like traffic violations or picking flowers in the park or whatever other lesser crimes run-of-the-mill folks like herself sometimes perpetrated. She couldn't even hear what transpired between the judge and the defendants—not at all like in the movies. Their conversations were conducted in hushed tones, and although Elaine could catch a word or phrase every now and then, she could not tell what the people who marched up to the bench were accused of or what the judge handed out as penalties.

Soon Elaine grew tired of staring at the back of the defendants and dared turn her attention to the judge himself. Somehow he did not fill her notion of what a judge should look like. His hair wasn't white but a rich chestnut brown, with what looked like a tinge of gray at his temples. His face and neck above his black robe were tanned; indeed, what she could see of him indicated a rather athletic look. The judge's loose black robe appeared to cover broad shoulders, and the hands folded in front of him were large and strong looking.

A mother with a baby balanced on her hip and a toddler in tow made her way to the front of the room in response to the bailiff's summons. Elaine wondered what the woman was accused of. Probably a traffic violation like her own. The judge didn't seem too upset with her. Elaine hoped he would adopt the same demeanor when her own turn came in front of his high bench.

Elaine decided since she was stuck here, she might as well try to get some work done. Gingerly, she reached for her purse and extracted a notebook and a date book from its voluminous insides, then carefully closed the bag and replaced it under her seat.

She looked over the date book first, checking to see what time the park-committee meeting was that night. She certainly didn't want to be late for that—not after all the work she had put in on her proposal for a fitness trail at the proposed park. Then she opened her notebook and worked on advance scheduling at the Fitness Center. The month of May was going to be a problem. One of her instructors was going on maternity leave, and Elaine had not been able to replace her.

It looked as if she'd be leading a few sessions herself, Elaine decided, although she scarcely had the time. With her television commitment and the park project plus her administrative duties at the exercise studio, she was really short on time.

Elaine always tried to lead at least one advanced class a session just to keep her own body in shape—it would hardly do for the physical-fitness expert to get flabby—but she left all the other exercise classes to her capable staff.

She absently drew squares to represent days of the week and jockeyed the names of her instructors about in the squares. Frank had college classes to work around. Sally needed to be home by the time her children got home from school. Sarah and Paul could only work evenings. Paulette and Rebecca worked weekends. Her assistant manager, Mark, wanted to take a week off.

But Elaine's mind refused to organize itself on the problem at hand. Her gaze kept wandering back to the judge. She found herself speculating about the man. How old was he? Was he married? Did he keep physically fit, or was there a "spare tire" under his black judicial robe?

After the second time of erasing Sally from the four o'clock session and taking Paul off a Saturday time slot, she gave up and openly watched the judge. He seemed so earnest as he leaned forward, talking to first one defendant, then another. There was nothing forbidding in his manner. It spoke more of concern.

Occasionally, he would even smile. Each time he did, Elaine felt her own lips curving into a smile. How foolish, she thought. He wasn't smiling at *her*; nevertheless, that expression on his face brought an involuntary matching response to her own.

She was fearful he might catch her staring at him, but the more she watched him, the more incapable she became of keeping her gaze from the man.

He was youthful but not young, Elaine decided. There were deep vertical creases defining the sides of his mouth and two smaller ones between his eyes, but his skin appeared firm and unwrinkled. She could judge better when she had her chance at the bench. He was attractive—good features, broad jaw, strong mouth, wide forehead, a nose that might be considered oversized on some faces but in keeping with the proportions of the rest of his face. She couldn't tell what color they were, but it was his eyes that most attracted her. They were expressive and perhaps kind of sad looking. Yes, sad looking and certainly sincere. Elaine judged what she called an individual's "sincerity level" by the eyes. She believed that no matter how carefully a person composed their expressions, if that expression was not a genuine one, the eyes would give it away.

The judge was genuine. The concern in his eyes was not contrived.

And that mouth! God, what a mouth. Why did she know just by looking that given the right set of emotions, this mouth could be a woman's downfall. *Her* downfall. She closed her eyes to rid herself of such unseemly thoughts. But by closing off the external world, an unbidden image propelled itself into her private internal one. His mouth again—on hers.

Elaine's hand went involuntarily to her lips, but not in time to quell the soft moan that erupted there. She felt the heavyset woman turn. Elaine knew she was being stared at.

It must be the lunch she'd skipped, Elaine decided. She was hungry, so hungry she was getting a headache—and having fantasies about a judge she had never laid eyes on before today. Just one more thing to add to her self-improvements list—eating meals regularly. After all, she certainly preached that message when instructing others about the road to physical fitness.

The courtroom thinned as one by one its occupants had their few minutes at the bench and marched from the room to pay fines or report to a court official, depending on the judge's dispensation of their case. The teenager sitting next to her was called to the bench and obviously lectured to. His time before the judge lasted longer than the other visits.

With the youngster gone, Elaine slipped into his seat to escape from the fleshy left arm of the woman sitting next to her that kept flopping across the armrest.

She realized her turn must be getting close. And she felt her body tense with expectation. Repeatedly, she wiped her damp palms on the twill fabric of her olive-drab pants.

You'd think I was waiting to see if I was going to get life or the chair, she admonished herself. *Relax.*

In spite of the anticipation, however, when her name was called, Elaine jumped. Her forgotten date book and tablet slid to the floor with a thud.

Not again, Elaine thought with chagrin as she bent over to scoop up the book and tablet. This really wasn't her day. Ordinarily she wasn't such a klutz.

She rose and made her way with as much dignity as she could muster to the bench. It was the judge's smile that undid her. This one was just for her.

His eyes were green.

"Did you find all your marbles?" he asked as he struggled to erase the smile and replace his stern judge's face. He almost succeeded, but his eyes still bore a tinge of merriment.

"Yes, sir," Elaine said, feeling a blush start at her neck and travel up her cheeks. What must he think of her? A real dingbat for sure. He'd probably give his legal colleagues a real laugh when he told them about the stupid woman who dropped a bag of marbles in his courtroom. But what did it matter what he thought of her? Just let him deliver his lecture, levy his fine and let her out of here. "I'm sorry about the marbles," she explained. "I bought them for my little brother, but I opened the sack to hold them up to the light. They look so wonderful when you— Anyway, I put the open bag of marbles in my purse, and when I dropped it, they went everyplace. But I guess you know that. I'm really sorry. I know people are not supposed to disrupt the courtroom. I know there are fines and things like that."

"Well, it's not a capital offense. And in your case, since it was accidental, I feel we can dispense with a jail sentence and even a fine."

He was making fun of her. Elaine didn't like that, but she couldn't blame him. Even if it didn't matter in the grand scheme of things what the man thought of her, she found herself wishing she could have made a different sort of impression on him. She wished she'd had time to stop in the ladies' room to smooth her hair. She wished she looked sleek and sophisticated right now instead of disheveled and embarrassed. And she wished she had been adult enough to resist opening that bag of marbles the minute she got them out of the variety store so she could hold them up to the sunlight like some whimsical child.

After examining her checkered driving record, the judge lectured her. Traffic laws were for her own protection and for the protection of others on the highway. People should allow enough time to reach their destination by driving within the prescribed speed limit. While one violation or even two might not be considered serious, she was acquiring a driving record that definitely demonstrated she was a habitual speeder.

Elaine half listened. She tried to nod at the appropriate times.

His hair was thick and wavy and healthy looking. It was indeed tinged with gray along the temples—wonderful clean hair that shone rich and brown even in the artificial light of the windowless courtroom. His brows formed an exquisite arch over those green eyes. They were a wonderful shade of green, leaning more toward a dark, brooding green flecked with brown rather than the bluish green of Elaine's own eyes.

I wonder what color eyes our children would have, Elaine found herself wondering as he patiently suggested that she try to allow herself more time to reach her destinations and therefore reduce her need to drive too fast. But what an absolutely stupid thought! Children. Even hypothetical ones. She didn't even know the man's name.

She tried to concentrate on his lecture. She really did drive too fast. She should be taking heed of what he was saying.

But even as he spoke, an image flashed across Elaine's mind, one of being in a car with him—a convertible with the top down, with her at the wheel, her hair whipping about her face as she raced with him down an open road. Faster and faster she wanted to drive with him until they were almost flying. The telephone poles and trees would pass by in a blur until at last they disappeared altogether as poles and trees and civilization were left far behind.

Would she have to call him judge when they made love, or would she know his name by then? She wished she could see the part of him hidden by the high bench so that she could better imagine how they would fit together.

What crazy, ridiculous thoughts! And totally inappropriate, Elaine fully realized. But yes, she'd like to take him places in her car and fit together when they stopped. A stranger. A beautiful stranger with the mouth she'd been wanting to kiss her for a hundred years.

Elaine drew in her breath, trying to relieve the constriction she was feeling in her chest. His brows knit together in concern.

"Are you all right?" he asked, leaning forward, his words sounding worried and private. She was mesmerized by the movement of his mouth. "I know this is upsetting for you."

His deep, sympathetic voice wrapped itself around her. Elaine felt caressed. *God, I'm going crazy,* Elaine thought. *What in the world is going on with me? You'd think I'd been raised by a race of women and was just seeing a man for the first time.*

But somehow that was the way she felt. She was smitten. She, of the superficial, "keep-it-light" philosophy in relationships, was under some sort of spell. She should be frightened. Elaine felt as if she should turn and run for her life. But all she could do was stand there and hyperventilate. She was going to die right in front of him. Her lungs had lost the ability to get oxygen from the air, and she was going to die of this man. On the death certificate they would have to write, "Cause of death: the brooding green eyes, the sensual mouth and the wonderfully caring voice of a municipal judge."

"Ms Farrell, do you need to sit down?" the voice asked.

"No," she lied, her voice a mere gasp. "Allergies. I've got allergies. Must be something in the air. It'll pass."

She knew he was going to dismiss her now. Frantically, Elaine looked at him once again, wanting to memorize the look of him, the feel of being in his presence, the greenness of his eyes, the delightful lines of his face. And his hands—she had been so busy with his mouth and eyes and hair that she had completely forgotten his hands. Hands were very important.

They were folded in front of him. There was a ring on the third finger of his left hand—a gold band.

No!

Elaine's mind cried out with the injustice of it. *No, please, no.* Maybe he just wears a wedding band to keep women away. She'd heard about men who did that. He just can't be married. The strong taste of disappointment rose in her throat. Married. Life's little joke.

It didn't matter, Elaine told herself. Even if the judge had been single, what difference would it make? The chances of her being able to maneuver an introduction were slim, and he might not even like her. She might not like him. It was just some weird combination of factors that brought on this wave of desire. Her hunger. Nervousness. The barometric pressure. Maybe she really was allergic to something. Regardless, Elaine realized he had better hurry up and finish with her, for she was overcome with an urge to sit down on the floor and weep.

Three months, Elaine heard him say. She was to come back in three months. If she had any other violations in that time period, he would take her license away from her.

She would get to come back was all Elaine could think. She would stand in front of him once more and be enveloped by his aura as he leaned close to judge her.

She got herself out of the courtroom without her knees giving way, without stumbling and without dropping her purse.

WHAT A STRANGE YOUNG WOMAN, Nathan thought as he watched her depart down the aisle of his courtroom. Even her manner of dress seemed somewhat bizarre to him. Nathan was used to beautiful women wearing fashionable *women's* clothing. Ms Farrell had been wearing a man's sport coat, collar turned up, sleeves pushed up, the waist belted snugly with a bright turquoise scarf. She incongruously wore the coat over what looked like a delicate lace camisole left over from the 1890s and a pair of what he could have sworn were military fatigue pants. High-heeled red pumps and hoop earrings completed her ensemble. Nathan had never seen an outfit quite like it, and he couldn't for the life of him figure out why such a getup struck him as absolutely charming. Perhaps it was because Ms Farrell was so lovely that her attire, no matter how dreadful, could not detract from her inherent good looks.

But then there was the matter of her peculiar behavior. For a moment Nathan had wondered if she was on drugs. It was not unusual for defendants to appear at his bench spaced out, and she had seemed disoriented at one point. However, he decided that her problem was of a different nature. Courtrooms and judges intimidated some people more than others. And that business of dropping marbles all over the floor. Was that ever one for the books! He'd seen heart attacks, concealed weapons, hysteria, screaming babies, passing out, throwing up and even an earthquake while presiding over a courtroom, but he'd never been invaded by rolling marbles. That really woke everybody up. What a bunch of startled expressions took over their bored faces—before the dead silence. He'd never seen anyone look so embarrassed as Ms Farrell had at that moment. Poor kid. And maybe she wasn't well. She'd mentioned a problem with allergies, although she certainly seemed healthy enough. Marvelously so. She fairly glowed with vitality and good health. Her body was slim and firm; her skin, smooth and glowing. Her mane of brunette hair was lustrous and thick— it fairly exploded around her incredible face.

Yes, she had definitely been upset about something. Nathan found himself wishing he could do more than speak comforting words. He had almost forgotten himself and reached out to touch her at one point, to offer a reassuring pat to her shoulder—or maybe a soft touch on her cheek. When he realized what he had almost done, he folded his hands firmly in front of him to ward off future urges. Judges didn't touch defendants. That was so basic, it didn't even have to be written down. But for an instant he had wanted to make contact with that smooth honey-colored skin. Even now as he thought about it, the tips of his fingers tingled with sensation as though infused with a memory of what might have been. Strange thoughts for him. He hadn't cared much about touching women for a long time—not since Marilyn had died. And even when he did think about such things, he'd never once had a desire to touch a woman in fatigue pants!

Marilyn would never have worn an outfit like that. Ever. And his daughter Rebecca wore only impeccably tailored clothing, as did all the women he associated with either socially or professionally.

But then, since he wasn't going to associate with that strange young woman, it hardly mattered what she wore.

He should have suspended her license. He would have been justified. But somehow he hadn't had the heart.

Instead, he gave her the longer version of his lecture and ordered her to return with an unblemished record in three months. He rather liked the idea of seeing her again. Why hadn't he said two months, Nathan mused as he looked down at the folder in front of him to check her first name. Elaine. Elaine Farrell. For some reason that name had a familiar ring to it. But he was sure he had never met her before. He would have remembered.

Reluctantly, he pushed the Elaine Farrell folder aside and turned his attention to the next case—something to do with a panty raid out at the college. Now that ought to be interesting! One certainly did get to see a different variety of law here in the courtroom than in the prestigious law firm of Atterbury, Berger and Stewart. Nathan's practice over the years had shifted more and more to tax work. His clients were primarily wealthy individuals in search of tax deductions.

In the year and a half Nathan had spent as a municipal judge, he had seen more segments of society than he'd ever dreamed existed. He had discovered he didn't particularly like sitting in judgment, but he had to admit that during his "politically expedient" term of looking at the world from the other side of the bench, he had learned a lot about how the rest of the world lived. His own world now seemed almost boring at times.

After all, one certainly didn't meet the likes of Elaine Farrell behind the hallowed doors of Atterbury, Berger and Stewart.

ELAINE SAT in the old station wagon for a time with her hands firmly on the steering wheel, somehow deriving strength from the feel of something solid. Geez, what happened to her in there? Never had she been so affected at first sight by another human being! She had

once shaken hands with the president of the United States
and another time had gotten Paul McCartney's auto-
graph. Those experiences had left her excited and
pleased, but she hadn't felt as if she were going to pass
out.

The judge had been very nice looking, but then, so
were lots of other men. For some reason, however, she
had been inordinately attracted to the man.

Elaine had long acknowledged her lengthy list of
character flaws, but she had always prided herself on
being in charge of her own emotions. Not that she wasn't
caring and affectionate, but she had learned a long time
ago always to keep a part of herself inviolate. It was safer
to only care so much, then draw a line. That way, no
matter what happened, a part of her was unscathed.

But she had wandered out on thin ice back in that
courtroom. One minute she was her same old self; the
next minute she was falling into a bottomless hole, and
all over some man she had never seen before, didn't know
anything about—and was *married*!

Married men were poison as far as Elaine was concerned. She fully planned to put this particular one from
her mind.

Chapter Two

Elaine signed her payroll checks and stacked her bills into two groups—those to be paid immediately and those that could wait. She looked up from the discouraging chore when Mark, her assistant manager, tapped at the open door.

"You better get changed," he warned. "Sarah hasn't shown, and it's only twenty minutes until time for Women's Aerobics II. And no, I can't take it. I'm not only booked, but the last time I led that class, two women complained about having a male instructor. Said it embarrassed them."

The diminutive man chuckled. "They needn't have worried. As I remember, the complainers were a pair of thunder thighs if ever I saw them. My attention was completely diverted by the little redhead in the second row. Not only was she beautiful, but she wasn't taller than me."

"You're making me jealous," Elaine teased.

"Look, boss lady, you know I would have taken up with you years ago if I wouldn't have had to spend the rest of my life staring at your neck. Lovely as yours is, I'm just not that into necks. But when a guy is only five feet four, there is a smaller pool of damsels to choose from. The five twos and under are the only ones who can wear any kind of heel on their shoes and still not tower over me."

"I keep telling you that you place far too much importance on height," Elaine said. "It doesn't really matter that much. You're a kind, considerate person and a great looking guy, with absolutely the most well-conditioned male body in the city of Heritage. And if I *was* five two instead of five seven, you still wouldn't ask me out. It'd be like taking out your sister, and you know it. Besides, why would I want to ruin a beautiful friendship and business association by going with you."

Mark glanced at his watch. "Enough talk, woman. Get your body into some tights and go lead that class of Thighs Anonymous."

"Oh, Mark, the park committee meets tonight, and I need to go over my presentation. You know how much I'd like to have my plan for a fitness trail accepted. You're just going to have to go in there and charm the ladies into submission. If Richard Simmons can do it, I'm sure you can, too."

"I would, Elaine, really, but remember this is the night I'm supposed to give a gymnastics demonstration at the grade-school PTA meeting. That's why I'm in my dress warm-ups," he said with a pivot to show off his smooth-fitting red-and-white exercise suit. "If we could get a gymnastics program going—"

Elaine waved him away. "Say no more. I'll manage somehow."

Mark was a former collegiate gymnastics champion. That was one of the reasons, along with his responsible nature and easygoing personality, Elaine had enticed her old high-school friend from his job with an athletic-wear manufacturer to come and work for her—in hopes of getting a gymnastic program started. Such a program would bring in more patrons and more much-needed revenue.

Mark had been a godsend. He was dependable and loyal, which was more than she could say for some of the part-time people she had hired. She was discovering that tardy instructors were one of the many problems she faced in operating the Fitness Center.

Elaine had not intended to teach any classes when she returned to the Fitness Center after her court appearance. She wanted to get home in time to look over her notes and plans one more time before the meeting tonight with the park committee. But that was not to be. It looked as though she'd be instructing her third class of the day. With a sigh, she rose and returned the checkbook to the safe, then started on her way to the locker rooms.

The Fitness Center had been in this location for six months, but she still had not gotten over its newness. Her own building—designed by her, owned by her, operated by her. It was a dream come true after years of operating her business out of a succession of rented buildings, starting with a refurbished garage seven years ago in Little Rock. Two years ago, when she had decided to move to Heritage, Missouri, to be near her parents and younger brother, Elaine felt that the time was right to move on to bigger things. She took the plunge, mortgaged her future to the limit and built a first-class establishment that incorporated the innovations she had longed for in her other locations.

And the Fitness Center was definitely "bigger things." This state-of-the-art physical-fitness establishment was a tremendous gamble, Elaine realized. And the verdict was far from in as to whether she would be able to make enough money to keep her business afloat. Sometimes she wondered if she should have stuck to remodeled garages. At least with those facilities there was not the stress of making huge bank payments each month and juggling the schedules of a large staff.

But as she walked through *her* building, she could not help but be proud of what she saw there. People of all ages and in various states of physical conditioning worked at the correct pace in a wide variety of activities. In a small studio there was an exercise class going on that was especially designed for individuals confined to wheelchairs. The newest addition to the center's program—a seniors' program for first-time exercisers—was going on in the larger studio. Elaine watched for a few minutes as two instructors worked with elderly individuals to tailor an exercise program that would bring them greater vitality and freedom of movement even at their stage in life.

It was free time in the weight room, and individuals who had already been checked out on the weight equipment were working out. Most of the racket-ball courts were in use, and at least a dozen people were jogging around the one-eighth-mile indoor track that circled the second-floor perimeter of the large building.

A support group of overweight individuals was gathered in the meeting room and was watching a slide show Elaine had devised to show them appropriate menu selections and portion sizes. What Elaine saw pleased her, but she had even more dreams for the future. She wanted to add a pool and a gymnasium for basketball and volleyball. She wanted to have more meeting rooms that could be used not only for the center's activities but for various self-help support organizations such as Alcoholics Anonymous and cancer-recovery groups. More than anything, Elaine hoped the Fitness Center could be a positive force in people's lives.

But then, Elaine thought with a sigh, as she stared at a stack of unpaid bills, it was time to forget about dreams and concentrate on keeping the reality afloat.

And that meant patrons. Lots of patrons. The Fitness Center needed more sessions, more people willing to pay to use her facility. The television program had helped. Three times a week, Elaine donned her leotards and worked out in front of the cameras of a local television station while she chatted with viewers about health concerns such as exercise, diet and a positive outlook. Her salary for doing the show was small, but already it was reaping rewards in the form of new patrons who were attracted to her program because of seeing her on television.

But she wasn't close to breaking even financially. And six months into her operation, she had expected to show a profit. Everything had cost more than she thought it would, and there had been problems—a lawsuit with the contractor over plumbing problems and a leaky roof, utility bills higher than had been projected and too many half-filled exercise sessions.

But even half-filled sessions had to have instructors, Elaine reminded herself as she quickly thrust her body into a red exercise suit.

The class was open to women of all ages physically fit enough to keep up with the establishment's Aerobics II classification. Elaine put them through fifteen minutes of stretching and warm-up exercises, then began the aerobics portion of the session. They did six routines of increasing intensity, then tapered off with a less strenuous routine, followed by a much slower cool-down number. At the end of the hour session, Elaine ducked out the door before she could be called on to answer questions or give individualized instructions about some of the routines. She hated to shortchange her customers, but she was going to have to shower in record time and get out of there if she was going to have any chance of making that park meeting on time.

She raced home to her apartment, needing to change into an outfit she hoped was more in keeping with the formality of the meeting than what she had been wearing earlier. She realized a tailored business suit probably would be an appropriate choice, but she ordinarily had no use for more sedate clothing and didn't own a suit.

She grabbed a narrow black skirt from its hanger and teamed it with a black sweater and broad-shouldered red jacket she'd found at a vintage clothing store. The jacket looked like something one of the Andrew Sisters might have worn in an old World War II movie. Elaine loved the way it emphasized the slim lines of her skirt. She belted the jacket with a wide purple belt and slipped her red heels back on, added some large gold disk earrings, grabbed her plans and raced out the door. She applied her makeup at stop signs. She brushed her hair as she hurried across the library parking lot.

And in spite of all her rushing, she was late. *Damn.* Late again after promising herself only this afternoon she was going to do better in that department. Her stomach was in turmoil as she rushed down the long corridor toward the meeting room. Such an important meeting and she was going to be late! That certainly wouldn't make a very positive impression on the committee.

Elaine very much wanted the committee entrusted with the Marilyn Miles Stewart Memorial Park project to be impressed with her and her plans for a fitness trail for the nearly completed park, but she realized she was competing with landscape architects and recognized physical-fitness experts. Her plan could very well be rejected in favor of one created by someone with academic degrees and a list of publications to his or her credit.

Elaine had no degrees. She had taken some college work as a special student in order to learn more about her chosen field. But she had never had the time or money actually to earn a degree with all the necessary hours and required courses. The only courses she had taken had been ones that taught her what she needed to know to direct physical-fitness programs, such as anatomy, physiology and the theory of exercise and recreation. But she hadn't had time for the liberal arts classes she would need to earn a degree. She regretted that and felt very one-dimensional. She knew a lot about one field and precious little about almost everything else, but that was the best she could do.

Elaine had given up on being well educated, but she was determined to be as knowledgeable about physical fitness as possible. She read avidly in the field and attended clinics and workshops. She felt she had achieved the status of self-made expert. Now she wanted others to recognize that knowledge. She wanted her design to be the one selected by the park committee. It would bring her and her business excellent free publicity. It would help establish her as an authority in her field. But most of all, it would bring $2,500, which was being offered for the winning design, into her empty coffers. And it might even provide the opportunity for her to do similiar work for other communities. A supplementary source of income would be a godsend right now. Oh, would it ever!

She paused in front of the double doors to the public meeting room, took a deep breath and pushed them open.

And there he was, sitting at the long table in front of the room. No black robes this time, but it was he nevertheless. The judge.

For an instant Elaine felt disoriented. Was she at the wrong place? Why was a municipal judge here? How could it be that she was to face that unsettling man twice in one day? What a weird coincidence—one her nerves certainly could have done without.

She realized she was being addressed by the man sitting next to the judge.

"May I help you, miss?" the heavyset man was saying.

"Yes. Is this the planning committee for the Marilyn Miles Stewart Memorial Park project?" she asked.

"You're at the right place," he announced. "You must be Elaine Farrell. I'm Jonathan Miles, project chairman. We've visited several times on the phone. Our meeting is already under way, so I won't take time at this point to introduce you to our members. If you'll just have a seat, we'll get to the presentations shortly."

Leaning her portfolio up against a chair, Elaine took her seat among a dozen or so other people sitting in chairs facing the committee members. She fervently wished someone else would come through the double doors so that she would not have the dubious distinction of being the last to arrive. She avoided looking at the judge and concentrated on calming herself. She guessed that judges engaged in civic-duty activities when they weren't officiating in a courtroom and conducting private law practices. But what rotten luck for him to be doing so on this particular project. She had already made a fool of herself in front of the man once today; now she seemed to be well on her way to an encore.

Elaine realized she was the only woman in the room. Four—no, five—others had large portfolios similar to hers propped beside their chairs. A bored-looking young man, rather informally dressed, was obviously a reporter and occasionally took notes on a narrow tablet.

A detailed report on the landscaping was now being read to the committee by a man who was apparently from the city park department. Elaine tuned it out and tried to concentrate on her upcoming presentation. But she knew the judge was looking at her. She could actually feel his gaze, and it was most disconcerting. Did he recognize her as the marble-dropping idiot who appeared before his bench today? Elaine had the uncomfortable feeling she was one of the day's more unforgettable defendants.

But she had to put thoughts of him and his damned green eyes aside. He had a strange effect on her this afternoon, but she had cured it with a Mars bar. Hunger. And nervousness. That's all it was. And if there was perhaps a bit of physical attraction thrown in, then the gold band on his finger took care of that. No more married men for her, Elaine said to herself, recalling the abrupt and painful ending to her last relationship. Of course, she hadn't known Eduardo was married. But somehow, as she looked back, she felt she should have guessed. His evasiveness, his unwillingness to commit to future plans, should have told her something. But she chose to believe what she wanted to believe.

The whole affair with the handsome Latin architect who designed her building had left her feeling angry and foolish and used and vowing never again to go out with a married man.

Elaine had found out quite by accident that he had a wife and three children in Mexico City.

Thoughts of Eduardo helped Elaine steel her heart against the disarming man whose gaze now sought hers. She avoided eye contact and concentrated on trying to decide whether to state her overall concept at the beginning of her presentation—before showing her drawings—or show the drawings as she went along.

She was pleased with the drawings. It had been very difficult to convey her ideas to the graphic artist she had hired, but after several false starts, they finally began to communicate. The drawings beautifully represented her ideas for the jogging and physical-fitness trail that was to wind its way around the perimeter of the new park. She even had a sketch that showed the overall plan of the park with the path incorporated into it.

The drawings had cost Elaine dearly; she had used money she could ill afford to lose if her gamble did not pay off. But as fine as the drawings were, she also wanted the committee to give its full attention to her overall philosophy for the trail.

She did not completely make up her mind how she would begin her presentation until the two landscape architects and a physical-fitness expert from the local college concluded theirs.

"Gentlemen," she began after taking her place behind a podium that faced the eight men, "never before in the history of our country have people cared so much about physical fitness. And as a result, the citizens of this nation are living longer, more healthy, more enjoyable lives. I commend the committee for the Marilyn Miles Stewart Memorial Park and our city park department for wanting more than natural beauty and playground facilities to serve the park."

Elaine moved to one side of the podium, not wanting anything between her and her audience. She took a step toward them, never breaking eye contact, and continued.

"And I'm sure you gentlemen would like a fitness trail in the park that would serve the largest number of people. You have proposed a one-and-one-half-mile trail. But do you realize that the majority of the people in this community could not run one and one-half miles, much less stop at all the proposed stations to do the prescribed exercises?

"Of course one could just not run the whole track and only stop at a couple of stations," Elaine said, trying to look at each committee member in turn. "That is defeating to beginning exercisers and does not offer them a comprehensive workout."

Elaine carefully explained that what she proposed was really three trails in one, with progressively strenuous stations. Each segment would offer a full range of exercise options and be complete unto itself. A participant could execute one, two or all three of the segments, depending on his or her fitness level. Even those less physically fit could have the satisfaction of completing a full segment.

The men seemed attentive enough but with guarded expressions. Elaine could not tell how her ideas were being received. And the judge seemed the most guarded of all. She took a deep breath and went on.

Finally, following her statement, Elaine showed her drawings, explaining the design of some of the stations and its assigned function as she did so. One station had steps to be climbed and descended a prescribed number of times. Another offered a rope ladder. There was a chinning bar and a parallel ladder to be "walked" hand over hand. She continued to glance from time to time at the faces of the men who had the power to accept or reject her plan, which represented such long hours of research and creative thinking on her part.

But their faces revealed nothing. They showed no more or no less interest in her presentation than they had in the others.

When she was finished, Elaine turned her precious portfolio over to the committee chairman and took her seat.

After the other three presentations had been made, the portly chairman cleared his throat.

"The committee will try to arrive at a decision during the next few weeks, and if our choice is agreeable with Judge Stewart here," he said, indicating the man to his right, "then we will notify you of the winning plan as soon as possible. Again, our thanks for your interest in our project."

Did he say Judge *Stewart*, Elaine asked herself. Stewart? The park was being built in honor of Marilyn Miles *Stewart*. Could the judge be related? Maybe she was his daughter? Or his mother? Or could Marilyn Stewart have been his wife? Of course Stewart was a common name. It could just be a coincidence. The judge's wife was probably at home waiting for him right now.

Elaine wracked her brain trying to remember what she knew of the woman whose memory was being honored with the park. As Elaine recalled, the city recognized the woman for her years of dedication to civic affairs, most especially her efforts to get a new civic-center auditorium funded and built. After the name had been decided the Stewart family elected to donate to the project. Their money was being used to add the physical-fitness trail to the original concept of the park. But what about the woman herself? Had she been related to the man at the front table?

Then Elaine had her answer. The chairman was bringing the meeting to a close, but he was interrupted by one of the other committee members.

"We appreciate your coming, judge," the man said. "I just want to say that this community owes a great deal to your wife. She had been trying to get a park built on the east side of town for years. We're real proud to be carrying out her wishes."

His wife! Poor man, he was a widower. But Elaine didn't really feel sad. In fact, she didn't feel sad at all.

Geez, what kind of a person am I, gloating over the fact that a man's wife is dead, she thought with a start. *My goodness, she must have been a wonderful woman if the city wants to name a park for her. That's really something! She must have been a very special lady. It's too bad someone like that is dead. Really too bad.*

Elaine knew at that moment, however, that she coveted Marilyn Stewart's husband. She not only wanted to win the contract for the fitness trail in the woman's memorial park; she wanted to win her husband.

I'm sorry, Marilyn, she thought. *I'm sorry you're dead. Honest. But since you are, you really don't need a husband anymore. If I don't get him, someone else will. And I promise to take very good care of him.*

Elaine waited until the last of the men in the room had finished going up to shake the judge's hand and exchange pleasantries before she took her turn.

She offered her hand. He took it. The sheer delight of touching him brought a sigh of pleasure to her lips. So that's how it felt, she thought, realizing how much she had been wanting some part of her body to touch some part of his. How could a handshake in a public place be so intimate, so personal? How could it be the most sen-

sual thing that had ever happened to her in her entire life?
But it was. She was *connected* to him.

This time she did not try to escape from his gaze. She
met it with her own.

Elaine was vaguely aware that they were blocking the
path of two men trying to navigate the narrow aisle between the rows of chairs. In unison, as though by prior
plan, she and the judge moved aside without disrupting
his firm hold on her hand.

"I left my marbles at home," she said.

"I noticed. And your fatigues."

"Yes. And you don't have your black robe. You look
nice. More human. More like someone who might ask to
buy me a drink. I'm sorry your wife is dead. Really, truly
I am. But since she is, I'd accept your offer if you made
it."

His mouth—that incredible, wonderful mouth—slowly
turned up at the corners in a grin, then parted in a smile.
Then he threw his head back and laughed out loud.

"And if I were to make this offer you're prepared to
accept," he said when he got his laughter under control
with an over-the-shoulder glance to judge how others in
the room had reacted to his jovial outburst, "where
would you suggest we go? I'm not up on the proper place
to take young ladies for a drink."

"Well, if you did, Play It Again Sam is a good place
and close by. The music's not too loud, and it isn't just
college kids. But I wouldn't want you to ask me if it
would make you uncomfortable. I'd certainly understand. Perhaps in three months, when I have to come
back to court and show you my clean driving record, we
could talk about it again."

"Since it would be very unethical for a judge to discuss a date with a defendant during court proceedings,"

he said, putting on an imitation of a stern judge's face, "I'd better ask you right now."

"And you wouldn't think I was too forward to suggest such a thing?"

"Well, what if I did think you were forward?" he asked, cocking his head to one side. "Would that bother you?"

"Yes, I think so," Elaine said hesitantly, wondering what in the world he must be thinking of her. "But how could you not think I wasn't being that way when I was."

"What do you say we continue this conversation at Play it Again Sam," he suggested, his eyes brimming with merriment. "Or else they're going to close up the library around us. And maybe you're not forward enough to want to be locked up in a library all night long with a stranger."

Elaine could feel her pulse race at the thought.

"Shall we go?" Judge Stewart said. Instead of relinquishing her hand, he tucked it over his arm, and they exited from the empty building.

He didn't know where the bar was, so it was agreed he would follow Elaine in his car. She was terribly conscientious about her driving, taking great care not to speed and to come to a complete stop at stop signs. She didn't even go through traffic lights on yellow.

"I'm really not a wanton hussy," she said as she slid into a booth and he took a seat opposite her. "I like to think I'm a reasonably nice person."

"And reasonably nice people don't suggest dates to someone they just met?" he asked in a teasing tone.

"Something like that."

"Well, please be assured that meeting you has been the most delightful experience I've had in some time. And your wanting me to ask you out is the most flattering. I

promise I will not regard you a wanton hussy or anything but a reasonably nice person. Now, that said, how
about a drink?''

Elaine was in love with his voice.

"One more thing," Elaine said.

"Yes?"

"I think I'd be very uncomfortable talking about your
wife right away, so can we put that off until another
time—provided we both are interested in another drink
on another occasion?''

"If you wish. But why does the subject of my wife
make you so uncomfortable?''

"Because when I first figured out you were a widower
and that ring on your finger served a memory and not a
living woman, I was glad. I'm feeling terribly guilty about
that—being glad. But I'm not glad she'd dead, just glad
you're not married. Does that make sense? I'd rather you
be divorced from her or never have married her in the
first place, and I'm not making any sense at all.''

"Yes, you are. I find that a very honest thing for you
to say. Now I'll share a bit of honesty about you. I really
didn't want to go to that meeting tonight. In fact, I had
already called to say I couldn't make it. But when I read
the agenda, I noticed a familiar name. Six people were
making presentations for the fitness trail. The other
names went right by me. But Elaine Farrell. Well, she
made quite an impression on me today in court. I absolutely couldn't resist taking a second look at that interesting young woman with the incredible clothing and
questionable driving record. So I gave up my nice relaxing evening and came to the meeting. And for a while
there I thought I'd wasted my night for nothing. Tell me,
Elaine Farrell, are you always late?''

"Practically, but I'm working on it, along with driving more slowly. Now, I'm ready for that margarita—as soon as you tell me if you have a first name other than judge."

His name was Nathan. *What a wonderful name,* Elaine thought. She wanted to say it out loud to feel it on her lips. She wanted to say it after he kissed her, after he made love to her.

Would they make love?

Elaine realized she wanted that. She wanted very much to make love with Nathan Stewart.

Chapter Three

The piano player pounded out forties tunes, including the one that inspired the club's name. The music provided a wonderful backdrop to their conversation, which seemed incredibly intimate to Elaine even though they were only discussing the park project or favorite movies or struggles of the American farmers to maintain family-owned farms. Like Elaine, Nathan seemed willing to avoid personal topics. They steered toward safe subjects. But something very personal was involved in the currents that passed between them.

Elaine found Nathan quite wonderful—intelligent, beautiful, in control. She loved the way the corners of his eyes crinkled when he talked. She adored the way he looked at her sideways and grinned when she said something funny. She admired his courtly manners and the way he took charge when the waiter came to their table.

Elaine felt both a participant and an observer in their conversation. She was enjoying their lively banter, but she almost felt that she was a third party at the table, watching them as a couple—speculating about the handsome fortyish man with the graying hair and green eyes and his younger lady friend with her brightly colored clothes and thick brown hair. The two certainly were enjoying each other. His eyes sparkled when he regarded her. She fairly burst with the excitement of pleasing him. They did not touch but kept leaning toward each other as though pulled inward by a magnetic field. Elaine could tell the two were terribly attracted to each other. She wondered if and when they would make love. Would they be as turned on to each other in bed as they were sitting at this tiny table in this dimly lighted room? Would they admire each other's bodies? Would they find boundless delight in sharing those bodies?

Elaine wondered about Nathan's body. Did he have hair on his chest, on his legs? Would it be tinged with gray like the hair on his head? Were his legs as muscular as his shoulders and upper arms? Was his stomach really as flat as it appeared in his clothes? And she wondered about his lovemaking. Would he be innovative in bed? Intense? Aggressive?

Elaine wanted to know. Somehow, at this moment, it seemed as though her whole mission in life was to discover the secrets of Nathan Stewart. She ached with wanting it.

In one of her mind's compartments, Elaine wondered if she had gone crazy. How could she be thinking such thoughts about a man she barely knew? It didn't make any sense at all. She just wasn't supposed to feel this way about someone she laid eyes on for the first time only hours ago. She didn't believe in love at first sight. Or at second or even tenth sight. Love was something that had to grow and be nurtured. It came when one got to know someone very well and found out what was lovable about that person. Maybe she was just in the throes of desire. Maybe it would pass.

But whatever *it* was, Elaine knew she was a goner. Her reluctance toward romantic entanglements seemed to have dissolved like salt in water. Caution seemed to have thrown itself to the winds. Maybe she should be concerned, but she didn't have time to worry about that now. She was too busy watching Nathan's lips form words, staring at his right hand picking up his Scotch and water, longing to unbutton his shirt and touch his chest, wondering about what he was thinking.

When Elaine could no longer stand the lack of physical contact with him, she asked him to dance. She felt his arms go around her to the mellow strains of "Stardust."

In her high heels, she was nearly the same height as he. Elaine liked that. It made their bodies fit together just right. She had known they would be a good fit. In fact, there was the most incredible rightness about the way their bodies molded against each other. It left Elaine in awe, filled with delight and excitement and anticipation. How dull her life had been until today. She had just been born. She was now alive. Ravishingly alive. It was very important that she relish each sensation and carefully concentrate on each move of Nathan's hard body, each soft breath on her neck, the aroma of his skin and the exquisite erotic feel of his hand at the small of her back.

Elaine was being transported—and taking him with her. She could sense his arousal. *Oh, how lovely,* she thought. *How very, very lovely.*

One song blended into another as their bodies continued to blend in perfect rhythm to each other. Elaine wasn't sure if they were the only people dancing; she couldn't open her eyes to look. But it felt as if they were alone.

When the music stopped, she could have gone on dancing. The melody in her head would have sufficed.

"What now?" Elaine asked in a small voice. "I have the feeling a heavenly chorus is waiting to perform."

"What do you want to happen now?" he asked, trailing a fingertip down her cheek to her mouth with a gesture that was almost reverent, as though he were touching something of great value.

Elaine waited to speak, needing first to concentrate on the exquisite sensation of his finger tracing the outline of her lower lip. She wanted him—truly wanted him. She was dizzy with wanting. Yet...

"I'm not sure," she answered, "or should I say there's a vast gulf between what I want to do now and what I think I should do."

"Which do you want to explain first?" he asked. His fingers were on her neck now, softly stroking.

Elaine leaned into his touch. "I *want* you to come home with me. But I'm worried about how I would feel after I got you there."

"What worries you?"

Now her shoulder was being caressed. Did he have any idea what he was doing to her?

"I would worry that we were going too fast," Elaine admitted, her eyes still closed, "that I had rushed you into something that might be wonderful tonight but hard to live with in the cold light of day, that you would think me brash, that you were still in mourning for your wife—whom we didn't talk about but probably should have—that maybe we should date a bit before we fell into bed with each other."

"And does my going to your apartment mean falling into bed?" Nathan asked. Now he was stroking her upper arm. Even there his touch was erotic.

"Wouldn't it?" she asked. Her eyes were open now. She was looking directly into those smoky green eyes.

He nodded. "Yes, I guess it would."

"And you're quite vulnerable right now, aren't you?" Elaine asked. "The pain is still very much with you. It showed in your eyes today in that courtroom. I knew you were sad."

And as she said it, the pain returned to Nathan's face. Such a subtle thing. It involved just the slightest readjusting in the tautness of the muscles around the eyes and mouth, but it was plain to see. For a while that look had lifted from his face, but her words had reminded him.

"I haven't been sad tonight," he said simply.

"I'm so glad," Elaine said, daring to touch his cheek with one tentative fingertip. "That pleases me more than you'll ever know."

He helped her into her coat, and they walked arm in arm across the parking lot. Elaine shivered in the cool night air. And there, beside her car, he kissed her. It was a kiss unlike any other. Her desire had been neutralized by the knowledge that their evening together was over, but his kiss pierced her with an overwhelming, painful poignancy. She knew if this man did not enter her life, it would cause an enduring emptiness.

She clung to him for a time, wishing his body could open up and absorb her so she would never have to be apart from him.

"I feel as though I should say something," he said hesitantly as he opened the car door for her. "But you're right. Things are happening awfully fast. So all I'll say is I'll call you tomorrow."

"Promise?" Elaine said.

"It's the most solemn promise I've ever made."

SHE DIDN'T GO HOME. Instead, Elaine headed for the Fitness Center, turned off the burglar alarm and let herself into the deserted building. Ordinarily, she would have found the empty building with its echoing hallways and deep shadows a little frightening. But she couldn't be bothered with fear tonight.

Going to her locker, she put on a pair of shorts and some jogging shoes. She pulled a sweatband over her thick hair. And she ran. Again and again she ran around the circular track. She ran because he promised to call her tomorrow. *Solemnly* promised! She ran because his eyes were the gray-green color of tree moss and his dark hair beautifully tinged with gray. She ran because the feel of his fingers against her skin ignited her. She ran because he kissed her and touched her soul. She ran because she didn't know what else to do about the emotion that welled up inside of her.

That such a man inhabited the same planet with her! In the same town. What if he had been born two hundred years ago? What if he were living in a monastery in Tibet instead of Heritage, Missouri? As she ran, she thanked whatever forces had arranged to put them in the same geographic location at the same point in time. If those forces had not, her life would have been over before it began.

For her life up to now had been but a preparation for this day, for meeting *him*. Nathan Stewart. His name had such a new sound to her. It did not yet match the man. In her mind, he was yet nameless—as an earthquake or cyclone was nameless but nevertheless an awesome force to be dealt with.

Elaine said his name out loud to get used to it. Then again.

The solid sound of her shoes hitting the rubberized track surface picked up the rhythm of his name and beat it out as she ran. Na-than Stew-art. Na-than Stew-art. Over and over. Her breathing became more and more labored, its rasping sound in perfect cadence with her shoes.

She didn't count laps. She didn't watch the large clock on the east wall. What did it matter? She ran until she quite literally dropped in a gasping heap on the track floor. Her lungs felt as though they were bursting. Her legs were so shaky they threatened to collapse under her as she used a side railing to pull herself to her feet. But it was the love that hurt. Elaine ached from the inside out with the raw, painful new love she felt for a man she had just met this day.

She shivered as her sweat-soaked body began to chill. Slowly, she got to her feet and headed for the locker room, her footsteps echoing in the empty building.

Elaine showered quickly, suddenly apprehensive about being in the deserted building alone in the middle of the night. She threw on a warm-up suit and hastily hung her clothes on a hanger, then hurried down the main hallway. Before she turned out the lights, she ducked into her office and checked the telephone directory for his address. She needed to know where Nathan lived, to have some notion of where he was at this moment.

She recognized the street name. Weatherford Drive. It was in *the* part of town.

Elaine hadn't realized she was going to drive by his house until she exited from the parking lot and turned left instead of right. But it wasn't far—only a mile or so out of the way. Then she could see the house where he was sleeping. That would help her longing.

High on a bluff overlooking the river, the neighborhood spoke of old money. New money lived elsewhere, in a neighborhood of more recently erected edifices with skylights and architectural innovation. But on Weatherford Drive, the mansions sat more solidly on their grounds, shaded by mammoth trees grown tall and sedate.

Nathan's Mercedes was alone in the circular driveway. The large Tudor-style house was dark except for a yard light that cast long shadows across the sloping yard and a glimmer coming from an upstairs window. Was he in that room, still awake? And thinking of her? What *did* he think of her? Maybe he thought she was the kind of woman who made a practice of throwing herself at men. Maybe, with hindsight, he was relieved he hadn't ended up in bed with her.

Elaine drove around the block, then parked for a time across the street, trying to feel the presence of the man inside. She concentrated on the glimmering light from the upstairs window. She realized what she was seeing was flickering reflections on the ceiling from a fireplace. A fireplace in his bedroom—how incredibly luxurious that seemed to her. She never had lived in a house that had a fireplace anywhere, much less in a bedroom.

But what was really significant was that the fireplace was lit. It was two-thirty in the morning, yet he was sitting there in the semidarkness, watching the dancing flames and— Elaine caught her breath. Could he be sitting up there thinking about her? Maybe their evening together had left him as confused and agitated as it had left her. There was another possibility, however. Elaine realized he might also be thinking about Marilyn. Maybe he was feeling guilty. But Elaine didn't want to consider that.

Instead, she tried to imagine what such a house would look like inside, but the images she drew on came secondhand from movies and magazine pictures. For she had never set foot in any place quite so grand. The house intimidated her.

Such a large house for one man. But then he hadn't always lived alone. Marilyn Miles Stewart had lived there with him. The bedroom Nathan was now sitting in, watching his flickering fire, probably had been their bedroom. Marilyn Stewart had been an outstanding woman. She raised money for a civic-center auditorium. She pursued a variety of philanthropic causes. She belonged to the class of women who did such things, and apparently she did it better than most. Her memory was much revered in this community, and this house had been her home. This neighborhood was populated by her kind of people. And her widowed husband was one of those people.

Elaine slowly pulled away from the curb, sorry she had come. Marilyn Miles Stewart would be a tough act to follow. Elaine feared she lacked the credentials.

AFTER THE THIRD TRIP down to the bar in his den to refill his glass, Nathan carried the whiskey bottle upstairs with him. He had long since shed his suit and coat and necktie. He supposed he should get undressed, but instead he rolled up his shirt-sleeves and poured another drink.

He couldn't stop thinking about her. He even found himself thinking about what it would be like if Elaine were here in this bedroom—first on the love seat in front of the fireplace, then on the king-sized bed. He became so caught up in his fantasy, he found himself building a fire. He hesitated, then struck a match and lit the kindling. Why not? He wasn't going to get any sleep, anyway. He might as well have a fire to keep him company.

He sat on the corner of his bed, his elbows on his knees, his hands dangling the half-empty glass between his legs. He felt as if he had been run over by a freight train.

He had never met anyone like Elaine Farrell. Never. She was the most disarmingly frank woman he had ever known. No games. No coyness. Just up front and honest.

And she was beautiful in such a totally unconventional way. Her unruly hair should have looked like a disaster area, but it didn't. Her mouth was unconventionally full but so appealing. And the way her lower lip curled out over her chin... Nathan took a deep swallow of his drink.

And then there were her clothes—her bizarre clothes, but charmingly so. He'd wondered what it would be like to remove her off-the-wall attire. Somehow he sensed that it would be a glorious experience. Was the skin on her body as smooth as that on her cheeks? He rubbed his forefinger with his thumb, remembering how it felt to touch her cheek. How would this firelight look reflecting off her pale flesh?

Nathan groaned. The sound startled him.

He was too old for raging hormones, Nathan tried to tell himself. But right now he felt like an infatuated adolescent.

It was as though she'd bewitched him.

Nathan instinctively looked over at Marilyn's picture, trying to restore his sanity. Marilyn. Cool, immaculate, elegant Marilyn. He'd missed her a great deal this past year. Their house, his life, were so empty without her presence, her constant flurry of activities. They had a good life together. Productive, orderly, calm. She had been a perfect wife for him.

But tonight, while he was with Elaine, Nathan had not thought about Marilyn. He had been totally captivated by a woman who was his dead wife's complete opposite. There was nothing orderly or calm about Elaine Farrell. She dropped things, she looked like a wind-blown gypsy with those bright wild clothes and her mane of hair, and she was so intense. When she looked at him with those totally honest, clear blue-green eyes, he could feel that intensity.

He had wanted to go home with her, but the gentleman in him said not to push. If he had insisted, would he be with her right now? Would he have his hands buried in that mass of hair while he possessed that wonderful pouting mouth? Would she be naked and moaning while he touched every inch of her with his hands, his lips?

Nathan's mind filled with images—passionate, erotic images. He shocked himself. Why in his forty-fifth year was uncontrollable passion threatening to enter his life? Sex had always been important to him, but it was usually kept in its place and not something he lost sleep over. Sex was neatly taken care of in his and Marilyn's life just like everything else.

Nathan drained his glass and got up for a refill. Then he paced back and forth in front of the fireplace, stopping occasionally to look at himself in the beveled mirror that hung over the mantel as though to make sure he was still the same man. He felt so different. He was agitated and frustrated and out of control—not at all like himself.

What in the hell was he going to do until morning? Television, maybe. He turned on the set and switched stations, settling on an all-night news station. A set of quints had been born in Shreveport. The secretary of defense made a strong statement about the fighting in the Middle East. An out-of-work plumber won a million-dollar lottery in New Jersey. A fifteen-year-old girl wonder was taking the tennis world by storm. But Nathan couldn't get interested in any of the news stories. That was all happening in another world. The only newsworthy person in his world was Elaine Farrell.

But Elaine was all wrong for him, Nathan told himself. He started making a mental list of all the reasons why he should not get involved with her.

First of all, she was too young for him. Elaine was probably still in her twenties. He had two children not much younger than she was. In fact, Elaine seemed more like a woman his son Robert would date.

And Nathan realized a woman like Elaine certainly wouldn't fit into his world. How could he escort a woman around who wore fatigue pants and conducted exercise classes?

But what a snob that made him sound like, Nathan thought with a start. Did he really care what Heritage's socially prominent citizens cared about his companions? While Marilyn was alive, appearances did get first priority, but that was something he did out of defence to her and her sensibilities.

So on to the next reason. Rebecca.

Nathan knew his daughter would never approve of Elaine. Robert might be accepting, but Rebecca was her mother all over again, and then some.

And there was this house. Such a responsibility. Marilyn had put so much of herself into this beautiful old home. How difficult it would be for another woman to live here.

Live here? *My, aren't we getting ahead of ourselves,* Nathan thought sarcastically. *Let's just say this house would be a difficult place for any female friend of mine to feel comfortable in.*

But most of all, there was the upcoming political campaign. So many people were counting on him to enter the race. Nathan was worldly-wise enough to realize Elaine Farrell would detract from his political image. He'd be okay as the widower of Marilyn Miles Stewart, whose father had served in Congress from this district. But just let him get involved with a foxy-looking young miss like Elaine and tongues would wag—unless he got her to tone down a bit. Or they could have a clandestine affair. But no. He couldn't even ask such a thing of her. Never.

Somehow, however, his list of reasons why he should not get involved with Elaine had no relevance to how he was feeling this moment. Nathan supposed it was a case of his heart ruling his head. Or a case of middle-age crazies. Or a delayed reaction to Marilyn's death. Or *something* that would eventually go away and leave him alone. Elaine Farrell was too wonderful a young woman for him to use. He'd just have to wait things out.

But what in the hell was he supposed to do in the meantime?

WHEN SHE LET HERSELF into her apartment, Elaine decided it was probably a good thing Nathan hadn't come home with her. First of all, her parrot—disturbed from his slumber—shrieked out his usual "What the hell?" the minute she turned on the light. The apartment had its customary clutter scattered about. And even when everything was in apple-pie order, it was really a very ordinary dwelling.

Funny how she looked at it through different eyes after her drive through "the better part of town." A year ago, when she had moved in here, the apartment had delighted her. One of four units carved from an older home, it had the charm of wooden floors and fluted moldings and casement windows. Elaine had combed thrift shops, garage sales and secondhand stores to come up with an eclectic array of furnishings, including a somewhat threadbare Oriental rug. Now the whole apartment looked a little threadbare to her.

"Shut up, Clyde," Elaine said absently as the parrot gave forth with the second of his two-part repertoire.

"Damn it! Damn it! Damn it!" Clyde shrieked.

Elaine dumped a little bird seed into the container on the side of the bird cage. Clyde cocked his head to one side, eyeing the seed suspiciously. "What the hell?" he said crossly as he hopped down to a lower perch. But the seeds were apparently deemed satisfactory, and soon the colorful bird was busily crunching away.

"Foul-mouthed old bird," Elaine muttered affectionately as she turned out the lights and headed for her bedroom.

She had already started to run a bath when she remembered she had just taken a shower at the Fitness Center. Sheepishly, she let the water out of the tub. "Not thinking too straight, are you, old girl," she said to her reflection in the mirror. "My, my, we haven't been this distracted for a long, long time. Must be some kind of man, this Nathan fellow."

Elaine nodded at the reflection. "Yes, some kind of man."

She changed into a nightgown and began to pace the floor. It was almost three o'clock in the morning. She should go to bed and get some sleep. There was her television show to tape at ten o'clock tomorrow morning, and she'd look like a wretch if she didn't get some sleep. But she doubted if she could sleep. She was afraid the instant her eyes closed a fantasy would come unbidden to her mind and insist on playing itself out. And while she was curious to see what her mind would do with its new fantasy hero, she was also frightened by the intensity of her reaction to this man. While she had avoided any romantic entanglements since Eduardo, she had her crushes and infatuations before. And she had even considered herself to be in love on occasion. All that, however, seemed like kid stuff now that she'd met Nathan Stewart. What she was feeling now was heavy-duty. Incredibly heavy-duty.

But it all seemed so impractical. What if she was wasting all this emotion on a relationship that was doomed before it began? She was no Marilyn Miles Stewart. That was for sure. She couldn't for the life of her see where she would fit into Nathan Stewart's life—or he into hers.

As Elaine feared, sleep refused to come. She counted sheep, mentally went over the muscle structure of the human leg and foot, pretended she was on a boat and imagined the rocking motion of the waves.

But her thoughts kept wandering back to Nathan. Her mind insisted on speculating about the touch of his fingers on her bare skin instead of stupid sheep jumping over their imaginary fence. Elaine curled her knees tightly against her body and clutched her pillow to her breasts in a futile attempt to ease the disquieting need that resided there like a set of congested lungs.

When the clock said four, she got up and poured herself a stiff shot of straight bourbon and downed it in three gulps. It hit her empty stomach like a brick. "Oh, geez," she said to her inquisitive parrot, "this is absolutely ridiculous."

"Damn, damn, damn!" Clyde offered in a medium-loud shriek.

"My sentiments exactly," Elaine said as she staggered back to bed.

This time, as she clutched her pillow to her stomach, she thought that at least the bourbon had given her something else to think about besides whether or not to attempt a seduction of Judge Nathan Stewart. After several more waves of nausea passed, Elaine could feel her body finally begin to relax. Maybe the booze would do the trick, after all, she dared hope.

She wasn't aware of falling asleep, but she realized she had finally done just that when she struggled to wakefulness. Not that she wanted to give up on her hard-fought battle for some sleep, but something was waking her up. A noise.

Knocking. Was that someone knocking on her door? Why knocking? Couldn't they use the doorbell?

But then Elaine remembered that the doorbell was broken. In fact, it hadn't worked for almost a month, and she hadn't gotten around to having it fixed.

Elaine looked at her clock. Six-fifteen. Now awake and somewhat alarmed, she struggled out of bed and into her terry-cloth robe. Who was it? What if something was wrong? What if something had happened to her parents? Or her brother? There was no good reason she could come up with as to why someone was knocking on her door this early in the morning.

Absently running her fingers through sleep-mussed hair, Elaine padded across her living room. Cautiously, she turned the dead bolt and with the chain lock still in place opened the door just a crack.

It was Nathan.

Her hands shook as she tried to unfasten the chain lock. Her heart thudded painfully in her chest. She dared not think why he had come. *Just open the door,* she told herself as she fumbled with the lock.

Elaine swung the door open so hard it flew out of her hand and slammed against the wall. "What the hell!" Clyde screeched from his corner. "What the hell! What the hell!"

They stood staring at each other across the doorsill. Nathan was still wearing the same suit he had on last night. The tie was missing, and the shirt was open at the neck and mussed. He looked tense.

"I couldn't sleep," he said. "No, actually I didn't try. I just sat on the edge of the bed and thought about you. And walked the floor and thought about you. And got slightly drunk thinking about you. And drove around the block out there fifty times thinking about you."

She opened her arms to him.

"I can't make any promises," he said as he engulfed her. There was such agony in his voice.

"I know," Elaine said as she buried her face against his neck. "I know."

Chapter Four

They embraced for a long time. Elaine drank in the feel of him, the aroma of him. She grew heady as the balance of her senses became upset with so much stimuli—and with the knowledge of what was to come. They had crested the top of a lofty mountain and were standing perched at the peak, about to plummet headlong into the shadows of the far side.

Elaine was experiencing so many emotions all at once—apprehension because she was entering a new relationship that promised to be more intense than anything she had ever felt before, gratitude that Nathan seemed to want her as much as she wanted him, and, she realized, relief to be getting the agony of waiting over with. For in the past twelve hours she had done a lifetime of waiting and wanting and not knowing what, if anything, was going to happen between them. No matter what awaited her in Nathan's arms, one way or the other, at least it would be over and she would know—know if she should somehow calm herself and get on with her life or if she was to be allowed to enter fully into a relationship with this man with whom she seemed to have fallen so hopelessly in love.

Elaine pulled away from the embrace first and took his face between her hands. "Whatever happens is all right," she told him.

"But I may be using you," Nathan whispered as though there were others with them in the small apartment.

"And I may be using you," Elaine told him in all seriousness. "Maybe it's all some sort of illusion or temporary insanity. But whatever it is, I'm ready to get off the carnival ride and find out if what I'm feeling is just an acute case of vertigo or something else altogether."

Then he kissed her. And in that kiss both conveyed their complete surrender to the forces that had brought them together. His kiss reached deep inside her and touched her soul.

Elaine knew she would not come away from Nathan unscathed. But even if she were to be granted foresight and realize that making love to him would bring disaster to her life, she probably would have been powerless to hold back from the intensity of their mutual passion.

For Elaine understood that Nathan was as out of control as she was. He had spent the night locked in a struggle with himself. His loyalty and love for his dead wife, his background, his family, his commitment to a life that had little to do with a woman who exercised on television and got speeding tickets—all that, and probably much more that Elaine did not know about, must have pulled at him dreadfully. She realized that his wondering if their lovemaking would be nothing more than a meaningless encounter caused him problems. He feared it would not be right to come to her, and he had tried not to. Elaine knew he had fought against his desire and lost.

Instinctively, even as she allowed him to slip her gown from her shoulders and gaze upon her naked body in the morning's half-light, Elaine realized that the reasons for Nathan's struggle would still exist after they made love. She knew that making love with him this morning might be the only chance in her entire lifetime that she could experience this man who had so awakened her emotions. But Elaine was wise enough not to tamper with the purity of the moment. She did not ask for promises that might be regretted later. She did not examine motives or ponder what the future might hold. She simply allowed her identity to fall away with her clothes and to become woman to this man.

Taking Nathan's hand, she led him to her bedroom. She was amazed that her hands did not shake as she unbuckled his belt and helped him slip his shirt from his body. But the time for nervousness was over. Her time with him could now be dedicated solely to wonder.

She watched as he sat on the edge of her bed to remove his shoes and socks, then stood to slip his slacks and underwear from his body. His chest and flat stomach were hairy, flecked with more gray than the hair on his head. He had a band of white flesh where bathing trunks had rested, but the rest of him was tanned. His thighs were muscular and strong.

He wanted her, his desire evident now, and Elaine stepped easily into his arms.

It was all so beautiful, like a ballet whose choreographer had understood the subtle importance of each movement. Elaine's neck arched backward, swanlike, exposing her throat to Nathan's kisses. Her arms rose slowly like a dancer's to entwine themselves around his neck. Elaine could close her eyes and see how they looked. They were a man and woman moving to the music of love and desire.

Elaine could not believe the absolute sweetness of Nathan's flesh against hers, the feeling was so erotic. It astounded her that one man's flesh could affect her so differently from another man's. But the feel of her bare skin against Nathan's was beyond belief. Intoxicating. Rapturous. She wanted to touch all of him. Slowly, to the cadence of their internal symphony, she rubbed her palms up and down his back, relishing the feel of his firm, bare flesh. The swell of his buttocks was as solid and unyielding as a wooden statue's, but Nathan was real, and he was making love to her, using his wonderful body to form a sexual union with hers. Elaine could not believe this was happening to her or understand why. But she certainly planned to hold nothing back from him. Nothing.

With a groan, Nathan swept her off her feet and placed her on the bed. He took a few seconds to stare down at her open and waiting body before lowering himself on top of her.

Elaine wanted him more than she had ever wanted anyone in her life, but far beyond that need was her desire to be whom Nathan wanted and needed. More than any physical craving was her wish to share herself with him.

"I haven't been with a woman in a long time," he gasped between their wild, breathless kisses.

"I know. I understand. It doesn't matter."

And it didn't matter. Elaine wanted too much to feel everything all at once—his lips, his tongue, his hands, *him*. But most of all, she wanted to bring him that gift first. She wanted to be totally aware of what was happening to him.

He came almost at once, burying his face in her hair and groaning as though a part of him had died—or been reborn.

Elaine cradled him in her arms, loving him completely. And when he tried to apologize for being so quick, she hushed him. And she silently offered a prayer of sorts—a thanks for being the first woman in a long time.

At first, Elaine thought he had dozed off, his body was so still. With great care, she lifted his head from her shoulder to her breasts, using their softness to better pillow his head. They lay like that, quiet, content. Elaine drew her contentment from him, willing her own desire into acquiescence for the time being.

But soon she sensed he was not sleeping. There was a tautness under her fingertips where they touched his back. Elaine didn't move, but she knew that Nathan's passion was returning and that this time her ardor would reach a climax. She knew that as surely as she knew her name, and her heart quickened at the thought.

Elaine knew that Nathan sensed the change in her, that he surely heard her racing heartbeat. He rubbed his cheek against her breasts, then pulled away to take a desire-swollen nipple into his mouth.

She could feel him growing hard against her leg and realized she was smiling. It was all she could do to keep from laughing out loud from the absolute joy.

This time Nathan was in charge. He took all the time in the world. It seemed he had decided to pleasure her as much as he possibly could. He ministered to her willing body until at last she could stand it no longer and begged him to enter her again.

It was she who came at once this time. And then again. And again. Elaine had not known she was capable of so much. She wondered, when it was over, if any other lover had ever taken a woman so far. She felt as though she had just experienced a miracle, and slowly, an overwhelming sense of gratitude filled her that she had been born just so she could experience this wonder, this man.

"Tears?" he said at last, touching her wet cheek. "Why tears?"

"Because you did that for me, and you're so beautiful."

NATHAN ALLOWED HIMSELF the luxury of lying in the bed and watching Elaine dress. She was self-conscious and kept looking at him with a shy little smile that made his heart turn over. Already an accusing voice deep within him warned that he could hurt this woman deeply, that he should get the hell out of this place and leave her alone before he did her permanent harm.

But her ivory body was so beautiful, and he felt young again. Young and lusty—almost as though he were in love.

Could he do that—fall in love with Elaine? Should he? But Nathan didn't want to sort out feelings now. He just wanted to enjoy this woman as much as she would allow.

He realized Elaine was concerned he might think her promiscuous, accustomed to inviting men to her apartment all the time. He didn't, but it wouldn't have made that much difference if she was. For Nathan knew that whatever had gone on in her life before, their coming together had been special to Elaine, just as it had been special to him. They had tapped some heretofore untouched reservoir in each other's sexuality. They had filled each other with wonder. He felt privileged to be here in her bed, privileged to have made love with her—even if he never saw her again. She had touched him deeply.

So what now, old man, Nathan asked himself. *Do you get up, pull on your pants and walk out of her life? Or do you really screw things up and get tangled up with her?*

Should he ask her out to dinner? Should he invite her to his daughter's engagement party or to the Carmichael's party Saturday night? Should he ask if he could come back here tonight? The thoughts warred as Elaine reentered the bedroom.

Her hair was washed and shining after her shower. It burst forth under the purple sweatband that circled her head. She pulled hot pink leotards on over a pair of purple tights. She was dressed for her television program, she explained—a physical-fitness show on one of the local stations. That meant anyone—any man—could tune in and see her moving her body around in that skintight garb. Nathan wasn't sure if he liked that idea.

She came and sat on the edge of the bed. "I have to go," she said. "Just make yourself at home. There's coffee in the pot, cereal in the cabinet, eggs in the refrigerator."

Nathan struggled to a sitting position. "When will I see you again?"

Elaine kissed his forehead lightly. "Look, Mister Judge Stewart of Weatherford Drive, I know your decision to come here this morning was a difficult one for you. I think you'd better do a little thinking about who you are and who I am before you proceed any further with things."

Nathan started to speak, but Elaine hushed him with a finger planted firmly over his lips. "What happened between us was so wonderful, I won't even try to explain it, but I'm grateful. It was the most beautiful gift I've ever had. It was a gift on my part, too—freely given with no strings attached. If we see each other again, it will never be quite that simple again. I just want you to think about things for a while. Okay?''

She didn't wait for his answer. With another kiss on his forehead, Elaine was gone.

Nathan closed his eyes to keep the image of her with him a while longer. He felt as if she had taken a part of him with her.

He could have dozed. It would have been easy to curl his body around the pillow that had held her head and drift away from wakefulness.

But the clock on the bedside table reminded him of responsiblity. He reached for the telephone and called his office to make sure he wasn't missing an important appointment. Nathan could tell that his secretary was puzzled when he offered no explanation for his tardiness and was probably thinking how very out of character such behavior was for the usually responsible law partner.

''You're booked pretty solid this afternoon, and you're scheduled to preside in court at three-thirty, but there's nothing I can't get you out of this morning,'' Mrs. Hopkins offered in her efficient-secretary voice. ''Don't forget your dinner engagement with the state committeeman and assorted potential political backers tonight. It's at the country club.''

''Right. Anything else?'' Nathan said, staring at a pair of red high-heeled shoes that resided in the middle of the bedroom floor where their former wearer had stepped out of them the night before. The red jacket Elaine had been wearing was hung over the back of a ladder-back chair in the corner. Her hoop earrings were on the bedside table.

''Your daughter called,'' Mrs. Hopkins informed him. ''She wanted to find out how the park-committee meeting went. She wants you to call her.''

"If she calls back, tell her I'll track her down later in the day."

Nathan hung up the phone and sank back on the pillow. He just wasn't in a mood to deal with Rebecca this morning. Or anyone else for that matter. He first had to get his fragile emotions in hand. How could he get up and go to the office as if nothing had happened when something quite remarkable had? Of course, Elaine had managed to go about her business. The events of the morning had not kept her from her appointment at the television studio. He wondered about that. Why couldn't she have stayed with him? He didn't want to have breakfast alone. He wanted to share the meal with her across the table from him. My, how perfectly marvelous that sounded— breakfast with Elaine! But then, she seemed to have felt a need to get out of his way. She didn't want him to say something that he might regret later, when the afterglow faded. What a remarkable woman she was! Truly remarkable.

He found himself surveying her bedroom as though to find some clue to her wonderfulness in the comfortable clutter surrounding him. Her headboard appeared to be the back of a park bench sanded smooth and stained in rich dark brown. Across the room was an old-fashioned vanity with a large round mirror attached. It reminded Nathan of a vanity his grandmother once had in her bedroom. On the other wall was a large old trunk that had been covered in a paisley-print fabric.

The vanity reflected a large, somewhat abstract print that hung above the park-bench headboard. Nathan studied the reflection for a time and decided it was suggestive of an assemblage of swans gathered at the water's edge. To the left of the bed, over the trunk, hung a framed print Nathan recognized as Degas's *Dancing*

Class, whose delicate line and subtle pastel coloring formed an odd contrast with the more contemporary bird picture. Yet as Nathan compared the reflected picture and the one hanging beside the bed, he realized they actually related rather well to each other. The composition of the two pictures was similar, with the graceful swan shapes grouped much like the dancers' semicircle in their dance studio. Very interesting, Nathan thought, realizing the two seemingly unrelated pictures had been deliberately brought together.

Intrigued, Nathan got up to discover what other surprises there were in Elaine's apartment.

As soon as he opened the bedroom door, he was greeted by an ear-piercing "What the hell?"

"Is that the only thing you know how to say?" Nathan inquired of the bird.

The parrot stood on one leg, cocked his head to the side and carefully eyed the stranger at his cage with inquisitive eyes of a vivid chartreuse. As though to answer Nathan's question, he jumped to another perch and offered a series of emphatic "damns."

For the next few minutes, Nathan examined Elaine's apartment. The high-ceilinged living room was spacious and appointed in an assortment of furnishings and accessories that seemed to have nothing to do with each other but somehow formed a charming whole. A 1940-vintage console radio sat beside an overstuffed armchair and matching ottoman the likes of which Nathan had not seen in years. A camelback sofa had been reupholstered in a green-and-cream stripe. Several old-fashioned wicker fern stands supported healthy looking greenery. But among all these relics were a futuristic chrome lamp that arched over the sofa, a coffee table formed by a thick slab of glass over a bright yellow plastic cube and walls decorated with several unusual abstract prints of an American Indian flavor. On the floor was an elderly Persian rug, its colors and pattern muted but still rich, placed alongside a Navaho rug whose geometric designs blended surprisingly well.

The small dining alcove that housed the parrot was furnished with a tiny white wicker table and chairs. The large window in the room was surrounded by a profusion of ferns hanging from wall brackets.

And there was clutter. Some was planned, like the basket of magazines, the collection of tiny ceramic parrots on the narrow chrome-and-glass étagère, the afghan tossed over the back of the sofa and the stack of floor cushions scattered about the coffee table. And some was unplanned, like the bottle of nail polish on the coffee table, the open newspaper lying across the ottoman, the open book—an Agatha Christie mystery—on the end table, bird seed scattered under the parrot's cage and a pair of decidedly scuffed loafers under a chair in the dining alcove.

The total effect was somewhat art deco and certainly original but most of all comfortable. Nathan realized that most of Elaine's furnishings were secondhand and that she probably had painted, refinished and recovered not just to save money but to express her special life-style and her own unique tastes.

The kitchen was tiny but bright, with checkered curtains, more ferns and a goldfish bowl on top of the small refrigerator. Nathan poured himself a cup of coffee and returned to the living room. He gathered up the newspaper and lowered himself onto the wonderfully large 1940ish armchair that had been reupholstered in a frieze covering in keeping with its era. All it needed was lace doilies over the back and arms to make it look totally authentic.

Oh my, Nathan thought as he sank into the large chair, propped his feet on the ottoman and leaned his head against the comfortably high back. They just didn't make chairs as they used to, or if they did, there certainly weren't any populating his house. He allowed his body a minute or two to settle in; then, out of habit, he started to scan the newspaper. The paper seemed vaguely familiar, but he held it in front of his face for some time, before he realized that it was yesterday's edition and that nothing he was reading had registered. His powers of concentration had escaped him. He was too aware of his surroundings and of the woman who lived there. Nathan folded the paper and put it on the coffee table, then simply sipped his coffee and contemplated Elaine Farrell.

His thoughts were a jumble. Nathan wondered when he could next make love to her. He wished he knew her favorite flower. He tried to decide how old she was. Did she always read mysteries? Had she grown up in Heritage? Where had she gone to college? He tried to decide whether he would rather go with her to Europe or the Orient if he ever had the opportunity to take her on a trip. And more immediately, where should he take her out to dinner tonight?

Elaine had said she wanted him to allow himself plenty of time to think things over before seeing her again. Nathan appreciated her intent but knew he could no more stay away from her now than he could give up eating. He was filled with her. He wondered if his mind would ever think about anything else. How could he make it think about anything so mundane as law or politics when it could recall the texture of her skin, the feel of his face buried in that incredible hair, the abandonment with which she made love? What had happened to him this morning was like something out of a book. Nathan didn't know a real flesh-and-blood woman could be that way. It overwhelmed him.

Not that he had planned to be celibate the rest of his life—nothing like that. He had grieved sincerely for Marilyn. He had loved and respected his wife very much. But she had been dead for over a year, and he was ready to get on with his life. Nathan assumed he would have relationships with other women, and he supposed he would marry again one of these days. In fact, he had just in the past month taken out two different women. They were lovely women, either one of whom could have slipped right into his life with scarcely a ripple—the type of woman everyone would expect his second wife to be. Yes, people would expect his second wife to be a duplicate of Marilyn in many ways. Until yesterday, Nathan realized he had assumed that was what would happen to him. If not one of those two women, then someone else. He was lonesome. His life-style and profession would be enhanced by a wife—a certain kind of wife.

Even Rebecca would have to approve of such a marriage, although Nathan knew that the notion of another woman in her mother's house was upsetting to his daughter. But Rebecca was a product of her mother's upbringing. Rebecca understood why her father, especially if he entered the upcoming political race, would need an appropriate consort at his side. And Rebecca definitely wanted her father to pursue a political career.

Now, however, Nathan wasn't sure if he wanted such a predictable future. Maybe he didn't want to slip into a relationship with an appropriate woman.

Suddenly *inappropriate* seemed quite exciting.

A watercolor of three perky daisies hung in the dining alcove. Nathan picked up the phone and ordered three dozen daisies to be sent to Ms Elaine Farrell at the Fitness Center. "And take her a dozen roses, too," he said. "I want the card with the daisies to say, 'I thought about it for a while, as you instructed. How about dinner tonight?' And put 'To a long and beautiful friendship' on the card with the roses."

After he hung up, Nathan remembered the dinner meeting with his political cronies tonight. Six of his congressional district's most influential men were gathering to discuss his political future. Damn! He'd have to take Elaine to dinner tomorrow night. But no, his children were arriving home from college for spring break tomorrow, and he was taking his daughter, his son and his soon-to-be son-in-law to dinner. The night after that was the Carmichaels' party. Maybe he should invite Elaine to accompany him to the party. Or should he? Perhaps he'd better get to know her better himself before he started expecting his friends to accept her.

Nathan wondered if he could just come back here after his dinner meeting and spend the night with her. But somehow it seemed insulting to ask that of her. Elaine deserved to be courted—to be wined and dined and treated well. He didn't want her to think all he wanted of her was time in her bed.

He called the florist back. "Change the card with the daisies," Nathan instructed the man. "Instead of dinner tonight, make it read lunch tomorrow."

Then he wandered out into Elaine's sunny little kitchen to see if he still remembered how to cook eggs. The parrot cursed loudly as Nathan passed his cage.

"Aren't you sweet?" Nathan said sarcastically, but inwardly he was thoroughly enjoying the crazy bird and his owner's offbeat apartment. In fact, he was having a marvelous time, he decided as he opened the refrigerator door. And was he even hungry! He honestly wondered if he had ever been so hungry in his life.

ELAINE HAD her regular Thursday-night dinner at her parents' modest house. Only three place settings at the table, she noticed as she came in the back door.

"Hi, Mom," she said, planting a kiss on Martha Farrell's thin cheek. "Dad's not going to be here?" she asked, knowing the answer already.

"He's been gone since day before yesterday," Martha said, her voice flat with resignation. "I called County Hospital, and they haven't admitted him."

How many years had it been, Elaine wondered. Since she was a child, it had been this way, but she never got over the pain of having an alcoholic father. At least she could remember him when he still held down a job and had dignity. She could remember when he taught her to ride a bike and helped her plant a garden. She could remember when he came to her softball games and took her for a hamburger afterward. Her brother, Tim, had only known his father as a tired alcoholic who would disappear for days on end and come home dirty and ill and asking for forgiveness. That made Elaine very sad indeed, because Vince Farrell used to be quite wonderful, and she knew that when he wasn't in an alcoholic fog, he loved his family very much.

"Where's Tim? I brought him a sack of marbles—very special marbles," Elaine said as she placed the depleted sack by Tim's milk glass.

"He's still at baseball practice. Should be here anytime," Martha said as she pushed a head of lettuce and a salad bowl toward her daughter. "And what's so special about the marbles?"

As she made a salad and helped finish preparing dinner, Elaine told her mother about the incident in Judge Stewart's courtroom, about the park-committee meeting, about the drink with Nathan afterward and about the boxes of flowers that arrived at her office that afternoon. Elaine didn't tell her mother just how far the relationship had already progressed, but from the way her mother kept looking at her, Elaine wondered just what she was giving away.

"He's a wonderful man, Mother. I can hardly wait for you to meet him."

"Are you going to bring him here?" Martha asked, indicating her immaculate but shabby kitchen and the equally shabby house beyond.

"Well, no, not right away," Elaine admitted. "I thought we could all go out to dinner someplace."

"To a restaurant? Honey, I don't think that would be a good idea, your father being the way he is."

"Well, maybe everyone can just come to my apartment," Elaine said. "I'll cook. I think you'll like Nathan, Mom. He's a fine man."

"I'm sure he is, honey," Martha said with a sigh. "And goodness knows, I'm ready for you to get married. I've rocked those sweet babies at the day-care center for two years now. I'd love to rock my own grandchild for a change. But isn't this judge a little old and a little grand for you? And what about his dead wife? Sounds like she must have been some fine woman, having a park named for her and all. Just remember, Elaine, it would be very difficult to follow in the footsteps of a saint. Don't set yourself up to get hurt, you hear?"

"Sure, Mom," Elaine said, wishing that her mother wasn't so pessimistic. She had looked forward all day to telling her mother about Nathan, but now she wished she had never brought it up. Her mother had managed in a very few words to verbalize many of the nagging doubts Elaine had refused to deal with after the flowers arrived. How her heart had gladdened at the sight of them and at their accompanying messages. Nathan wanted to see her again! He was wonderful. Life was wonderful. She could breathe again. She felt like running or dancing or singing—anything to accommodate the surge of energy that had burst through her.

But this evening, as Elaine turned her energy to mashing potatoes, she could feel her mood taking another swing. Although Nathan's age didn't worry her, her mother was right in other ways. He *was* rather grand. And sainthood would indeed be a tough act to follow. How strange that she had worked so hard to design a fitness trail for a park that memorialized a woman who had become, in a sense, her competition. Well, not competition exactly. After all, the woman was dead. But Elaine feared that if she did establish a relationship with Nathan, she would forever be compared with Marilyn Miles Stewart. His children, his colleagues, his friends, the man himself, would always be comparing her to the woman who came before her.

"I didn't mean to put such a damper on your good spirits," Martha told her daughter with a hug as the two women stood surveying the table and waiting for Tim's arrival.

Elaine returned her embrace. "Oh, Mother, I know you're just looking out for me—like always. I'll try to hang on to the good sense I acquired at my mother's knee, okay?"

"Timmy's coming," Martha said, cocking her head to one side.

"How can you tell?" Elaine asked.

"By the sound of his bike tires on the gravel."

Seconds later, Tim came bursting into the room. "Hi, Mom. Hi, Laine. What's for dinner? I got two hits in practice and caught two fly balls. Coach says I'll get to play a lot. You coming to my games, Laine?"

"Wouldn't miss them for the world," Elaine said, mussing his hair and thinking how much more cheerful this shabby room seemed with the sparkling presence of her eight-year-old brother.

Then she watched his face as Tim took in the table set for three. He looked over at her and shrugged. "He's been gone for a couple of days. Hope he's okay."

"I'm sure he is," Elaine said, her heart aching for the boy. Such a good kid, he was. He deserved another kind of father. "There's a package for you," she said, pointing to his place.

His smile revealed two missing teeth. "Hey, neat marbles," Tim said exuberantly as he opened the small sack. "Thanks."

"Well, just keep them in your pocket," Elaine suggested. "I'm sure your teacher wouldn't appreciate them rolling all over the schoolroom floor."

The meal was nice—nothing fancy but good food well prepared. The aroma of spices and warm bread filled the air. The kitchen—like the rest of the house—was old and run-down but clean and homey. Elaine felt comfortable here.

She wondered if Judge Nathan Stewart ever ate in the kitchen of that house over on Weatherford Drive. Somehow it didn't seem likely.

Chapter Five

Nathan arrived at the restaurant a few minutes early. The hostess seated him by the large stone fireplace. Nathan appreciated its brightly burning fire and the coziness it lent to the Old English decor of the restaurant. It was unseasonably cold outside, and the wind blowing across the river was raw. April was half over, but winter wasn't ready to give up yet. In fact, Nathan had noticed some blowing snow as he drove over from his office.

He sipped on a cup of coffee and waited, wondering if Elaine would be on time for their luncheon date. By her own admission, she often ran late, and he realized that her lateness was a trait that could one day annoy him.

Punctuality was important in Nathan's world. Of course, he admitted, there had been others—secretaries, servants, law clerks and a wife until Marilyn's death—to keep him operating on schedule. In fact, Mrs. Hopkins, his secretary, had discreetly interrupted his last morning appointment to remind him of his 12:30 luncheon engagement. Nathan's life was arranged so that all he had to do was take care of business. Time-consuming details were taken care of for him.

And what about the world of Elaine Farrell? She lived modestly, and no housekeeper maintained her three-room apartment. Other than that, he really knew very little about her except that she owned her own business and had an exercise show on a local television station. Well, no, that wasn't quite true. He did know a few other things about Elaine. He knew that she had a small mole on her right hip, that her skin was like silk under his fingers, that her hair had the most wonderful lemony, clean-hair smell when he buried his face in it. And Nathan knew that Elaine had touched him deeply. Since yesterday morning, he thought of her constantly, alternately telling himself to cool it and wondering how soon he could make love to her again.

The political meeting last night had done nothing to solve his dilemma. Nathan had finally committed himself to making the race for the state senate, and he wasn't quite sure how Elaine fit into those plans.

For months now, Nathan had resisted all entreaties that he declare for the senate seat from his district. Of course, becoming a state senator had been part of his and Marilyn's plan. First the judgeship to get his name better known among the voters, then a couple of terms in the state legislature, and eventually a congressional race.

But Marilyn's death had taken the wind out of his sails. Without her at his side, the idea of spending the next six months of his life involved in a political race did not seem very appealing, although Nathan believed he could serve the people of his district creditably if elected. He considered himself above the vested interests that so often interfered with an elected official's ability to serve his constituents fairly, and it was certainly time to oust the incumbent. Frank Billingsly had been there five terms and managed to accrue a great deal of power and money. Just thinking about the old buzzard made Nathan's blood pressure soar.

"And Lord knows it's time someone did," offered Jonathan Miles, Nathan's brother-in-law and chairman of the board of Heritage's largest bank. "Billingsly's doing nothing but holding up progress. Take that school-land thing, for example. And he's organizing the opposition to the governor's industrial-trust proposal to provide low-interest loans of state money to qualified communities to build industrial parks. The trust is probably a lost cause this session, but if we could get Billingsly out next November and our own man in to reintroduce the bill, we should be able to get the ball rolling again. Now that the military base across the river has been all but shut down, we are looking at zero economic growth in Heritage unless we get that bill passed and attract industry to this city."

"Of course, a lot of citizens in this community would applaud Billingsly on his stand on the industrial-trust issue," Nathan pointed out. "In spite of the Chrysler bailout by the federal government, there's a lot of opposition to tax money being used to support private enterprise. And not everyone in this town is interested in growth. Some people like the town just the way it is."

"I don't think you're aware of what that trust would do for this community, Nathan," Jonathan said as he pushed his chair back from the table and lit a cigar. "State money could be used to develop the industrial park in this city that we've been talking about for years. Max here tells us that one of the nation's largest manufacturers of calculators and personal computers would give the go-ahead on a Heritage plant if we provided the land and tax incentives. That could mean hundreds of jobs to this community. I don't see how anyone representing this district could possibly be against such a bonanza."

"You have the credentials," insisted Max Duncan, president of the local chamber of commerce. "Your own family and your late wife's family are known in this district. Your father-in-law was a congressman. You won your judgeship handily. Thus far, you have made few political enemies. Your work on the Governor's Special Commission on Education earned you a lot of admirers. And you're a tax man. We need someone in the statehouse who can write a tax bill favorable to new industry and offer a rational voice against some of those so-called tax reforms being proposed by the right-wing riffraff."

"Riffraff? That's a little strong, Max. And if you're after a tax expert, why not Clark Rutherford?" Nathan was curious to know. "I think a lot of people would consider him a logical choice for the office. He's served in the state legislature for two terms and certainly was instrumental in blocking the new well tax all the oil people were so much against."

Rutherford was being groomed for Washington, Nathan was informed. The news didn't set particularly well with him somehow. Rutherford was not a man Nathan personally admired, but he apparently had the support of the men in this room.

Nathan hadn't quite realized just what kingmakers these men were. They had mentioned past choices for other races, most of whom had won. He wasn't particularly comfortable with the idea of political races being decided by rich cigar-smoking men over their brandy, but he realized that was the way of it. They were the men who got things done in this community. And Nathan wholeheartedly agreed that it was past time to do something about Frank Billingsly's stranglehold on the district, not so much because of the industrial-trust issue—Nathan wasn't quite sure how he felt about that issue—but because of other things he knew about the man.

Nathan had long been aware that the incumbent state senator from their district had built himself quite a power base and had used it to make himself a wealthy man. Two years ago, the senator—who had close political ties with the state corporation commission—just happened to turn up owning a large tract of land near Springfield that was purchased by American Electric for a plant. And Nathan had learned through his colleagues at the law firm that there was more than a strong possibility that Billingsly was involved in a dummy corporation that had acquired land later purchased by the state for a correctional facility now being built in Custer County.

And many of Billingsly's pals seemed to end up as tag agents or on the state payroll. Nathan was certain the crafty old politician received a sizable kickback from such people. Such practices sickened him. Politics should not be a game played for personal gain.

Yes, the idea of ousting Billingsly was an attractive one. No doubt about it. And Nathan appreciated the confidence this group of men placed in him. Maybe a new challenge was precisely what he needed to get his life going again. Over the past months he had felt like a ship caught in the doldrums. A lethargy overtook him at times that he couldn't seem to shake. It would be nice to be absorbed in a new cause.

But Nathan still needed convincing. He threw out other names. What about Elizabeth Jenson? Or Charles Cramer? Or Reverend Michaelson. Each person Nathan mentioned as a potential candidate, however, had too many liabilities to please the group.

"We want a winner," his portly brother-in-law told him. "We don't want to put our money and our reputations behind a loser."

That was when Jonathan had come up with the clincher. He got up and walked around the table to stand beside Nathan. "You know this is what Marilyn would have wanted you to do," he said with a kindly hand placed on Nathan's shoulder.

Jonathan was right. Tears stung at Nathan's eyes as he thought of Marilyn and her dreams for their future. He remembered how proud she had been when he was elected municipal judge. Somehow, knowing she wouldn't be with him if he was elected to the state senate had up to now taken away much of Nathan's enthusiasm for the race. He would have been running at least in part for Marilyn.

Nathan often thought that Marilyn should have been the one to enter public life. She had the organizational skills needed to run campaigns. She was intelligent and knew Missouri politics inside out, and she was more of a public person than Nathan was. Since her father was a former congressman, Marilyn had grown up in the political arena. In fact, at one point Nathan had tried to get Marilyn to run for the city council, but she wouldn't consider it. The notion of womanhood that she been raised with and adhered to throughout her adult life did not condone women such as herself entering politics other than as a volunteer working for her preferred candidate. Strange. Marilyn had been able to organize a fund-raising drive for her various charitable and civic projects like a professional. She managed to get wings added to the church's educational building and day-care centers established far better than Nathan could himself. But there was a line Marilyn would not cross over. She worked her miracles from the power base supplied by wifehood and family. And she had devoted her energies and considerable talents to her husband's future—a future of which she was no longer a part. How unfair life could be.

Nathan felt a strong sense of obligation to keep alive his and Marilyn's shared dream. She would have expected it of him. And in spite of the fact that there was a lot he didn't know about politics, he was qualified for the job. He knew tax law. He was not motivated by hopes of personal gain and was independent of special-interest groups. He would give it his all. The challenge, he realized, was not without excitement.

He agreed. He would run for the state senate.

There was much backslapping and handshaking and plans for upcoming strategy meetings. Nathan was on his way. A spirit of camaraderie and optimism filled the small room.

But even then, as the toast was being offered, he had been thinking of Elaine. Where did she fit into all this? He certainly hadn't been in any doldrums since he met her. His secretary had commented on the spring in his step. Elaine had put it there and filled Nathan with something that was missing in his life—a sense of anticipation. Was he entering a future that had no place for her, he asked himself.

When the celebration finally ended several toasts and drinks later, Nathan desperately wanted to drive straight to Elaine's apartment, to see her, to be with her. But his inability to project Elaine's place in his future prevented him from seeking the comfort of her arms. The next time they made love, Nathan wanted to be certain he wasn't just using her. He had to be sure his intentions toward the young woman were honorable.

But it was almost twelve hours until their lunch date. Nathan had wondered if he had the strength of character to endure twelve more hours without her.

He did endure, however. The brandy and the exhaustion from a totally sleepless night took care of his desire. He had slept as if he were drugged.

And now the wait should be about over. Very soon he would see Elaine again. Nathan almost hoped he would be disappointed by their luncheon date. Now that he had made love to her, maybe he could calm down and be more objective about her. Maybe it *had* simply been a case of middle-age crazies. His life would certainly be less complicated without her.

Nathan checked his watch. Elaine was now officially late. It was 12:35. He nodded at a few acquaintances and stared absently at the menu, although he already knew what he would have. He always had a hot roast-beef sandwich when he ate lunch here. He wished he had brought his briefcase. If he'd known he was just going to be sitting here, he could have gone over some briefs. He checked his watch again: 12:41.

The waiter returned to refill his coffee cup. As the man moved away, Nathan saw her. Elaine was standing by the door, her gaze searching. She was wearing a cream-colored cape and black boots. A bright red scarf was hanging around her neck. Her lustrous hair was wind-blown and scattered with snowflakes.

Nathan appraised her admiringly as he waved to attract her attention, but his heart didn't turn over until she smiled.

Oh, that smile. Just for him. Radiant. A little abashed because of her tardiness. She jauntily tossed her scarf over a shoulder and came striding toward his table. She seemed impervious to the turning heads. The diners looked first at her, then checked to see whose table she was heading for before turning back to stare at the flamboyant young woman with the spring in her step and the smile on her face. Nathan knew there was envy in the stares of the men in the room. Nathan found himself not quite believing that such a vibrant, exciting woman was going to lunch with him. It was all quite overwhelming. And confusing. And worrisome. But so wonderfully exciting! He felt twenty years old. He sat taller in his chair. He wished he had brought her flowers.

Nathan rose and helped her off with her wrap. Elaine kept the red scarf around the neck of the fluffy white sweater she was wearing with a pair of black slacks. The slacks were tucked into the top of her high-heeled boots. Thin silver bracelets jingled lightly on her slim wrist as she adjusted her scarf.

He seated her beside him instead of across the table. "You look absolutely marvelous," he said as he pushed in her chair. He was unable to resist the urge to put his hands momentarily on her shoulders. A whiff of her fragrance reached his nostrils. The sweater was soft and furry to his touch and he could feel her collarbone. He allowed a thumb to stray under the scarf and brush against the skin on her neck.

"Thank you. I could say the same for you." She looked up at him, acknowledging his touch with her eyes.

Nathan sat down. Their knees met under the table. She did not draw away. That pleased him. He never dreamed sitting knee to knee could be such a turn-on, but then everything about her turned him on. It made him suspicious. No one could be that wonderful.

"I saw your television show," he said, not knowing on which part of her to feast his eyes. For an instant he wished he had seated her across from him so he'd have a better perspective. But then their knees wouldn't be touching.

"And?"

"And I think you have the most delightful fanny I've ever seen in a pair of tights."

"Does it embarrass you?" she asked.

"Your fanny?"

"No. The fact that I do that on television. Exercise in tights. Some people consider that provocative and in poor taste."

Nathan started to make a joke, but he could tell she was serious. "Embarrass me? No, I was jealous thinking of all the men who were getting their kicks watching you, but I think you do a fine job. Not just the exercising. Your commentary was excellent. You really know what you're talking about, don't you?"

"I try. I've taken classes, read a lot."

"My secretary tells me you've built up quite a following with your show. Local celebrity and all that."

"A little, I guess," Elaine said with a small shrug. "People sometimes recognize me on the street or in stores. I guess that's part of what I mean about embarrassing you. I mean, here we are in a public place, and some of these people may be asking what Judge Stewart is doing with the 'exercise girl' from television."

"I think the only thing anyone is thinking is how lucky that old codger in the three-piece suit is to be with that lovely young woman in the sexy high-heeled boots."

Elaine laughed. Nathan liked making her laugh. He felt as if he'd been given a prize. But he also felt a little deceitful. It had crossed his mind that someone might be wondering about him and the "exercise girl." Not that he was embarrassed; he hadn't been deceitful about that. Nathan was delighted to be here with her, but he realized that some people might think them an inappropriate pairing, that Elaine wasn't his social equal. And they would assume that he couldn't possibly be serious about her, that it was just a sexual thing between them. People might look at the likes of him dating the likes of her and nod their heads knowingly to one another. "The judge has got himself a real looker to play around with. Ever see her on television? Great body. Imagine he's set her up in a little love nest someplace." Nathan knew that's what people would be thinking, because that's what he would be thinking himself if he had seen one of his peers with Elaine. Such thoughts made him uncomfortable, partly, he realized, because he wasn't sure how close to the truth they were. Of course, he hadn't set her up in a "love nest." She wasn't a kept woman, but making her one had crossed his mind. Some men used such arrangements as an alternative when marriage wasn't appropriate.

"Actually, the show has been very good for my business," Elaine was explaining. "I don't get paid much for doing it, but it's generated clients—not enough, but we would have really been in trouble without it."

"Business not too good?" he asked. He liked the way she looked right at him when they talked.

"Probably as good as I can expect after only six months in the building but not good enough to stay out of the red. But I'm working on it. One thing I'm never short of is ideas. Not all of them work, however."

"Well, do you have any idea what you'd like for lunch?" Nathan asked, realizing the waiter was heading their way. "I always have the hot roast-beef sandwich. It's very good."

"You *always* have it?" Elaine questioned.

"When I come here for lunch, yes."

"What about the other things on the menu. Aren't they any good?"

"I really don't know," Nathan admitted. "I guess I've never tried them."

"Judge Stewart, it sounds to me like you're in a rut."

Elaine smiled up at the waiter. "We'll both have the fresh poached salmon—with hollandaise on the side. And bring lots of fresh lemon. New potatoes instead of baked. Sautéed zucchini for the vegetable."

Nathan was somewhat taken aback. No woman had ever ordered his lunch before. But he loved the mischievous glint in her eyes, and he realized fresh salmon did sound delicious. Elaine was right. He was in a rut—about lunch and almost everything else in his life. At least he had been until the day before yesterday. He wanted to remember that day. The day he started climbing out of the rut. The day he met Elaine.

He asked her to go to the Carmichael's party with him tomorrow night. She raised an eyebrow. "You sure?"

He nodded. "Absolutely."

"At the club? The *country* club? No, I don't think so."

"Please. My daughter will be there with her fiancé. I can introduce you to her and to my friends."

Elaine wanted to say no. She wasn't ready for that scene yet. His daughter! Evening clothes at the posh Heritage Golf and Country Club. Introductions to friends. But how could she tell him no? Elaine doubted if she could deny him anything.

"Can we make love afterward?" she asked, her clear green eyes so open and honest.

"Absolutely!"

Nathan rejoiced. She liked him! This desirable woman really wanted him to make love to her! The knowledge made him heady. Nathan felt all the reservations he had about a relationship with Elaine being shoved into the back closet of his mind. Somehow he would make things work for them.

Somehow.

"I have a family dinner tonight," Nathan said. "But why don't you come by my house for a nightcap after you close? I'll be back by ten or ten-thirty. I'm not sure I can wait until tomorrow night to see you again."

Elaine smiled but shook her head no.

"Why not? I fix a pretty fair brandy Alexander," Nathan said.

She put her hand over his. "Not tonight. I'm not ready for your big house with all its memories. I may never be, Nathan. Don't expect too much out of me. I'm the daughter of a mechanic and come from the wrong side of the tracks. Let's do the country-club bit first and see how we manage, then take it from there."

"The house probably isn't nearly so intimidating as you think," Nathan said.

"Yes, it is. I've already checked it out. Let's save Weatherford Drive for another day, okay?"

SATURDAY WAS A BUSY DAY at the Fitness Center, especially on the track and in the weight room. On weekends, Elaine and her staff ran a full schedule of exercise sessions that could be attended on a drop-in basis. People took advantage of weekends to work out.

And this Saturday, Elaine was trying something new. On a trial basis, the Fitness Center was offering light lunches and snacks—green salads, fruit salads, sandwiches, soup, juices—to sell to the patrons following their workouts. She had rented tables set up in the front lobby, brought the food in and coerced her reluctant staff into helping put together the salads and sandwiches. "If this works, I'll hire someone to run the food service. And I'll add breakfast. We can start opening at six, and people can exercise, shower and eat breakfast before going to work.''

The day had been frantic. The food-service idea looked promising. If only she could come up with enough moneymaking ideas, maybe she could get the business operating on a profitable basis.

Throughout the day, as she tore lettuce, cut up fruit, led classes, enrolled new members, demonstrated weights and answered the phone, she thought about the evening ahead. And she pondered what in the world she would wear.

Elaine was apprehensive about the evening and really didn't want to go. She wished she and Nathan could do something less demanding, like a movie and a hamburger, but she could tell that the party was important to him. And in a way it was a vote of confidence on his part that he wanted her to accompany him. Her being with him at such a function would alert his friends to his interest in her. That flattered Elaine, but it frightened her too. She wasn't ready for a coming-out party.

What did people wear to big parties at country clubs, Elaine wondered over and over, mentally going over all the garments in her closet. Nathan had said evening clothes. She didn't own any, but she did have dressy outfits she had worn out in the evenings. One of them would have to do. She supposed it was probably a blessing that she was so busy today; otherwise, she would have done something dumb like rushing out to charge a new outfit she couldn't afford and would still not measure up in any way to what the other women would be wearing at the party.

Elaine realized she would have to manage for this occasion as she had always managed. She could not afford expensive clothes. But she had discovered vintage clothing stores a long time ago, and she'd found some real treasures at thrift shops, at garage sales and at the army surplus store. She had made a hobby out of it. Often such garments were of a higher quality than anything she could have afforded new. It was amazing the labels one sometimes found in such clothes, and often all they needed was a mandatory trip to the cleaners and perhaps some mending or alterations, which Elaine could do herself. She had learned to rely on color, well-chosen accessories and what she hoped was flair. That was what she would have to use tonight. For her only choices were to create something out of her own closet or not go.

As usual, she was rushed for time. She left the Fitness Center later than she intended that evening. And she didn't dare drive home without stopping for gas. Her gas gauge had been on empty since yesterday. Then she had to stop at the florist for her rose. When she exited onto the freeway, fifty-five miles an hour seemed impossibly slow. She had to remind herself repeatedly of her resolve not to speed anymore.

She arrived at her apartment with less than an hour to work a miracle before Nathan arrived. She showered, dried her hair and applied her makeup. The outfit she had mentally conjured up consisted of black crepe evening pants paired with a black camisole that had once been some woman's undergarment. The camisole was trimmed with crocheted inserts and border. Elaine wrapped a red scarf around her waist cummerbund style and added her trustworthy red heels. She pulled a cream-colored fringed stole out of her bottom drawer and surveyed her outfit in a full-length mirror.

Nobody would mistake it for a Dior, Elaine realized, but her outfit would have to do. She added some dangling earrings of jet beads, pushed her hair back over her right ear and pinned the rose there.

Nathan's knock came promptly at 7:30. Clyde elected to use his "What the hell?" greeting for the occasion.

The look of admiration in Nathan's eyes was reassuring. Elaine gave Clyde some sunflower seeds to shut him up. She poured Nathan a glass of wine in a dime-store glass with only one small chip on its lip and hurried back to her bedroom to change purses and check her reflection one last time. A little more eye shadow. Fluff her hair out a bit more. After all, schoolgirl was hardly the look she was after. A spray of perfume. And now she needed a wrap other than just the stole. Her cape would have to do.

"I've never ridden in a Mercedes before," Elaine commented as they pulled away from her apartment house. "Or been to the country club. Or dated a wealthy man before."

"You're a very interesting young woman," Nathan said, looking at her sideways. "Most people would act blasé and not admit their lack of experience."

"What would be the point of that?" Elaine asked in a puzzled voice. "I am who I am. I was born poor. I was raised poor. And with all the money I owe, I guess I'm poorer now than ever. Do you want me to pretend otherwise to your friends? I can't do 'Vassar girl.' It isn't in my repertoire."

"You don't have to pretend anything at all," Nathan said in a serious tone. "I want you to be yourself, Elaine Farrell, period. You'll knock 'em dead. And just to keep the record straight, I'm not all that wealthy. I make a comfortable living, but the big house and all the trappings are a drain.''

"'Trappings' like this place?" Elaine asked as they pulled up to the well-lighted portico of the sprawling country club. "It looks like a movie set," she said as she took in the dazzling white facade of the huge white-columned brick building. She had only caught glimpses of the building through a tall hedge before; now she realized just how grand it was.

A uniformed doorman came racing forward to open the door for her, and soon she and Nathan were marching arm in arm across the spacious marble-floored foyer.

David and Jessica Carmichael greeted them as they entered an elegant room filled with people in evening clothes.

Every woman in the room had on an evening gown. Elaine's heart sank. Evening pants obviously weren't "in" among the country-club set. Well, she'd always believed in being different, she told herself. Tonight, however, was one night she would rather have blended in.

Elaine's impression of the room and its occupants was one of opulent elegance. The room sparkled with crystal chandeliers and mirrors. White-gloved waiters were circulating with trays laden with sparkling glasses of champagne. The whole scene looked like something out of *Town and Country*.

Jessica Carmichael's pearl-and-ruby necklace could have paid the debt on the Fitness Center. Her jewel-encrusted dress was probably worth more than a new station wagon.

"Jonathan tells us you're ready to toss your hat in the ring for the state senate race," David Carmichael told Nathan over a handshake. "That's great news. You can count on my support."

The bejeweled hostess gestured to two women helping themselves to glasses of champagne from a waiter's tray. "Rhonda, Lauren. Come over here and meet Nathan's friend. Elaine Farewell, this is Rhonda Stratton and Lauren Boswell."

"Farrell," Elaine corrected. Nobody paid any attention. Lauren drifted away, and Rhonda exchanged brief, impersonal pleasantries with Elaine, then went straight for Nathan.

Elaine met a confusing parade of people. Nathan insisted on keeping her tucked at his side in spite of the hostess and Rhonda's periodic attempts to lure him away. Two or three people commented that Elaine looked familiar.

"You've seen her on television," Nathan explained. "She has the exercise show."

"I love your rose," one matronly woman commented. Elaine wasn't sure if the woman was being sarcastic or complimentary. She thanked her—just in case.

A plump woman in black taffeta and ruby earrings launched into an explanation of how long she had known Nathan. "Marilyn and Nathan and I graduated from St. John's together. Marilyn was a dear friend—a fine, fine woman. Such a tragedy. Did you know her?"

And suddenly there was the daughter. Rebecca. Small, blond, self-assured, resplendent in blue velvet. Home from college for spring break. A handsome fiancé in tow.

Elaine's presence at her father's side seemed to take Rebecca by surprise, but Elaine had the feeling that not too many things cracked the poise of the sophisticated young woman. And indeed, after a momentary widening of the eyes, Rebecca recovered beautifully.

"Have you known my father long?" Rebecca asked politely.

"No, I just met him last Wednesday," Elaine said down to the much shorter Rebecca. Elaine always felt overly tall next to such small women. She wondered if Marilyn had been small.

"Oh, I see. Are you a new client?" Rebecca prodded.

"I met your father in court."

"You're an attorney, then?"

"Well, I did meet him in a legal capacity. But no. I'm not an attorney. I drive too fast and had to appear before him."

"And he asked you out during court?" Rebecca asked with a puzzled frown.

"No, actually, I asked him out after a committee meeting we both attended," Elaine said, realizing the conversation was not going well. Nathan hadn't heard. He was talking to Rebecca's fiancé. That was just as well.

Rebecca abruptly turned her attention from Elaine to her father. "Everything is all set for our engagement party," she told her father. "I told Bryan I was sure you would be delighted to escort his aunt. She's widowed, you know. A lovely woman. His mother's younger sister. I know you'll enjoy meeting her."

Rebecca's remarks seemed designed to prevent her father from bringing a date of his own choosing to the engagement party. *She's afraid he'll bring me,* Elaine realized.

"And, Daddy, can you speak to Robert for me?" Rebecca continued with a pretty pout.

"What's your brother done to displease you now?" Nathan asked. His tone was not amused.

"He insists that he's worn a dinner jacket for the last time. Will you tell him he has to dress right and behave himself at the engagement party?" Rebecca asked, tucking her arm in her father's and turning her back to Elaine.

"I'm sure you and your brother can work something out," Nathan said, patting his daughter's hand. "Now if you'll excuse us, there's some more people I'd like to introduce Elaine to before dinner is served."

At dinner, Elaine was seated at a table with Rhonda Stratton. Elaine didn't bother to correct the woman when she introduced her around the table as Irene Farewell. Nathan was seated at another table—on Jessica Carmichael's right. He looked at her helplessly across the room and lifted his wineglass to her, offering a mute apology. Elaine smiled and nodded.

"Your outfit is very interesting, dear," Rhonda said in a brassy voice. "Did you make it?"

Chapter Six

Elaine had never felt so out of place in her life. What made her think that a put-together outfit of secondhand garments could ever make the grade with such people? What made her think she had any business at such a party?

She toyed with her food while she manufactured a way to escape. Could she simply excuse herself, leave the room, call a cab and go home? No, she would have to tell Nathan first. She could insist she had a headache but that he should stay at the party.

Telling him, however, would entail going over to his table. Elaine was reluctant to call attention to Nathan in that manner. She didn't want to embarrass him in front of his friends any more than she already had.

She bent her head down, plucked the rose from her hair and dropped it to the floor. No one at the table seemed to notice. The men on either side of her discussed the oil depletion allowable across her as though she weren't there.

The other two men at the table were talking about the crisis in the Middle East. They had their geography wrong. Iraq did not border the Persian Gulf, but Elaine didn't bother to correct them. Rhonda and the other two women at the table launched a discussion of an upcoming Junior League charity gala. It was going to benefit the art museum. Should it be a champagne brunch or an evening wine and cheese? A harp or a string quartet for background music? Their conversation seemed designed to exclude Elaine.

Elaine felt as if she were invisible.

Her untouched salad was taken away and replaced by a dinner plate. Roast lamb. The smell nauseated Elaine. She desperately wanted to leave.

"Excuse me," she mumbled, and started to push back her chair.

Nathan was there behind her. He pulled back her chair and took her elbow when she rose.

"I have to leave," she said.

"I know." His mouth was tense, angry. "I've already offered our regrets."

Elaine wondered if she could get out of the room before tears poured out of her eyes. *It's not important,* she told herself. *It's not worth getting upset over.*

But she couldn't kid herself. The night had been so very important. It was a trial run into Nathan's world, and she had failed miserably. The dream of her and Nathan together had been a nebulous one but in a very short time had become lodged at her center. And now the dream had been torn away from her. Elaine felt wounded and empty.

Nathan told the doorman standing guard over the grandiose front lobby to send for his car.

"You don't have to leave. Just call me a taxi," Elaine insisted.

Nathan ignored her words. "I'll get your wrap," he said.

The uniformed doorman eyed her strangely. *He's probably trying to decide who let me in,* Elaine thought.

Nathan returned, wearing his overcoat. He placed the cape over her shoulders and propelled her toward the door, but Elaine held back. "Please. There's no need for you to leave. Just get me a taxi," she begged him again.

He shook his head.

As they stepped out the door, Nathan's Mercedes pulled under the portico. Nathan tipped the attendant and opened the door for Elaine.

He drove one block, then pulled over to the curb in front of a house that could have passed for a hotel. Nathan reached over and pulled her into his arms. "Oh, God, Elaine, I'm so sorry. How dreadful that must have been for you."

She cried.

He stroked her hair and kissed her tears—which made her cry all the more. Such a wonderful man she had fallen in love with and could never have.

"I don't belong there," she said between sobs.

"It doesn't matter. Believe me, it doesn't matter." His words were soothing. His breath was warm against her skin.

"I've gotten your shirtfront all wet," she said in a small voice.

"Forget it. Are you going to be okay?"

"Sure. I'm tough." She pulled away from him and sat with her hands in her lap.

"Can you ever forgive me, Elaine? I should have known better than to take you there."

"I should have known better than to go. We're both wiser now, aren't we? You can take me home now."

They drove home in silence. There didn't seem to be much else to say.

At the door to Elaine's apartment, Nathan put his hands on her shoulders and turned her to face him. "I want to come in," he said.

Elaine felt herself stiffening. But before she could refuse him, Nathan put a finger on her lips. "Not for what we talked about yesterday at lunch. I just want to hold you in my arms for a few minutes."

She knew the tears were about to start again. Concentrating very hard on keeping them at bay for just a minute longer, Elaine said, "That would just make matters worse. Good night, Nathan."

THE LAMP BY HIS CHAIR made a pool of light in the large room, leaving the shelves of books bordering its walls in shadows. Nathan leaned his head against the high back of his chair and sipped at his brandy—a Courvoisier, which was one of the best, as was his custom. He thought of the bottle of corkless wine from which Elaine had poured him a glass earlier in the evening. She had never been able to afford the best of anything.

He wondered what Elaine would think of this room, of this house, which was so much a part of him. It was a fine old house that spoke of tradition and prosperity. Could she ever feel comfortable here? Would she ever want to?

Nathan had thought of inviting her to his home tonight but knew he would have to postpone her first visit since Rebecca was home from college. But he needed to have her reaction to his home, just as he had needed to take her among his friends tonight. His friends had made her dreadfully uncomfortable. Would his house do the same?

"Waiting up for me?" Rebecca asked jokingly from the study door. "I'm a big girl now, remember?"

She took off her coat and laid it over a chair. "A little dark in here, isn't it?" she said, and without waiting for an answer, switched on a second lamp. "Actually, I'm kind of glad you're still up. I'd like to talk to you."

"And I with you," Nathan said, watching his daughter seat herself in the wing chair that matched the one he was occupying. He remembered when she used to come into this room carrying her picture books. "Read to me, Daddy," she'd say, scrambling up into his lap. And he would hold her plump, sweet little body close and feel so blessed to be the father of Rebecca.

"You look more like your mother all the time," Nathan commented, putting his empty brandy glass on a marble-topped end table.

"Thank you," she said softly. "I know you mean that as a compliment."

"Oh, indeed I do," Nathan said firmly. "Your mother was a beautiful woman—and a fine person. I was just thinking that in all the time I spent with her, I never once heard her be rude to anyone."

Rebecca looked down at her hands for a minute, then threw back her head, her eyes challenging. "And you think I was rude tonight to that—that woman?"

"Her name is Elaine. And yes, I think you were rude. You might as well have said, 'Don't you dare come to my engagement party!'"

"Well, I don't want her to come," Rebecca said defensively.

"Then you never should have brought it up."

"Are you terribly unhappy with me?" Rebecca asked, her eyes taking on a brighter glisten.

"With you and a lot of other people," Nathan said with a sigh. "I guess I never realized before tonight what a bunch of snobs we all are."

"Daddy, I don't think that's fair. Those are lovely people, our friends. They were Mother's friends, too. They knew Mother and respected and admired her. And then you bring that woman—Elaine—among them. No one really knew quite what to do. She was dressed all wrong. I heard people say she was just an exercise girl on a local television station. Everyone was talking about you, Daddy."

"I'm sure they were," Nathan said. "I should have had better sense than to subject her to that crowd. Well, let me tell you something, Rebecca Stewart, that young woman has more character than the whole motley crew put together."

"And am I one of the motley crew?" she asked, her chin tilted upward.

"Tonight you were, honey. I wasn't too proud of you."

Rebecca said nothing for a long minute. But finally she said, "I'm sorry I was rude to your friend. And you're right. Mother was never rude. She had more class than that. I shall try to be more like her in the future."

Her tone was sincere enough, Nathan decided. His daughter was not an unkind person, just a young woman who had been raised in a very sheltered and elitist world—the same world in which he himself had lived very comfortably until now. He leaned forward and patted her hand.

"Are you going to keep seeing her?" Rebecca asked.

"I don't know," Nathan said. "She probably won't be interested after tonight. The whole evening was pretty traumatic for her."

"I don't want to sound like a snob, Daddy. Really I don't. But she didn't belong. If you want to—well, to *see* her, why don't you do so privately?"

"That's the one thing I absolutely won't do," Nathan said angrily. "I'll either see her openly, or I won't see her at all."

Rebecca stood. Looking down at him, her lower lip trembling, she said, "If you really care about the way she feels or about the way I feel, you won't subject either one of us to any more embarrassment."

Nathan took his daughter's hand—a beautiful manicured hand adorned with an impressive diamond engagement ring. He brushed his lips over its soft skin. "Is that how my being with Elaine made you feel? Embarrassed?"

"Oh, Daddy," Rebecca said, crumbling to her knees in front of him and offering her other hand. "I'm getting married soon. This is *my* time—maybe the most important time in my life. I want everything to be perfect. It's bad enough that Mother's not here with me—with us—to share it all. But to have people whispering that my father is carrying on with someone so inappropriate for him—it will spoil everything."

"Do you care so much about what people are saying, Rebecca? What if they're wrong?"

"Well, are they? Surely you aren't serious about her! Good grief, you've only known her since Wednesday. And she's all wrong for you, Daddy. She's too young. She comes from a different background. She wouldn't belong in my mother's house!" Rebecca said with a gesture encompassing the book-lined room and the house beyond. "And if you aren't serious about her, then— well, I call that 'carrying on.' Remember when you used to lecture Robert and me about inappropriate behavior? Well, now you're going to let Robert come to my engagement party in jeans, and you've allowed yourself to become an object of gossip."

"Rebecca, I'm not going to let gossips dictate how I live my life. And as much as I love you, I'm not going to let you do that, either. I'll do my best to get Robert in a tux, but I'm not making any promises about Elaine. Now quit acting like a victim of some tragedy and go to bed."

He kissed his daughter's unbelievably smooth forehead. So young, she was. He remembered when Marilyn's forehead was that smooth.

What a mess, he thought as he turned off two lamps and headed up the stairs. *I've managed to get them both upset. My daughter and my—*

His daughter and his what? Girlfriend sounded too adolescent. Woman friend sounded too impersonal. Elaine was his lover, he decided. But he didn't like that word, either.

Lover. That was an interesting term. It was used to refer to a sexual liaison and not necessarily to two people who were in love.

Was he in love with Elaine? Nathan honestly didn't know. He had never doubted he loved Marilyn throughout their life together. But even when he courted her, he couldn't remember being as captivated by Marilyn as he was by Elaine. Elaine assaulted his senses from all directions. She was the most disarmingly vibrant, honest woman he had ever known. And there was the sexual thing. He was incredibly attracted to her. He couldn't stop thinking about her. The times during the past few days that Elaine wasn't actually in his mind, he was clearing his mind of other thoughts in preparation for thinking about her. At age forty-five, Nathan found himself more sexually turned on than he had ever been in his life. But through all his sexual excitement he realized there was a great deal more involved. He wasn't sure if he loved her, but he genuinely liked Elaine Farrell. And he admired her as a human being. He admired the way she had managed her life and struggled to make something out of herself.

True, he had known her only a short time. True, she was much younger than he was, though the fifteen years that separated their ages was not as many as he had at first supposed. True, she was from a different background. And she would never feel at home in the house he had shared with his wife during most of their married life.

None of that bothered him terribly, however. Oh, it was all important, but those were surely things that two intelligent people who cared about each other could come to terms with. Still, the knowledge that his dating Elaine had embarrassed his daughter bothered him. In spite of his remark about not letting Rebecca dictate his life, he didn't want to spoil her wedding or alienate her from his life.

He tried to see Elaine as Rebecca and the others at the party might have seen her tonight. He realized her outfit had not cost the small fortune needed to purchase each of the gowns worn by the other women, and there were no jewels at her throat. But she looked so fresh, so lovely. Surely the others recognized that. Elaine wasn't one of them, though. They thought he had shown poor taste in bringing his young companion to their party. To their way of thinking, it might be acceptable for him to ''see'' someone like Elaine privately—have a clandestine affair with her—but never allow her to intrude on their carefully monitored existence. They considered Elaine beneath him, Nathan realized, when all the time he was wondering if he could ever live up to her.

How would they have treated her if she was his wife, Nathan wondered. Quite differently, he decided. And somehow that made him mad. Elaine shouldn't have to marry someone like him in order to be treated respectfully. In many ways, Nathan admired her more than he admired those of his class who had been born with the so-called silver spoon in their mouth. She had always worked, Elaine told him, since she was fourteen years old. Everything she had, she had earned herself. Everything. Nobody had ever given her anything. But Nathan was beginning to realize those kinds of accomplishments didn't matter to the Carmichaels or the Strattons or the Boswells of the world—or even to his own daughter.

He felt like a blind man who had just been granted sight. There was so much he had not seen before.

MARK WAS SITTING on a hall bench waiting for her as Elaine came out of the small exercise studio. He looked like she felt—miserable.

"Thanks for coming in, Mark. I'm really short-handed tonight. I hope you didn't have plans with Ms 'Five Foot Two, Eyes of Blue.'"

"No. That didn't work out. She's shallow. And besides, I found someone else."

"Oh, when did this happen?" Elaine asked, sinking down beside the small man and drying her brow with the towel hanging around her neck.

"Last night," he said with a heavy sigh. "I was sitting there at Billy Boys, sipping my Perrier and lime, when I heard this laugh—the sweetest, most charming, sincerest laugh in the whole world. Like crystal bells, I swear. I knew as soon as I heard it that I would love the woman who laughed that way."

"And did you?" Elaine asked. "Was it love at first laugh?"

"Yes," Mark said with a second sigh. "I turned around, and our eyes met. Her eyes. Navy blue. I swear. I've never seen such eyes in my whole life. They were rimmed with lashes this long," he said, holding his thumb and index finger an inch apart to show the length of the woman's lashes. "And they weren't fake, either. I know fake when I see them."

"So what happened?" Elaine asked, knowing from his dejected attitude that it wasn't good.

"I introduced myself. She'd even heard of me," he said with a shake of his head, as though he still couldn't believe it had happened. "A gymnastics fan. We had instant rapport. It was absolutely incredible. I've never experienced anything like it. We talked and talked. We both knew we wanted to see each other again."

"So why the long face?" Elaine asked. "You look awful."

"She stood up."

"Oh," Elaine said, understanding. "She's tall."

Mark nodded, his eyes closed. His face was a tragic mask.

"Oh, Mark, I'm sorry. But are you absolutely sure you can't love tall? Maybe you should reconsider your criteria."

"You think it's funny, don't you?" he challenged, his eyes flying open. "You've always been just right. You can't understand how it feels to be different."

"Don't be so sure. I had a rather heavy dose of being different Saturday night," Elaine said, remembering how it felt to be wearing cheap pants in a room filled with expensive gowns, to be socially unacceptable among a group of the community's socially elite. It was painful just to think about it. "And I don't think your situation is funny. I'm sorry if I gave you that impression. It's

probably just as well you came to work. It'll help take
your mind off your misery. And I really appreciate it. I
don't have another sit-up left in me. I'm on my way to the
showers.''

"Oh, I almost forgot," Mark said as he pushed himself up from the bench with great effort. "There's a guy
in your office who wants to enroll in a fitness program."

"Well, why didn't you sign him up?" Elaine asked.
Trying to charm a new customer was the last thing she
wanted to do right now.

"He says he wants to see Ms Farrell," Mark said.
"He's probably seen your sexy body on television and
fallen in love with you."

Elaine took a halfhearted swipe at him with her towel
and headed wearily for her office. After leading her
fourth aerobics class for the day, she was exhausted. But
Sally had taken her maternity leave early, and Elaine decided she would just have to find the time to lead a few
more of the classes herself. If she led them, she didn't
have to pay someone else to. And when she was working
up a sweat, she didn't think about Nathan so much. She
hoped her exhaustion would help her sleep. Sleepless
nights were the pits. And if she could just discover how
to stop thinking about him when she was awake and not
exercising.

She toweled off her moist forearms, then pulled the
sweatband from her forehead and combed at her hair
with her fingers as she entered the anteroom to her office.

The man was sitting with his back to the door. Dark
hair. Dark suit. "I'm Elaine Farrell," she said as she
rounded her desk. "How can I help you?"

The man was Nathan.

Elaine sank into her chair. She felt as if a medicine ball had just hit her in the gut.

"Hello, Elaine," he said softly. He looked tired, but no man ever looked so fine. It hurt just to look at him.

"Why have you come?" she asked.

"To see you. And to make sure I will continue seeing you, I'd like to enroll in an aerobics class," he said. "And perhaps buy a membership to use your weight room and track."

"It won't work, Nathan," Elaine said. "Surely you know that after the other night."

"I know a lot of things after the other night, but that isn't one of them," he said, looking at her intently with those moss-green eyes. "I'm not ready to give up yet. There is something pretty special going on between us, and I'll be damned if I'm going to let the snobbery of my erstwhile friends prevent me from seeing the woman I most want to see."

"How was the engagement party?" Elaine asked pointedly.

Nathan looked away for an instant. "I had a talk with Rebecca. She won't be rude like that again."

"Your daughter was exactly right in making sure I wouldn't show up at her party. I would have been an embarrassment to her, and I wouldn't have belonged any more than I belonged at that party Saturday night. I don't want to cause trouble with your daughter or alienate you from your friends. And I don't want to sneak around in order to see you, either."

"All that aside," he asked, "how do you feel about me? Have you thought about me at all in the past two days?"

Elaine wondered if she should lie. In this instance, dishonesty seemed like the best policy. She'd just tell him to bug off and be done with it.

But when she opened her mouth, all that came out was a sigh. She rubbed her temples with her fingertips. God, why did life have to be so damned confusing?

"I have never been so crazy about any man in my life," Elaine said. "I have made myself physically ill thinking about you. I have not been able to eat for these past two days. I can't sleep. Damn you, Nathan Stewart, it hurts. But I have my pride. As much as I want to be with you, I will not be the doxy of some uptown lawyer who's entering politics and would have to keep the likes of me under wraps—which is what you would have to do, you know? I don't have expensive clothes. I don't put on champagne brunches to benefit art museums. I work for money. I do gauche things like exercise on television and sweat."

For emphasis, she dabbed at her now-dry neck and shoulders with the towel.

"Let's start over," he said simply.

"What do you mean?" Elaine asked.

"Start over," he repeated. "Low-key. Slow things down. No country clubbing. When we go out, go to neutral public places like restaurants, theaters. I won't inflict my daughter on you again for a while. You don't introduce me to your family or friends. We just get to know each other. Find out if we even like keeping company with each other. Keep it as uncomplicated and un-hurried as we possibly can. Maybe even no sex—for a while, if that makes you more comfortable. Then if something permanent is meant to happen, it will evolve."

"Do you really believe that?" Elaine asked, daring to hope.

"I think so, Elaine. It's the best I can come up with right now. I just know that the idea of not seeing you again is totally unacceptable. And I've made my own list of all the reasons why it's not a good idea, but even if I had come up with a thousand reasons, it would not counterbalance the need I have to be with you. Even right now—in spite of the awkwardness of our situation—just being in the same room with you makes me feel so alive, so full of possibilities. Remember at lunch on Friday when you said I was in a rut? Well, you were right. Until I met you, my entire life had been one long rut—a luxurious one, to be sure, but a rut nonetheless. You've changed my life, Elaine. I'm a different person because of you, and even if I never saw you again, I don't think I could climb back down in my rut. I don't think I could ever look at my life through quite the same set of eyes."

"That may be true in some ways, Judge Nathan Stewart. Maybe you won't have the same entree for lunch every day, but you are who you are. You've built a life being that person. Your children know you as that person. So do your friends, your associates. Others depend on you to stay true to that person. I'm sure you lead a very satisfying life that you would miss if you changed it very much. My dad always used to say, 'If it's not broken, don't fix it.'"

"If you're telling me to go away," Nathan said, "you can save your breath. I'm not going to. Even if you won't go out with me, I'm going to become a patron of your business. I'm going to send you flowers and candy and write inept, mushy poems praising your charms. I will call you constantly. I will even learn to play the guitar and serenade you from under your bedroom window if necessary. So you might as well give up and give my plan a try."

Nathan leaned forward and extended his hand. "How about it, Elaine? A deal? Neutral places in public. Uncomplicated. No families. No promises. Just enjoy each other. Find out if there's a future for us out there."

Elaine eyed his offered hand, then slowly gave him hers. Solemnly, they shook hands. "A deal," she said. "How could I possibly win an argument with a lawyer, especially when I don't really want to?"

Nathan let out a sigh of relief. "Well, let me tell you, I argued some big cases in my life. But I never wanted to win an argument more than that one. Now, your assistant said I should make an appointment for a fitness evaluation before I can sign up for any of your programs."

"Oh, that won't be necessary," Elaine said with a sly smile. "I've already checked your physical fitness. You'll do."

Nathan grinned. Then he threw his head back and laughed. "God, my life was dull before I met you. You are one adorable woman, Elaine Farrell."

Chapter Seven

The agreement made, Nathan and Elaine became cautious. They treated their relationship as if it were some sort of precious crystal vase—so delicate, so easily shattered, so in need of protection and careful handling. When they first met, they had proceeded with abandon. Now they were backing up, starting over and proceeding with great care. For both now more fully understood just how much was at stake.

At the end of her week of spring break, Nathan's daughter, Rebecca, returned to finish her senior year at Tulane University in New Orleans.

"I know you've been awfully lonesome this past year," she told her father as they waited for her boarding call in the airport coffee shop, "and I hope you find the right woman someday to help ease that loneliness. I just want you to find someone who's worthy of you."

"Rebecca," he said irritably, "it's my life."

"I know, Daddy," she said, a hurt look veiling her brown eyes—her mother's eyes. "But I do think you do owe it to Mother to have her successor be a woman of quality."

"If by 'a woman of quality' you mean Bryan's aunt or some other widow of social prominence, then don't count on it," Nathan said in a tone that invited no argument. "Now, quit worrying about me. You worry about getting through your senior paper and finals. Don't let all these wedding plans interrupt your studying."

Nathan felt obligated to offer that little fatherly counsel, but he knew that although plans for Rebecca's June 30 wedding were foremost in his daughter's thoughts these days, she would manage her academic responsibilities competently. Like her mother before her, Rebecca was a very responsible woman. She always managed beautifully.

Nathan walked his Rebecca down the concourse, experiencing a father's pride in such a poised and elegant daughter. However, he kissed her goodbye and waved her onto the airplane with a certain degree of relief. At least temporarily, he would not have to deal with his daughter's disapproval of his choice of female companionship.

True to his word, Nathan began courting Elaine. The first date of their redefined relationship was a movie, followed by pizza and video games. Elaine couldn't believe Nathan had never played video games. "Oh what a sheltered life you've led!" she teased as she showed him how to play PAC-MAN and Donkey Kong.

Nathan was intrigued. "Could I make a living at this?" he asked. "I'd give up law in a flash if this paid."

"You'd have to get a lot better," Elaine said as she beat him for the fifth time at PAC-MAN. "I don't think you're ready to turn pro. You'd have to take lessons from my brother. He's a whiz kid when it comes to video games."

Their next date was dinner at the elegant Sky Terrace atop the Heritage Sheraton. At Nathan's insistence—"I'll come dress you in it myself if necessary"—Elaine wore the same outfit that had caused her such pain at the Carmichaels' country club party. Nathan provided the rose. And after a few apprehensive minutes and several admiring glances from male diners and waiters, Elaine realized she looked just fine.

Along with the dates, there were the daily flowers. Mrs. Hopkins was accustomed to ordering any flowers sent by her employer. In fact, she often reminded him of appropriate occasions for flower sending and at times had sent flowers from him on her own initiative. When Nathan announced he wanted flowers sent to Ms Elaine Farrell at the Fitness Center, Mrs. Hopkins was curious, wondering why in the world Mr. Stewart would send flowers to someone who worked at an exercise studio. When he requested that this be done every morning, Mrs. Hopkins was shocked.

"*Every* morning," She questioned, her lips forming a thin disapproving line.

"Yes, every morning," Nathan said gaily. "They needn't be overwhelming—just a daily remembrance. A few roses, or some carnations. Whatever you think is nice."

Mrs. Hopkins was even more startled by her employer's behavior when, a few minutes later, he opened the door between their offices, came strolling over to her desk and sat down in one of the chairs facing her desk. Never once in twenty years had Mr. Stewart come into her office and sat down rather than call her into his.

He cancelled his request about the flowers.

"It just occurred to me," Nathan said, locking his fingers behind his neck and casually tipping the chair back, "that having flowers ordered by one's secretary and delivered by an impersonal florist doesn't seem very thoughtful. I'd like this to seem like a more personal gesture. Therefore, I have decided I will select and deliver the flowers myself.''

Mrs. Hopkins realized her mouth was open. She closed it, then primly questioned whether he had time for such an activity, reminding him of his full schedule, especially now that he was going to have to start campaigning. ''You have a busy six months ahead of you, Mr. Stewart. Your calendar is already fuller than it's ever been.''

''It won't take long to run to the flower shop and pick up a flower or two,'' Nathan assured her. ''I can do it on my way to work out at the Fitness Center.''

''I'm sure the Fitness Center is a fine facility,'' the matronly secretary offered diplomatically, ''but don't forget the weight room and indoor track in the basement of this very building.''

''But there's no instruction in the basement, Mrs. Hopkins,'' he said as he rose from the chair. ''What I need is a good instructor. And don't go crazy with that calendar. Regardless of what Jonathan Miles tells you, I don't want any evening engagements for the next month. I realize the banquet trail awaits me. But not yet. There's a young lady I want to wine and dine first.''

And he took time for a cocky wink before he strolled back into his office. A wink! From Judge Stewart. Mrs. Hopkins was shocked.

Nathan selected a tiny bouquet of violets and presented them to Elaine during his first visit as a patron of the Fitness Center. He arrived with a single yellow rose the second day. And thereafter, he usually found time for a quick stop for a flower or two—roses, daisies, carnations—whatever caught his eye that day. It became a ritual Nathan enjoyed, especially at the end of the first week when he began to shift his stop from the florist to the greenhouse in search of more varied botanical fare. The owner of the greenhouse thought Nathan strange—not wanting to buy a whole plant but willing to pay for the privilege of plucking one stem and blossom from a geranium or mum or azalea plant.

"Now what's the name of that one?" Nathan would ask repeatedly while walking up and down the rows of plants basking in their trays in a glass-enclosed world.

"Would those grow in my yard," he asked, pointing to a tableful of cheerful pansies. "Why don't you send about ten dozen of them out to my house? I think I'll plant them in the bed by the front door."

Late that afternoon, Nathan's gardener dropped his cigar when he rounded the corner of the house and saw his employer kneeling in the dirt, planting pansies. "Here, Mr. Stewart," he said, rushing over to Nathan's side. "You'll be getting your slacks dirty. I'll do that."

But Nathan didn't budge. He was fascinated at having his hands in dirt. He was sure he must have made mud pies or played in the dirt as a child, but he didn't remember. Side by side, Nathan and his elderly gardener filled the bed with a blanket of colorful pansies. Nathan decided they were his favorite flower.

"I saw some kind of ground cover under some bushes in front of the courthouse," Nathan told the gardener. "Grows real close to the ground and has a spike-shaped cluster of purple flowers and lots of purple in the leaves. I'm going to find out what it is, and maybe we can plant it over there under the lilacs."

"That would be ajuga," said the man, nervously tugging at the straps to his overalls. "I'll see to it, sir."

"Fine. I'll help you put it out," Nathan said, staring at the dirt under his fingernails.

The gardener couldn't wait to report to Mrs. Murphy, the housekeeper. "He's hardly ever taken a walk in the yard before, and now he wants to plant ajuga," the gardener said, shaking his head and relighting his cigar. "He even talked about a vegetable garden on the back side of the swimming pool. Imagine, replacing the English ivy and azaleas with tomatoes and squash and green beans! Lovely view that'll be from the summerhouse! The missus never would have put up with something like that."

"The missus wouldn't have stood for what he's done in the house, either," reported Mrs. Murphy, stirring her cake batter with increased vigor. "He wouldn't let me have all the furniture put back after Miss Rebecca's engagement party. Said he liked the rooms better not so 'full of stuff.' Imagine; Mrs. Stewart's beautiful antiques and he wants to store some of them away in the attic. And he wants me to start opening the drapes in the living room in the daytime 'to let the sunshine in.' But letting the sunshine in is goin' to fade that beautiful carpet sure as I'm standing here. If one is going to live in an elegant home like this, it appears to me they have an obligation to take care of it and keep it up proper."

The gardener agreed. No question about it.

ELAINE SUFFERED some good-natured teasing from her employees about the daily supply of fresh blossoms for her desk. But periodically throughout her day, she would look at them and smile. Such a charmingly foolish thing—a floral tribute hand delivered every day by the judge himself. Adoration was okay, she decided. She had been liked before, maybe even loved. But no one had ever adored her before, and Elaine wanted to savor it.

Enjoyment did not come easily to Elaine, however. She found herself mistrustful—not of the adoration itself but of its permanence in her life. Suddenly her life had become a lovely symphony, but Elaine couldn't completely relax and take pleasure in it, because she was afraid the music would end, and she knew how sad she would be when that happened. The prospect of an eventual silent void tainted her delight in the virtuosity. Although she knew that Nathan sincerely cared for her at the present time, deep in her heart she feared that he would come to his senses eventually and put the Elaine Farrell episode in his life behind him. What if the best she could hope for was that Nathan would someday remember her fondly and wonder whatever happened to that nice Elaine Farrell?

The more Elaine was around Nathan, the more she read about him in the newspapers and watched him on the local television news programs, the more she heard what others had to say about him, the more she realized he was a person who could go places in the world of politics. She decided that if she had any character at all, she would send him away right now and never see him again. That would, in the long run, be best for both of them. Her hanging on would only increase the eventual pain she would have to endure when he ended their relationship—as he would surely do eventually. Her presence in Nathan's life could only serve to hold him back. He needed another woman like his Marilyn at his side. Elaine realized that. Nathan's daughter realized that. Nathan himself, however, seemed to be enjoying a period of delusion. Elaine was weak. She knew she would never send him away. She would let him adore her temporarily and try to think as little as possible about the day when they would go their separate ways.

Her life proceeded at a hectic pace. While her business continued to grow, the Fitness Center still did not meet its operating expenses. The day was rapidly approaching when Elaine would have to come up with more money for debt service, and she doubted very seriously that the bank would grant her another loan or extend her current ones. There wasn't even enough money for her to pay herself a salary check this month, and her savings account was almost exhausted. She thought longingly of the money to be awarded for the winning design of the fitness trail at the park being built in memory of Nathan's wife. How she could use that money! Elaine wondered why the park committee was taking so long to respond. She wished she would hear one way or the other. Even if the award went to someone else, she'd like to know so she could quit thinking about it.

Elaine tried to assume as much of the work load at the facility as she possibly could. Already shorthanded before Sally took her maternity leave, Elaine was now doing the work of two full-time instructors—plus taking care of administrative chores, taping her weekly television show, and making a growing number of public appearances to advocate physical fitness and therefore enhance the image of the Fitness Center. Her television show had made her a local celebrity of sorts, and she was in demand for demonstrations and talks at shopping malls, church or civic groups, or sporting good stores. Such appearances were good public relations for her business and generally brought in at least one or two new clients—sometimes more.

And she saw Nathan every day. His call would awaken her in the morning. His voice over the telephone was the last thing she heard before she went to bed at night. He brought her flowers when he came for his daily workout. If he couldn't take her out at night or at lunch, he would come by very early and take her to breakfast.

Elaine was busier than she had ever been in her life. She herself realized she was overdoing. The breakneck pace was taking its toll. Her assistant manager frequently pointed this out to her. "You look tired all the time, honey," Mark would tell her, "except when the judge comes around, and then your face lights up like the Fourth of July. You need a vacation."

Elaine laughed at the thought. A vacation! As though she could afford a bus ride to the next county, much less a vacation.

Clark Williams, the station manager at the television station, chastised her for losing weight. "You're sure not filling out those tights like you used to," he complained. "You're supposed to look physically fit, remember, not rundown and skinny."

"How about if my assistant takes over the show—at least temporarily?" Elaine asked. "He's starting a gymnastics program at the Fitness Center, and I'd like to promote him in the community. He's an NCAA champion gymnast and would probably spark a lot of interest in the show."

"No way, Elaine," the director told her firmly. "You can have him on as a guest, but the show is yours. That was our bargain. I don't know if you realize it, but the Sunday-morning airing of your show has the number-one rating in its time slot. That's unheard of in this community for a locally originated show. I've even had some interest expressed in syndicating the show, and that would mean money for both you and the station. In fact, we are planning to launch a promotional campaign for your show sometime in the next few weeks. We'd like to put you on the twelve-thirty talk show and the evening news doing segments on health and exercise—and use your picture on some schedule placards to put up around town. Needless to say, before we have you photographed, I'd really like you to stop working so hard and get a little meat on those lovely bones. You're looking a little faded these days.''

Elaine's mirror also let her know she wasn't looking so good. Selecting what she wore on dates with Nathan was a painful procedure. Every outfit seemed to emphasize her thinness. And she, who had always been somewhat casual about makeup, found herself taking extra pains before she went out with him to cover the darkness under her eyes and add extra color to her cheeks. It was always worth the effort. His every look was a compliment. In his eyes, she was beautiful beyond belief. And indeed, she always felt prettier and more special when she was with Nathan.

But the constant exercise took its toll on her body no matter how much she seemed to eat. And it was difficult to get a good night's sleep. She would usually sink into bed exhausted and fall asleep at once. In the middle of the night, however, she would awaken. Between Nathan and the threat of bankruptcy, a full night's sleep eluded her.

What if her business failed, she worried constantly. What would happen to her family, who so depended on her monthly checks to make ends meet? Elaine wanted to do more for them, not less. She wanted to send Tim to baseball camp this summer and buy her mother a dishwasher. But most of all, she wanted to get ahead enough financially so she could afford to send her father to one of the private clinics for alcoholics. Elaine knew her mother had given up on ever reforming him, but Elaine still carried the hope that someday Vince would dry out and be a father to Tim.

Tim continued to be the one bright spot in his mother's life. And Elaine, too, loved doting on her nine-year-old brother. She found herself longing to introduce Tim to Nathan. She was so proud of her brother and knew Tim and Nathan could be great buddies. But she and Nathan had agreed. No families for now—nothing to complicate their tenuous relationship.

"So how come you don't bring your young man—or I guess I should say your gentleman friend—over to meet your family?" Martha Farrell asked her daughter as they sat side by side in the bleachers, waiting for Tim's first baseball game of the season to begin. "I hope you're not pretending to be something you're not, Elaine. He does know about your poor relations, doesn't he?"

"Yes, Mother," Elaine said, zipping up her jacket against the chilly north wind that often ignored the calendar during a Missouri springtime. It was no day to be sitting out, and she tried not to think of all the work that awaited her back in her office, but neither she nor her mother would have considered missing the game. "Nathan knows about my family. And you'll meet him soon enough. His daughter was giving him a hard time about me, and we decided that for now we're going to keep our families out of things—at least until we figure out if we're going to keep seeing each other."

Both women clapped as the team came trotting out on the field for their warm-up. Tim looked in their direction and waved. Elaine thought he looked adorable in his uniform—*and just look at him throw that ball.*

"Elaine, are you sure you know what you're doing?" Martha asked. "I just can't for the life of me see how a young woman who exercises for a living is going to fit into the circles that man travels in. Is he going to ask you to get rid of your trendy clothes and get a tamer hairdo?

Will he expect you to stand beside him wearing a nice proper little navy dress and hat and smile sweetly while he tells his supporters, 'Thank you for voting for me'? And if he does want you, is that what you want to do with your life? You've worked awfully hard, Elaine, to have your own business and be who you are. You've developed your own style about the way you dress and the way you walk and laugh. A politician's wife, you're not. You're used to a certain kind of life; the judge is used to a certain kind of wife. Maybe you two can come to terms, but I just don't want you to get hurt, 'Laine. And I'm afraid that's just what you're asking for.''

Elaine was afraid her mother was absolutely right. However, the term ''hopelessly in love'' had taken on new meaning for her. Her love for Nathan did seem hopeless, but she also seemed powerless to do anything to end their relationship. As long as he would ask her, she would see him. And when sex reentered their relationship, Elaine would welcome it. She was ready for Nathan to put gallantry aside, although she doubted if she had the energy these days to be very sexy. But the thought of their bodies together or of their holding each other without the barriers of clothing or propriety was a beautiful one. Elaine wanted the pleasure of his loving. She wanted to make some memories with him. She knew how precious those memories would be to her in the years to come, especially if they were all she had left of Nathan.

Would memories be all she had left someday?

Probably.

But as the days went by, Elaine realized there was a stubborn little corner of her soul that refused to give up its belief that true love could conquer problems, that if two people loved each other enough, things somehow would work out. She found that hope does indeed spring eternal in the human breast, that there is the soul of a romantic hidden away inside even the most pragmatic realist. If she could just love him long enough and strongly enough and deeply enough, maybe... Just maybe...

All her life Elaine had made things happen. Nothing except the love of her family had ever been given to her. She had been a seeker and a doer. She understood at a very young age that the world was never going to beat a path to her doorstep, that whatever she wanted out of life would have to be sought out and fought for.

And what she wanted was Nathan. She would be willing to fight for him, but her mother thought Nathan would want another kind of wife. *Could I change,* Elaine wondered. Dressing more sedately wouldn't be so awful. She could cut off some of this mane of hair and opt for a more subdued hairdo. And she could enroll at the university and get serious about working toward a degree. She could read more books and learn more about politics and art and music and whatever things the wives of men like Nathan were interested in. She could give up her television program and start drawing back from her image of Heritage's exercise lady.

With such thoughts in mind, when the three men from American Fitness showed up at her office, Elaine wondered if providence had taken a hand.

"Would you be willing to sell the Fitness Center?" a Mr. Dunn asked her after some preliminary small talk about trends in equipment and the weight-lifting craze.

"I really haven't given it any thought," Elaine answered in all honesty. "The past seven or eight years of my life have been working toward the goal of having an establishment like this. It's my baby, you know. I designed it, I built it, I've sweated blood over this business."

"Yes, I'm sure you have," agreed the older of the two men, William Rubin. "Basically, we like what we see. You have some very innovative things going on here—the weight-control, exercise-package concept, the meals offered right here in the building, the support groups, the programs for the elderly and handicapped, the drop-in classes on the weekends, the lectures and films. You're a very clever young woman, Ms Farrell."

"Yes," agreed Mr. Dunn. "It appears you've managed to make the facility almost like a club or social outlet for your regular customers. We like that. We have been considering putting in a facility in Heritage for some time now. But as we observed the Fitness Center, we began considering the possibility of buying your establishment. Of course, we'd make some changes, but basically we like what we see. With an increased advertising budget, increased parking and a few luxury touches such as steam rooms and whirlpool baths—things like that— we think the business could be enhanced."

Mr. Dunn leaned forward in his chair, his voice compelling. "I'd like to see you sell us the Fitness Center and come to work for American Fitness as a consultant and spokesperson. Jim and I would like to see some of your ideas incorporated into our other studios. And we've seen tapes of your television show. I see no reason why you shouldn't be doing that as a nationally syndicated show. You do an excellent job."

"Is this a package deal?" Elaine asked. "Would you still like to buy my business even if I didn't go to work for you?"

The two men looked at each other. Jim Dunn shrugged. Mr. Rubin nodded. "Yes. Quite frankly, however, we want both you and the business. I'd wish you'd think about the wonderful opportunity that is being offered to you, Ms Farrell.''

''I'm quite flattered, gentlemen. I don't think I'm interested in selling the business or in working for you. But quite naturally, I'd be curious to know just what price you're talking about.''

The price Mr. Dunn quoted was impressive—too much for Elaine to turn down without serious consideration.

She promised to visit with her lawyer and accountant, then get back to them within ten days.

After the men had taken their leave, Elaine leaned back in her chair and closed her eyes. Sell the Fitness Center? It would be like selling a part of herself. She had worked so hard for so long to have a facility like this. However, of late she had been wondering if maybe she was business person enough to make it work. And then in walk two men ready to assume her indebtedness and pay her a considerable amount of money for her equity. She could do the things she wanted to do for her family. She would have some breathing room. It would no longer be necessary for her to be the TV exercise girl. Maybe she could become a more appropriate woman to be seen at Nathan's side. She could buy some expensive, conservative clothing. They would be more public about their relationship—become engaged, get married.

Would it be so awful to change her life-style in order to be more acceptable to Nathan and his friends, family and associates? And in spite of what her mother thought, she could become the background wife going to teas and waving sweetly to campaign crowds if it meant being with Nathan.

As attractive as such a fantasy seemed, however, Elaine was wise enough to know she had really better think through all the ramifications of such a move. First of all, she'd better make certain Nathan really wanted her on a permanent basis before she did anything drastic.

It was tempting to pick up the phone and ask Nathan what he thought of her selling her business. But she didn't. Before she offered that as a possibility, she'd better make sure that's what she really wanted.

With great effort, Elaine forced herself from the chair. Just one more class to lead and she could quit for the day. Nathan had wanted to take her bowling tonight, but she had declined. "I've got such a busy day ahead of me," she told him over the phone. "I'll be too bushed. How about just coming over for an omelet and television?"

Nathan was silent for a minute. Then he announced, "I've got a better idea."

Elaine waited. "Well, what is it?" she asked. "Or am I supposed to guess?"

"Nope. It'll be a surprise."

"Nothing strenuous, I hope." Elaine knew how tired she would be by this evening.

"Milady will not have to lift a finger," Nathan promised.

"Please tell me I don't have to dress up."

"Jeans will do nicely."

That evening, Elaine made the mistake of sprawling on her bed the minute she walked into her apartment. Nathan's knock woke her up. Clyde let out a stream of damns.

"Oh, my gosh!" she said as she opened the door and saw him standing there looking freshly scrubbed and quite handsome in a pair of neatly pressed jeans and a white crew-neck sweater. "Is it that late? I fell asleep."

"No problem. Your warm-ups are fine. Nobody will see you but me, and I find you beautiful no matter what state of disarray you're in. I can tell you're really beat. But a warm meal, a glass of good wine and some soft music will be good for you, and I promise to bring you home as soon as you start turning into a pumpkin.''

"At least let me comb my hair," Elaine said, hurrying off to try to make herself presentable.

"Okay, but hurry up. I'm starving."

Elaine surveyed her tired self in the mirror. A disaster! She really should change into something more attractive than faded sweat clothes. But on second thought maybe she wouldn't. That worn-out person in the mirror was her, too—every bit as much as the well-turned-out self she had been careful to show Nathan over the past weeks. It suddenly seemed honest to let him see her this way, too.

She had showered at the Fitness Center after her last class, but she took the time to splash cold water on her face. After a quick application of some color so she wouldn't look as though she belonged in a sick bed, she brushed her hair and fluffed it into place.

Nathan was talking to the parrot while he waited. "Come on, Clyde old man," he was saying when Elaine came into the living room. "It's really very boring to have such a limited vocabulary. Let's try 'pretty bird.' Or how about 'God bless America'?"

"He's hopeless," Elaine announced as she came from the bedroom. "When I first got him, I tried and tried. Even made recordings to play, repeating things over and over. But he's stuck with his two lines for almost three years now."

"I don't like to think that anything is hopeless," Nathan announced, taking her in his arms.

Elaine leaned her body into his, and he let out a sigh of pure pleasure.

"Oh, my darling Elaine," he said, his lips close to her ear. "I can't tell you how incredibly nice it feels to have you in my arms."

"Oh, yes," Elaine said with a sigh of her own. "I don't know about you, but I'm getting a little tired of all this proper-courtship routine. When do you plan to drag me off to a cave and have your way with me?"

He told her with his kiss. Tonight. Such longing, such promise of the night to come, was concentrated in their kissing. She felt as though she were pouring herself through her mouth into his. She held nothing back now and would hold nothing back when they returned here later in the evening to make love. Maybe he would spend the night. She would like that—waking in the morning with him at her side.

Her weariness left her like smoke on the wind. Her whole body was filled with anticipation. It was tempting to make love now, not to wait. But by unspoken agreement the decision was made to wait. Their meal, their conversation, their wine—all would be a prelude to love-making. It was to be a special evening. Elaine's heart rejoiced. She put all thoughts of the future from her mind and vowed to live just for tonight.

Arm in arm they walked to Nathan's car. And soon they were heading west, out Kansas Boulevard. Elaine became suspicious when Nathan turned onto Riverview.

Her heart sank when he turned down Weatherford Drive.

"No, Nathan," she implored, putting her hand on his arm. "I'm not ready for your house yet."

"You won't ever be," Nathan said, pulling her close and stroking her hair. "Let's get it over with. Let's bury Marilyn's ghost and get on with our lives. Besides," he said, holding her away so he could look at her face, "*I* am the chef for the evening. You are about to be the first victim of my new cooking career."

"Oh, Nathan, I don't know..." Elaine said, regarding the formidable house and desperately searching her mind for a good excuse to avoid entering it. "I don't belong in there."

"Nonsense. It's my house and I've invited you. Now don't be such a ninny. I wouldn't think of letting my afternoon in the kitchen trying to bake a cake go unappreciated. And besides, there won't be a soul around except you and me. What's to be afraid of?"

The marble-floored entry hall was two stories high, with an elegant stairway curving around the most beautiful crystal chandelier Elaine had ever seen. Just the entry hall was bigger than Elaine's entire apartment.

There *was* another soul in the house. The housekeeper was bustling about the kitchen in a blue uniform covered by a crisp white apron. "Oh, Mr. Stewart," she said, "I decided to set the table before I left. I used Mrs. Stewart's luncheon Spode, since you're just having omelets. I opened the wine so it could breathe, and the French bread is buttered and warming in the oven. Are you sure you don't want me to stay and prepare the omelets for you and your guest? And what about a tossed salad?"

The woman eyed Elaine over Nathan's shoulder. Elaine realized her faded warm-ups were being scrutinized. Her expression asked very clearly what sort of woman came to dinner at the Stewart mansion in warm-ups?

"I appreciate your wanting to help, Mrs. Murphy," Nathan said firmly, "but as I explained to you, *I* would like to prepare the meal myself. Good evening."

They watched in silence as Mrs. Murphy went to the pantry, retrieved her sensible brown coat and put it on.

"You're sure" she began, trying one last time to stay in command of her kitchen.

"*Good night*, Mrs. Murphy," Nathan said.

He installed Elaine on a kitchen stool, poured her a glass of wine and began his preparations. "No, I don't want you to help," he said before she had a chance to ask. "I had a trial run this afternoon," he confessed. "I went through a dozen eggs before I finally got something that remotely resembled the picture in the cookbook. Mrs. Murphy was frantic before I got out of here. She's very proprietary about her kitchen. I'm making a chutney omelet. I had one once in New Orleans and remember how really tasty it was."

Elaine watched Nathan bustle around. He was thoroughly enjoying himself with his newfound pastime. Never cooked a meal before! Incredible, Elaine thought. Absolutely incredible—as was this kitchen. One could cook for an army in here with the array of utensils hanging from the ceiling, the huge walk-in pantry, the biggest refrigerator she had ever seen. But at least it was a kitchen. She felt more comfortable there than she would be in the other rooms of this overwhelming house.

Mrs. Murphy had laid a lovely table, complete with a bouquet of daffodils and candles in brass holders. So this is an informal setting, Elaine thought, wondering what in the world the housekeeper's version of a formal one would look like.

Elaine helped Nathan carry the food into the elegant dining room, with its silk wall covering, crystal sconces and antique mahogany furniture. The table was resplendent with crystal goblets, ornate silverware and expensive china.

Nathan moved her place setting from the length of the large table to his end of the table. Elaine wondered if he wanted to be close to her or if it bothered him for her to be sitting in the place his wife formerly occupied.

She ate as much of the meal as she could. Strange how the salad and the bread and the omelet all shared the same tastelessness. What she did manage to eat revealed a pattern of dainty bluebells on the cream-colored china—"Mrs. Stewart's luncheon Spode."

Chapter Eight

After dinner, Nathan gave Elaine a tour of his home. She learned that the house was more than eighty years old and was one of the first homes built in the area called Osage Hills, which covered a series of small bluffs that overlooked eastern Missouri's meandering Missouri River. Marilyn Stewart had inherited the house from an aunt. Marilyn herself had grown up two blocks east of Weatherford Drive in a house that her brother Jonathan now owned. And Nathan's parents also owned property nearby until they retired and moved to southern California.

Nathan told Elaine that he and Marilyn had moved into the house shortly after their marriage; over the next several years Marilyn had devoted herself to renovating and redecorating the stately mansion.

Elaine was especially taken with Marilyn's garden room, which had been built on the back of the house. Even at night, it was an enchanted room, with walls formed of clear glass interspersed with panels of jewel-toned leaded glass. The room was filled with a profusion of tropical plants—some bearing exotic blossoms—and furnished with dainty white furniture made of filigreed wrought iron. At the room's center was a small rock-lined fish pond with a tinkling fountain.

"It's a work of art," Elaine said as she looked in wonder around the unusual room. "I've never seen anything quite like it."

"Neither have I," Nathan admitted. "Marilyn designed it and had it built. It's quite remarkable the way she used the leaded-glass panels as part of the glass walls. She salvaged most of the panels from an old church that was torn down over in West Plains. Nighttime really doesn't do the room justice. Wait until you see it in the sunlight."

Once again, Elaine stood in awe of the incredible Marilyn Miles Stewart. Was there no end to the woman's accomplishments? As Elaine took in each detail of the wondrous room, she almost wished she could find some fault with it. But there was none. The room was exquisite.

"Who has the green thumb?" Elaine asked. "It must be quite a job to take care of all these plants."

"I have a gardener," Nathan said, "and a plant service that rotates the house plants."

"You must be very proud to live in such a house," Elaine said sincerely.

"Yes, I suppose," Nathan said without a great deal of conviction. "It is spectacular but awfully big and lonely for one person—and terribly expensive to keep up. A house like this is a real financial drain and probably should be inhabited only by the truly wealthy, which I'm not. We never could have managed at all if Marilyn hadn't poured the money she inherited from her parents into the house. It gave her pleasure to entertain here and she entertained so well. Rebecca's a lot like her mother in that regard. She had her engagement party here in the house and handled it beautifully. Her wedding will be here, too—right here in the garden room, as a matter of fact. She and her mother decided on that years ago while Rebecca was still a little girl.''

Elaine took one last look at the impressive room before following Nathan through French doors into the formal living room. She couldn't imagine a more beautiful setting for a wedding and could see why Rebecca had dreamed since girlhood of having hers in the garden room. Elaine herself had dreamed of a beautiful wedding when she was a little girl but soon had given up such youthful dreams. She wasn't very old when she realized her wedding probably would be a more spartan affair. Most likely, she'd put on her current best dress when the time came and go with her intended to a justice of the peace's office.

''Where do you go to relax?'' Elaine said, suppressing the urge to whisper as she was led around the imposing formal living room with its brocade-covered settees and ornate Hepplewhite chairs.

''Either upstairs in my bedroom or in here,'' Nathan said, escorting her to his study.

The study was not so formidable as the rest of the downstairs. With wall-to-wall books and leather-covered wing chairs, it looked like a place in which one might read the evening paper or have an after-dinner brandy.

Nathan opened two sliding panels that hid a mirrored bar. He poured brandy in two sparkling snifters, but instead of drinking in the study, he insisted on going upstairs. ''I've dreamed too long of having a brandy with you on the sofa in front of my bedroom fireplace. I certainly don't plan to let the opportunity go by now that I actually have you under my roof.''

Elaine followed him across the marble-floored entry hall and up the grand staircase with its mahogany banister and balustrade that wrapped itself around the curving wall. A magnificent crystal chandelier hung down the center of the oval hall.

Their footsteps were muffled by the thickest carpet Elaine had ever walked on. At the top of the stairs was a grandfather clock that stood at least seven feet tall and sounded the hour with a magnificent echoing chime. As they walked down the long upper hallway, Elaine avoided looking at the gallery of family pictures and instead peered in a series of bedrooms that looked as if they belonged in *Gone with the Wind*.

Such a house! Elaine recognized that Marilyn Stewart had done an incredible job decorating the house. Signs of her impeccable taste were evident at every turn. Elaine could not imagine a more beautiful place in which to live. Such care and money had been lavished on the old mansion in order to restore it to its turn-of-the-century elegance. The artwork, the antiques, the stained-glass windows, the Persian rugs, the ornately carved woodwork, all had an air of authenticity. Elaine felt as if the rooms should be cordoned off and viewed from the doorway over velvet ropes.

Nathan's bedroom was handsome but less ornate and less imposing than the other bedrooms. Some of the furniture was even contemporary. Elaine wondered if the room had always looked this way. Somehow it didn't match the rest of the house. Had Nathan changed it after his wife died, or had the decor of their shared bedroom been formulated by Marilyn Stewart's concern for her husband's comfort?

The room looked as though someone actually spent time there. Magazines filled a brass stand. The sofa looked as if it were designed for sitting rather than perching. The king-sized bed was covered with a green comforter and backrest pillows. And the fireplace lent an almost cozy look to the room in spite of its high ceilings, corniced draperies and heavy woodwork.

Nathan placed the brandy snifters on a glass-topped coffee table in front of the sofa. A fire had been laid, and in short order Nathan had it lit and burning brightly.

The fire was nice. The brandy was mellowing. The man beside her was special beyond belief. Elaine realized she was supposed to be enjoying a prelude to lovemaking. She knew Nathan wanted her to join him soon in the large bed. He told her how he had lain there night after night, thinking of her, wanting her there with him. And she herself had longed for him, too. Sometimes when Elaine recalled their time of lovemaking in her own bed that incredible morning when he came to her, her knees would go weak with the intensity of that memory. She would have to pause and close her eyes in order to regain control. The early-morning hours were when it was the worst, when her desire for Nathan became a raw, agonizing need.

But along with the need there was also dread. Elaine knew that when they resumed their physical relationship, she would never be able to reclaim her life. Perhaps it was too late already to find any sort of peace or happiness or fulfillment in the future if and when Nathan left her.

She realized, however, that such thoughts were academic. She would never resist him. Elaine had known that when the time was right, she would give herself over to him totally. She was incapable of another response.

And even now, in the house of his beloved, saintly wife, the feel of his arm across her back poured a myriad of sensations throughout her body. That aching need that had become a part of her since meeting Nathan began multiplying and intensifying. Her impatient body knew that fulfillment was close at hand. She felt its opening. Her body was ready, waiting, demanding.

Elaine understood why Nathan had been insistent on bringing her here, why he wanted to make love to her here. He wanted to prove to her that the memory of his dead wife would not be an obstacle to their love. He needed to do that for her, and Elaine was touched.

But it seemed the memory of his dead wife was more of a problem for her than it was for him. Elaine was in awe of the woman, of her home, of her accomplishments, of the high regard in which she was held by her family and friends and community, of her elegance and breeding, of her education and wealth. Elaine knew that in so many ways she herself paled in comparison to such a woman. If she should marry Nathan, she would always be ''the woman Nathan married after his wife died.'' She would never be accepted into his world. She would always be remembered as the girl who had exercised on television. People would shake their heads over her—and remember what a fine woman Marilyn had been.

And Elaine knew that this house—this incredible museum of a house—could never feel like home to her. She would always be an interloper here, she thought as she looked around the handsome bedroom. Always.

Her gaze stopped at one of the bedside tables. She stared at it for a minute, pondering. The matching table on the other side of the bed was populated with a lamp, a clock and a stack of books, making its mate look strangely empty with only a lamp on its polished surface. Elaine knew why. The empty table must be where

Nathan kept his wife's picture. He had put it away in anticipation of Elaine's visit to this room.

She could almost feel the look of puzzlement on Nathan's face as she wordlessly rose from his arms and went to the empty table. The picture was face up in the drawer.

So that was what she looked like, Elaine thought.

She picked up the colored picture in its heavy brass frame and for a long minute stood there staring at it, mesmerized by the patrician forehead, the delicate features, the softly curling blond hair, and the wide-set, intelligent eyes of Nathan's dead wife.

Elaine hadn't realized Nathan was standing beside her until he gently took the picture from her hands, returned it to the drawer and turned her to face him. "Don't do this to yourself, Elaine. Marilyn was a fine woman, but she's dead. You're alive. You're here with me, and more than anything else in the world, I want to hold you and love you and make you know how glad I am to have you in my life."

He brushed her hair back from her forehead, then softly traced the features of her face. "So lovely," he said as to himself, "and so very dear. I don't know if it helps any, but the bed is new. I bought it last week. It's *our* bed."

What a shame she was not wearing velvet robes for him to remove rather than utilitarian warm-ups, Elaine thought, as Nathan—with great ceremony, as though she were a princess or a high priestess—slid her clothes from her body.

"You're too thin," he said as he held her nude body to his still-clothed one. "I knew you were losing weight, but I refused to think it was significant. Is it because of me? I'm putting you through hell."

With such tenderness, he made love to her. Elaine wondered if it were possible to die of tenderness. He treated her with reverence, as though she were an object of worship. No part of her body was left untouched—or unloved.

Elaine knew that at another time their lovemaking would take on a different complexion, that she would take a different role, but on this night nothing was required of her but that she allow him to love her. She closed her mind to their problems and opened her body to him. She thrilled to his kisses, to his touch, to his ministrations, all the while thinking that no other man could be for her what Nathan was. Ever. It was as if her body had been waiting for this one man to awaken it. It was because she loved him—totally. Her skin loved him. Her fingers loved him. Her breasts, her lips, her tongue.

Afterward, however, with their warm, moist bodies entwined, Elaine closed her eyes and saw the face in that picture. Nathan had put it back in the nightstand, but Elaine could *feel* its presence emanating from the drawer like an invisible force field.

Go away, her thought cried out, addressing the presence. *Leave me alone. Please, leave me alone.*

How long after she left would the picture be reinstated to its place on the table? How did one compete with a dead woman?

That love could hurt so much had come as a great shock to Elaine. She had not known.

ELAINE AWOKE to Nathan's gentle shaking. "Hey, sleepyhead, it's morning," he said. "Time to eat."

She opened her eyes to the morning and to Nathan's form, silhouetted against the window, holding a large tray. It seemed she was to have breakfast in bed.

"Oh, my," she said in wonder. "And I'm not even sick. I feel like a princess."

"You are a princess. I hereby apply to be your consort. I'd like to spoil you and wait on you and bring smiles to that lovely face."

He put the tray down on the nightstand, then sat down on the bed beside her and took her hand. "Come live with me, Elaine. Share my bed every night. I want you here with me."

Her vision blurred as her eyes filled with tears. How could she tell him? How could she make him understand?

"Men in your position don't do things like that, Nathan—live with women. You're a public figure. You're running for a political office and will be held up for public scrutiny at all times. And think of your family, of the embarrassment it would cause them."

"Elaine, don't be a prude," he said between the kisses he was planting in her palm. "People live together all the time these days."

"Not men running for public office," she said, pulling her hand away. "You know that, Nathan. You're just full of wonder right now. Your heart is ruling your head. Let's just enjoy each other for the time being. I don't think you're ready for any permanent or semipermanent arrangements. Right?"

Nathan got up and walked across the room. He stood with his back to her, looking out the front window of his magnificent house—out at the other magnificent houses in this neighborhood of Heritage's rich and powerful. Elaine was right, he thought. Bringing her here to live with him would be frowned upon in the neighborhood. Jonathan and his other political associates would have a fit. Rebecca once again would be humiliated.

And while Nathan found himself not really caring what some other people thought, he did not want to embarrass his daughter. He also realized he had a certain obligation to Jonathan and the others who were supporting him in this political race. But most of all, he dreaded the embarrassment that Elaine would be subjected to if she came here to live. Even Mrs. Murphy, out of the sense of loyalty she felt for her dead mistress, would do her best to make Elaine uncomfortable. Just now, when the housekeeper had fixed him a breakfast tray for two, she had done so with a disapproving scowl and pursed lips for a woman had spent the night in "Mrs. Stewart's bedroom." While Nathan could admire the woman's loyalty, he realized servants could sometimes be the worst snobs of all.

Of course, he could fire Mrs. Murphy, who had worked for him ever since the day he and Marilyn brought one-week-old Rebecca home from the hospital. And he could say to hell with his daughter and to his friends of long standing. He could alienate himself from his peers. But he could not eliminate the discomfort that would certainly be Elaine's.

There was another option, however. Marriage. But would that really change things? Perhaps undercurrents of unacceptance would always be there. What if Elaine would always be made to feel like an outsider in his world? For the first time, he fully realized how miserable he could make Elaine. It frightened him. When two people fell in love, it was supposed to make them happy, not mess up their lives. What about love conquering all? Was that just a romantic myth?

He turned back to her and drank in the sight of her in his bed. He desperately wanted her to be there again tonight and tomorrow night—for all of his nights. She was so very precious to him. Elaine had returned a sense of anticipation to his life. She overwhelmed him with her sensitivity and her caring and her beauty.

She made him feel brand-new.

"All that beauty, and wise, too," Nathan said reluctantly as he picked up the breakfast tray from the table and placed it on the bed beside her. "But I'm just putting the issue on the shelf for the time being. I want you here with me, and I refuse to believe there aren't solutions. I'm a lawyer, remember. A lawyer's job is to find solutions."

ELAINE WAS GOING TO NEED her car later in the day, so Nathan dropped her by her apartment to pick it up instead of taking her straight to the Fitness Center. "I'll be in late this afternoon for my workout," Nathan said. "I have a political meeting later tonight, but I'd like to have dinner with you first."

"Fine," Elaine agreed. "Let's just get some carry-out Chinese and take it to my place."

She clung to him before taking her leave. How wonderfully clean and manly he smelled. How good the solid bulk of him felt in her arms. Oh, how she loved him. Would times of parting always be this difficult for her? Even though she would be seeing him again this same day, she felt that a piece of her was being pulled out of her middle. It was a physically difficult thing to do—to let go of him and force herself to get out of his car. But the day awaited her.

When she opened the car door, her purse rolled out into the gutter. It was unzipped, and several items poured out.

Elaine shook her head. "You'd think I'd learn," she muttered.

"At least there were no marbles," Nathan kidded. "Need any help?"

Elaine shook her head, blew him a kiss and watched him pull away before she reclaimed her possessions from the gutter and hoped the rest of her day went better than it had so far. First Nathan's offer for her to live in the family shrine and then dumping her purse in the street.

The rest of the day was also filled with problems.

For starters, the custodian hadn't shown up. The building was still dark, and the air conditioners had not been started, making the building hot and stuffy. The floors had not been swept. The bathrooms needed cleaning.

"I'm a gold-medal-winning gymnast," Mark protested when she handed him a push broom.

"The floors or the bathrooms? Take your choice," Elaine said.

Mark quickly grabbed for the broom. "And I don't do windows, either," he said. "Now tell me, how does this thing work? Which is the front and which is the back? Do you push or pull?"

Leaving Mark to his sweeping, Elaine rolled up her sleeves and tackled the bathrooms.

She was calling the employment agency in search of a custodian when Mark informed her of a problem with one of the air-conditioning units. He couldn't get it to switch on, which meant cancellation of some of their classes. The warranty on the unit, Elaine soon discovered, covered parts but not labor. The estimate from the repairman was horrendous and wiped out any hope of profit for the week.

One of the patrons in her weight-loss class came in to complain. The woman insisted she hadn't missed an exercise session and had followed her prescribed diet religiously but had still not lost weight. While working at the new food bar, Elaine had observed the woman's bad eating habits firsthand but realized it would do no good to point out her dietary infractions to her. The woman seemed honestly to believe that she "ate like a bird." Elaine refunded her money and watched the woman leave in a huff, her fleshy bottom jiggling furiously in spite of her snug-fitting leotards.

After leading the morning classes, Elaine worked in her office, trying to juggle bills. It was the unforeseen expenses like the air conditioner and the increase in her liability insurance and the fine from the county health department over her serving meals without a food permit that left her account so empty.

Well, she had a permit now and was in food service in a bigger way than she had ever intended, and that brought a whole new set of headaches—health regulations, food storage, licensed food handlers. Her income on the food service was barely meeting her costs, but it was becoming such a popular feature of the Fitness Center that she dare not discontinue it.

She found herself thinking once again of the offer from American Fitness. She could sell out and be done with all the headaches. But then what? Work for that company and travel around the country? Or find another job here in Heritage? Start all over? Be the employee instead of the boss? Elaine knew that she might have to consider such a move. Selling her business, however, was not what she wanted. She would like to be able to make the Fitness Center a success. She believed in her concept, and she believed that the quality of people's lives was improved by better physical fitness. Her whole identity was wrapped up in the center and in the recognition it had brought her in the community. It was only when Nathan came into her life that she began to question the identity she had created for herself and wish she presented a more sophisticated image to the world. Before that, she had been rather proud of herself.

NATHAN INVITED his brother-in-law to lunch, but as usual, Jonathan claimed to be too busy to eat out and insisted Nathan join him in the plush dining room First Federal Bank provided for its high-level executives and their guests. On the top floor, it provided a breathtaking view of the city.

"You got my message about those League of Women Voters' candidate forums?" Jonathan asked as he seated his large bulk in the oversized chair that was kept at the corner table always reserved for the bank president's exclusive use.

Nathan nodded.

"Well, don't dismiss them just 'cause it's the ladies," Jonathan said with a wink. "They're holding one this week, and then they will hold another later in the campaign. There will be full media coverage both times. You'll need to have a prepared opening statement. And the boys and I can coach you a bit on suitable answers to the most likely questions. I understand Billingsly and the other candidates will also be there."

"I have nothing but admiration for the League of Women Voters and would never 'dismiss' any of their activities," Nathan said, not bothering to conceal his irritation. "And I believe I can manage to answer their questions without any coaching."

"Oh, I'm sure you can," the banker said with a nod of his large head. "It's just that this industrial-trust thing is quite sensitive right now, and it would be better if you talked around that a bit."

"The bill that was defeated at the last legislative session is public record," Nathan said. "And any bill introduced next session would also be. Just what is so sensitive?"

"People are just doing a lot of speculation about where an industrial park might be located if the bill passed this time around and the city was to qualify for industrial-trust funding. There are a lot of 'ifs' right now, and the less specific you are about the whole subject the better. You don't want to be held accountable for something that later turns out was not the best approach. Now I understand there's prime rib, Boston scrod or chicken salad on today's menu. What are you hungry for?"

The food was superb as always. And their table was visited throughout lunch by various bank executives who expressed their approval of Nathan's latest political decision and promised to back him in the upcoming primary. Nathan had the feeling that the little parade of vice-presidents and board members had been arranged, but most of their comments seemed sincere enough.

Finally, over coffee and sherbert, Nathan could broach the subject he wanted to discuss with his brother-in-law.

"How's the park project going?" Nathan asked. "I thought the committee would have selected the winning design for the fitness trail and made the award by now."

"Well, that's a rather delicate subject," Jonathan said, avoiding Nathan's eyes by paying careful attention to the stirring of his coffee.

"Delicate? What do you mean by that?" Nathan demanded. "It was obvious that Elaine Farrell's proposal was head and shoulders above the others. What's delicate about rewarding the most deserving design?"

"You're going out with her. Right?" Jonathan said between mouthfuls of sherbert.

Nathan nodded. "What does that have to do with anything?"

"If she receives that cash award, it will seem like the competition was fixed, like she got it because of her special relationship with you."

"Well, you're the chairman of the committee," Nathan said pointedly. "It'd be up to you to make sure everyone understood why she was getting the award—because her design was the best. She deserves that award, and she needs the cash. You do admit that her design is best, don't you?"

"It was an excellent proposal," Jonathan said, accepting a second dish of sherbet from the waiter. "I see no reason why we can't pay her a little something for her ideas and then incorporate them into the winning design."

Nathan threw up his hands in a disgusted gesture. "In other words, rip off her design but just see she doesn't get credit for it! I wouldn't allow that, Jonathan. I demand that you give her the credit and the money."

"Settle down, my friend, and listen to reason," Jonathan said in a voice Nathan found patronizing. "A lot of people would find it rather tasteless for your mistress's design to be chosen for the fitness trail being built in a park honoring your dead wife. If you were a private citizen, you would be perfectly justified saying to hell with those people, but you're not a private citizen. People will take note of the situation. Billingsly controls the *Herald*, and you know our local scandal sheet wouldn't pass up the opportunity to do a smear on you. Choosing Elaine Farrell's design would not be at all good for your campaign. It would embarrass your and Marilyn's children. And it would certainly embarrass Ms Farrell herself to have everyone thinking she got that award because she slept with the man who not only donated the money she won but who was married to the woman in whose honor the park was being built.''

"Look, Jonathan, I know how hard Elaine must have worked putting that proposal together. And it would mean so much to her professionally to get that award.''

"No, it wouldn't," Jonathan said firmly. "Not now. How could it help her professionally when it appears the reason the exercise girl won against all those professionals was because of her special relationship with you? Are you dense, man? How many more times do I have to explain it? Granted, it's unfair, but hell—that's life. Now the best plan is to make the award to someone else and do nothing to call attention to Elaine Farrell.''

Nathan felt physically ill. He pushed the dish of sherbet to one side and took a sip of water. Poor Elaine. He certainly hadn't done her any favors by getting involved in her life. None at all.

"And while we're on the subject of Ms Farrell," Jonathan continued, "I really wish you'd just see her privately and not keep parading her around in public. Even if she were an appropriate woman for you to be seen with—which she is not—you're offending a lot of folks who would have supported you because of Marilyn. Getting publicly involved with any woman erases the political asset you derive from having been married to my sister. Let's get you elected; then you can date—but not the Farrell woman. Hell, old man, it's all right to have a cutie on the side. But for God's sake, stop flaunting her. Rent a pretty little apartment and visit her there.''

"Jonathan, sometimes I wonder how a perfectly lovely woman like Marilyn could have grown up in the same family with someone as disgusting as you," Nathan said, fighting to keep his voice level. "You can take your advice and shove it. I will be seen in public with whomever I choose. And if you don't like it, get yourself another candidate.''

The portly banker leaned forward and grabbed Nathan's arm. His breath smelled of cigars and onions. ''Look here, Nathan Stewart, what's the point of running in a race if you don't win? And if you're going to win, you've got to give the voters their illusions. Why do you think Jackie Kennedy never smoked in public or FDR always got himself propped up in front of the podium for a speech rather than deliver it from a wheelchair? Sometimes we have to use little dishonesties to root out even greater ones. Now when you weigh getting Frank Billingsly out of the state senate with having to be a little discreet with your lady love for the next few months, which is more important?''

Chapter Nine

As Elaine led the Aerobics III dance students through their paces, she took pleasure in the contemporary beat of the music and in the sight of so many women in such fine physical condition. Many of the women had progressed markedly from a lower fitness classification in the months since Elaine had opened the Fitness Center.

Her star pupil was a fifty-year-old woman who had joined both the exercise program and the weight-loss program in the center's first week. Mildred Perkins had lost thirty-five pounds and progressed from the "special" class designed for people with minimal physical conditioning to a class for those with top physical conditioning who could withstand a full hour of vigorous exercise. Mildred even had led several of the classes on a fill-in basis, and Elaine very much wanted to ask her to join her staff as an instructor. What better testimonial to individuals no longer young that physical fitness was achievable than to have someone like Mildred as their instructor? However, with her present shoestring operation, Elaine couldn't possibly increase her payroll at this time.

"'Flashdance,'" Elaine called out, announcing the next routine. "Jog in place until the music starts."

When the music began, Elaine led the group through a routine that included dance steps and calisthenics. She had discovered that many people, especially her female patrons, enjoyed this form of exercise more than any other. It was lively and graceful, and the music made the task more fun. They found it more appealing than swimming laps, running or other forms of aerobic exercises that were intended primarily to condition the cardiovascular system but also offer improved vitality and muscle tone.

"You're looking good," she called out as the music ended. "Take your pulse. Next is 'Magie Lady,' the new routine I taught you last time. Start with samba forward four, pony back eight—then the skip sequence. Go through it with me. Keep moving! Keep those hearts pumping!"

As she quickly went through the steps of the new number, Mark and a slender young woman in a smart-looking hot-pink suit and high-heeled sandals came in the back door and took a seat on the small bleacher along the side wall, apparently to observe the class. Mark was pointing out features of the gym to his companion, and Elaine at first thought the woman was a prospective patron.

But as she worked the class through the vigorous routine that included repeated jumping jacks and high kicks, Elaine realized that Mark and the well-dressed woman were not strangers to each other. Mark's behavior to the woman was more animated than usual, and he kept touching her arm as he talked to her.

Why, he's coming on to her, Elaine realized, and she's tall! She wondered if the woman could possibly be the love-at-first-sight dream girl he had been mooning about a couple of weeks ago.

When the class ended, Elaine grabbed a towel to wipe the perspiration from her forehead and headed to the back of the gym. Mark and the woman rose to meet her.

In her high-heeled shoes, Mark's attractive companion was almost a head taller than he was. But there was no mistaking the adoration in his eyes—and in hers. They held hands while Mark made introductions.

"Elaine, I'd like you to meet Millie Martin. Millie, this is my boss, Elaine Farrell."

Elaine tried to act normal, but all the while she was thinking, *I just don't believe this—Mark and a tall woman!*

The two women shook hands while Mark launched into a rapid history of Millie, who was a model with a local agency and had once been a highschool gymnast and could still do flips like a champion. Millie clung to his hand and looked down at him with loving eyes and a shy, sweet smile while he said wonderful things about her.

"Well, I just wanted to show Millie the building and for you two to meet each other. Millie and I are going out to dinner now at the Candlelight Inn," Mark explained. Then, as though suddenly remembering his manners, he hastily added, "Do you have plans, Elaine? Would you like to join us?"

Elaine declined his invitation, realizing she was being invited out of politeness and that the two had an evening in mind more romantic than taking Mark's boss out to dinner.

She walked as far as her office with them, then watched them go arm in arm across the lobby. Elaine couldn't get over it. Mark, who was so self-conscious about his height that he had never dated a woman who wasn't at least two inches shorter than he was, now had fallen in love with a model who was several inches taller. Love seemed to have cured the biggest hang-up in his life.

She wished love could cure her hang-ups the way it had Mark's, Elaine thought as she unlocked her office door and sank into her desk chair. She loved Nathan so totally. When they were together, she was happy, and the world was wonderful and rosy. But when they were apart, the rosiness went away, and she saw things as they really were. There seemed no solution to the vast gulf that separated his life from hers. Nathan's position in the community, his political ambitions, his responsibility to his family, his background—all demanded a different sort of woman than Elaine to share it with. It seemed to her she had two choices: to try to become the woman Nathan needed or to give up any hope of sharing a life with him. And if she did try to change, to become a more acceptable sort of companion for Judge Nathan Stewart, Elaine had no guarantee it would make any difference. Maybe she could never make herself acceptable. Her father was fond of saying you can't make a silk purse out of a sow's ear. But even if she did manage such a feat, Elaine had no notion of whether Nathan wanted her in his future. Maybe she was simply a present-day diversion.

Once again, she thought of the offer from American Fitness to buy her business. Should she give up everything for which she had worked so hard and revamp her life? Would it make any difference? Elaine feared that no matter how much she changed, she always would be a misfit in Nathan's world. Just as Mark had ultimately to accept that he was short and there was nothing he could do about it, maybe it was time she accepted once and for all that she was the product of a blue-collar home and someone who would never fit in with the folks on Weatherford Drive. She really wouldn't even want to—

except for Nathan. But living the rest of her life without him was too grim even to think about.

Her thoughts went around and around. Elaine felt as if she were riding a perpetual merry-go-round. She went crazy thinking about her relationship with Nathan and trying to find some sort of solution that would allow her to continue being with him and sharing her love with him.

The only solution, however, that seemed to present itself with any frequency was an impermanent one. She could continue to have an affair with Nathan until he realized that it was not the way he wanted to conduct his life. Of course, there was the possibility that having an affair was all Nathan had ever wanted of her. After all, that first morning he had said he could make no promises. And he had made none since then. He had not spoken of love or of marriage. Elaine was certain that Nathan cared for her with a great intensity, that he needed her physically, that he enjoyed her company, that she was very special to him. But did he even consider her when he thought of the future?

In fact, if she believed what his brother-in-law had so earnestly told her just the night before, Nathan's relationship with her could well be ruining his future.

The heavyset banker had come to the Fitness Center and spelled this out for Elaine pretty graphically. In between puffs of a huge cigar, Jonathan Miles told her what other people were saying—how no one could understand why any man who had been married to Marilyn Miles Stewart now could be involved with an "uneducated little tramp."

"Of course, I know you're not a tramp," Jonathan assured her in an oversympathetic tone Elaine found patronizing, "but people can be cruel. And tell me, Ms Farrell, can you honestly see yourself as Mrs. Nathan

Stewart? Can you see yourself giving teas for the society matrons? Can you see yourself chairing committees and hostessing important social functions? Can you be the kind of woman who always knows just what to wear, how to act, what to say? Just think of Nathan's first wife, my beloved sister, Marilyn. She was a born lady, and she was raised for that sort of life. Her life-style complemented Nathan's in every facet. In Marilyn's way, she was just as respected in this community as he was and just as well-known. Her picture and stories of her projects and social activities appeared with great regularity in the local newspapers, and she was out and about the community so much with her clubs and committee meetings and philanthropic projects. Do you want people always to be comparing you to her?''

Elaine heard the man through, then said coldly, ''How charitable of you to acknowledge that I'm not a tramp. Please forgive me if I don't seem suitably grateful for your kindness. Now, I want you and your cigar to get out of my establishment. And don't ever come back—unless it's to sign up for a fitness class.''

She had been more angry than hurt at the time. How dare he come here and say things like that to her and then ask her not to tell Nathan about his visit! But now as Elaine thought over his words, tears filled her eyes, and anguish pushed painfully against the walls of her chest. Nathan had never discussed the future with her. For them, it did not exist. Nathan obviously knew that. Maybe it was time she accepted it, too. But oh, how it hurt. It was more than she could bear. Just to think of a life without Nathan brought a horrible aching heaviness to her chest and painful constrictions to her throat.

Elaine fought against the pain the only way she knew how—with work. She pulled out the work schedules for her staff and attempted to make some sense out of them. She needed to discover a way she and her meager staff could get through another week. But she couldn't think about anything except Nathan. If only he would call. The sound of his voice would reassure her. She would know that at least for another day he was still hers.

She shuffled the papers around listlessly, knowing that the schedules had to be done before tomorrow evening. Maybe she could do them after dinner. Dinner? She didn't want to eat. She wasn't hungry. She wasn't anything except in love.

Elaine found herself wishing she had another exercice class to lead. Physical exertion was the only thing that promised any relief from her tortured thoughts, but no other classes were scheduled. She was free for the rest of the evening. She reached for the phone to call her mother. At least she could go to see her family, she decided. But there was no answer.

Tim must have a ball game tonight, Elaine thought as she replaced the phone in its cradle. *Now what,* she wondered, staring down at her messy desktop.

It was several seconds before she realized someone was standing in the door to her office. When she raised her gaze to her visitor's face, she drew in her breath sharply.

In spite of his tattered attire, Elaine knew immediately who he was. The shape of his head, the wide-spaced green eyes, the square jaw and the full, well-formed mouth were his father's. The young man was Nathan's son.

"I know. Don't tell me. I've heard it all my life. I look just like my dad," the young man said with an endearing, somewhat crooked smile. "Robert Miles Stewart at your service. My friends call me Robby."

The young man's courtly bow seemed incongruous with his ancient, patched blue jeans, a lumberjack plaid shirt that looked as if it had survived a couple of generations of wear and dusty cowboy boots that looked as though they had never been subjected to a coat of polish. He held a sweat-stained cowboy hat in his hands.

"How do you do, Robby Stewart?" Elaine extended her hand and received a warm handshake in return. "What can I do for you?" she asked.

"Oh, just satisfy my curiosity, I guess," he said, lowering his lanky frame into the chair facing Elaine's desk. "My sister has been after me to help her 'do something' about Dad. I'm home from college for the summer, so I thought I'd mosey on over to meet 'the problem.' But you are hardly what I expected."

Elaine liked him. She dared to ask, "And just what did you expect, if you don't mind me asking?"

"A scarlet woman. That's what I was expecting to find. You should be wearing red sequins and have long red fingernails and false eyelashes out to here," Robby said, kiddingly indicating an outrageous distance from his own eyelashes. "And here I find your basic wholesome-looking, downright pretty miss in athletic warmups. She seems a little young for my old man, but then, I've known him all my life, and maybe he doesn't seem so old to you as he does to me."

"But I'm sure your sister has told you all of my shortcomings," Elaine said. "And I don't say that sarcastically, either. She has a case, Robby. I hardly fit into your father's life-style and family. In fact, the *problem* is trying to find the courage to bow out of the picture gracefully and save everyone further embarrassment."

Robby seemed to be pondering her statement for a minute, then abruptly asked, "I wonder if you'd allow the black sheep of the Stewart family to escort you to dinner. I understand Dad's got a meeting tonight with Uncle Jonathan and his cohorts, so you won't be spending time with him, and I know a little truck stop out on the highway that serves the best chicken-fried steak with creamy gravy in the whole state—unless of course you'd rather go for something a little more uptown and gourmet.''

"You'll excuse me if I look a gift dinner in the mouth, but why are you asking me out?'' Elaine wanted to know. "If you want to tell me all the reasons why I shouln't be going out with your father, I already know them—and some I'm sure you never thought of. I don't need to be taken out to dinner to be instructed about those things."

Robby held up a hand in protest. "Hey, I just want to get to know the nice lady. I haven't let my sister pick my friends since kindergarten, and my dad told me he admires you very much. And you look like you could use some country cooking to me."

She was unsure. Robby Stewart seemed appealingly nonthreatening. But Elaine was so tired and emotionally strung out. Why should she inflict upon herself the stress of spending the evening with one of Nathan's children?

"Come on, Elaine," Robby said, flashing another one of his crooked grins. "I don't cuss or chew around ladies. I take off my hat indoors just like my mother taught me. And some folks think I'm pretty fair company."

"Are you sure you grew up on Weatherford Drive?" Elaine asked with a disbelieving shake of her head.

"Thanks for asking," he said. "Lord knows I've tried my best to live it down. Now, what about dinner?"

Elaine felt a smile of acceptance tugging at her lips. Nathan had joked affectionately to her about his "country and western" son, but Elaine had not realized

Robby Stewart would be so completely the opposite of his sister. He was like a young Willie Nelson—unconventional, outspoken and altogether charming.

Elaine told Mark she was leaving and was soon heading down the road in Robby's muddy pickup truck. When Elaine commented on his vehicle, he said with a chuckle, "I have a 'respectable car,' but I like to drive the truck when I know my sister's going to be around. It irritates the hell out of her for me to park the truck in front of the house. I drove through a few puddles yesterday on purpose just to make sure it was good and dirty. And did you notice the coon tail on the radio antenna? She'll flip over that. I can just hear her now—'Robert, *really...*'"

"You and your sister don't get along very well, I take it," Elaine commented.

"We have our differences, to be sure," Robby admitted. "She has her good points, but I fear Rebecca is a snob. And she is about to marry a snob. And I suppose they will raise a couple of little snobby children. If I didn't look so much like my father, I'd swear I didn't have any of that blue blood running in my veins, that I was a foundling they took in or got mixed up with some other kid at the hospital. I think, somehow, the silver spoon I was born with was tarnished. Lord knows, my dear mother tried to make me straighten up and fly right."

Robby was silent a minute, and when he continued, his flippant tone was gone, replaced by a more serious one. "I used to worry a lot about how I disappointed her. I wouldn't go to the little dances and tea parties she organized for us kids. I played in the band instead of the junior symphony. I played football and baseball instead of golf and tennis. I got myself kicked out of private school so I could go to public. Then when I got older, I did uncouth things like drink beer and go to a state university instead of to a more elite institution of higher learning. But Mother and I had really started to work things out. Of course, she still wished I'd fall in love with a debutante and rejoin the fold, but she was beginning to stand back and look at things from my perspective. That park she wanted built on the east side was a concession in a way to my point of view. It was her way of letting me know she also realized there was a world outside of Weatherford Drive, that there are people in the world who have never been to the symphony and didn't play tennis or bridge or golf. I admired her for it. I think she was entering a transition period in her life. Oh, I don't think she ever would have given up society but I think she would have added some genuinely worthy causes to her lists of charities.''

"You miss her very much, don't you?'' Elaine asked softly.

"Yeah,'' he said. "I really do. My mother put up with a lot from me, but I never once doubted that she loved me—very much. I try not to be bitter about her death, but I really resent not getting to have an adult relationship with her. I think we were both beginning to figure out that we were good for each other, that we helped each other strike some sort of a balance in our lives.''

Elaine watched as Robby unashamedly wiped tears from the corners of his eyes.

"Oh, I think the balance will stay with you,'' she offered, realizing with a pang of jealousy that she had to add "good mother'' to Marilyn Stewart's growing list of accomplishments. "Your mother may be dead, but you're still her son and always will be.''

"You may be right," Robby said thoughtfully as he pulled his truck onto the Interstate. "She wanted me to go to law school—all the men in her family had been attorneys. And now, despite all my earlier protestations to the contrary, I've decided to go to law school when I finish my undergraduate degree and become an attorney, after all—not to enter the family firm, however. I'd like to be a country attorney out in a small town, or if I stay in Heritage, work for Legal Aid and do lawyering for the everyday folk instead of just one who can afford to pay large retainers. Dad did the Legal Aid bit for a while, you know."

"No, I didn't."

"Yeah, it was considered an appropriate way for young attorneys to get experience and fulfill their *noblesse oblige*!" Robby said as he sped in and out of the heavy rush-hour traffic. "He didn't enter the law firm started by the grandfathers until he'd been out of law school a few years. First he did Legal Aid, then he started getting heavily into tax work. He's now considered quite an authority on corporate taxes, but I think he always kind of missed general law and the drama of the courtroom. I think one of the reasons he was willing to run for municipal judge was to get himself back in the courtroom and be involved more with mainstream law."

"If he likes courtroom work, why doesn't he just change the nature of his practice?" Elaine wondered.

"I guess it's not that easy. You get a lot of clients who depend on you. You get a family and a big house and a certain life-style that requires a big income. I think I'll opt out of the big-house scene and the uptown life-style myself. Leave that sort of stuff for my sister," he said as he parked his pickup among the rigs in front of Fred's Truck Stop and Cafe. "Now, soon as we get inside, I want to hear about what sort of life-style you're going to opt for."

The cafe was a study in red-and-white checks; the tablecloths, the napkins, the curtains and the waitresses' aprons were all made of red-and-white checkered cloth. An old-fashioned jukebox was playing a Wayland Jennings tune. The drivers of the trucks parked outside sat on stools in front of the counter. Elaine and Robby sat at one of the tables.

Elaine followed Robby's lead and ordered the chicken-fried steak, which was listed as the specialty of the house, and a beer.

"That's what I like," Robby said with approval. "A beer-drinkin' woman. How did my father get so lucky?"

"Oh, Robby, you and I both know that what your father needs is a sherry-drinking lady. It seems to me the best thing I could do for him is go away. I'm just complicating his life at a time when he needs to concentrate on other things. I had a visit the other night from your Uncle Jonathan, and he spelled it out to me pretty clearly just what people are saying about your father and me and just how much our relationship is damaging Nathan's chances in the upcoming race."

Robby let out a low whistle. "Uncle Jonathan! You poor kid. Does Dad know that pompous old fool has been bothering you?"

"Oh, good heavens, no," Elaine said, grabbing Robby's arm, "and don't you tell him, either. I don't want to cause more family problems than I already have. I'm sure your uncle was just doing what he thought best and that he had your father's best interest at heart."

"Don't be so sure," Robby said. "Men like Jonathan Miles only have one person's best interest at heart—their own. I couldn't believe it when I found out Dad had announced for the state senate race. Last time I talked to him about it, he indicated he'd done a lot of thinking since Mom died and decided politics wasn't his thing—that he would complete his term as municipal judge and then find some new direction in his life, maybe go back to general law instead of all that tax stuff. But Uncle Jonathan, I'm sure, put a real guilt trip on him. 'Who else can oust Billingsly?' 'The future of this community rests in your hands.' All that kind of stuff. No telling what he told Dad. And my father takes responsibility seriously. *Very* seriously. Unless I miss my bet, my uncle wants to make sure my father is elected to the state senate because in doing so Dad would neutralize a longstanding political enemy who happens to be the incumbent. And I wouldn't be surprised if there weren't another reason or two why Uncle Jonathan wants Dad elected that have nothing to do with what's best for Nathan Stewart."

"You sound like you don't quite trust your uncle," Elaine said.

"Maybe I don't," Robby admitted. "You see, I've had a couple of run-ins with Uncle Jonathan in the past, and I don't have as high an opinion of him as the rest of the family. He puts on his pious 'I'm just trying to do what is best for this family' posture, then tries to get a guy's mother to send him to military school so his behavior won't embarrass the family. Or he tries to get her to convince her son to quit going with a girl because her dad's been in prison and because it supposedly casts a shadow on the family's reputation. What is really going on is that Jonathan doesn't want *his* power position as the godfather of this community jeopardized or tarnished in any way by family members. You've got to understand, Elaine, that bankers like Jonathan Miles don't run for office themselves, but they often are the behind-the-scenes power brokers in many communities.''

Elaine waited for the waitress to place their beers on the table, then responded, ''I really don't know what sort of man your uncle is or in what spirit he offered me his advice, but he's right. I don't belong with your father.''

''My dad is crazy about you,'' Robby protested. ''He looks ten years younger and twice as happy as the last time I saw him. You're good for him, Elaine. I can't say the same for Jonathan Miles or political races or even my own sister. You know, when he first started telling me about you, I hoped he was going to say he had decided not to run for the senate and marry you instead. I thought maybe you would bring a change of direction to his life. I still hope you do.''

''Why's his changing directions so important to you?'' Elaine asked.

''Because I think he's earned the right to be happy. I think men like my father often get so tied down by doing what is expected of them that they don't leave any time in their lives for themselves. He's paid his dues. You know, he told me when he's walking beside you, he feels like skipping—that he even has skipped a few steps on an occasion or two. Well, I want you to keep my father skipping, Elaine Farrell. I think he needs you a hell of lot more than he needs political races and corporate law.''

''But political races and corporate law are his life,'' Elaine protested. ''They represent who and what he is. So I make him feel frivolous and happy sometimes. But he would soon resent me if I kept him from his life's calling. Your father is infatuated with me right now. But I think that in his heart of hearts he knows it's not a long-term arrangement. We just spend time together, Robert.

I hope I've given him some happy times, but no mention has ever been made of the future."

Elaine couldn't stop the tears from filling her eyes. She searched her purse for a tissue and finally gave up and dabbed her eyes with a checkered napkin.

"It's no infatuation for you, is it?" Robby asked gently.

Elaine shook her head no. She didn't trust herself to speak.

"Drink your beer, honey," he instructed. "You need it."

Robby raised his glass to her. "Here's to Elaine, who's more of a lady than any woman I know."

ELAINE DROVE aimlessly about after Robert dropped her off at her car, not realizing she was heading for Weatherford Drive until she turned down the street. She went around the block twice before she pulled into the circular driveway. She didn't park in front of the imposing house. Instead, she pulled into the service area behind the house.

The house was dark. Neither Nathan's Mercedes nor Rebecca's red sports car were parked in the driveway. But she rang the doorbell, anyway, before using the key Nathan had insisted she keep with her but which Elaine was certain she would never use.

She wandered through the elegant home, sitting first in one room, then the other, as though trying them on for size. She tried to picture herself graciously greeting people in the grand entry hall, overseeing a gathering in the large living room, directing people to their seats in the dining room, pouring after-dinner coffee in the study from the ornate sterling-silver coffee service. "One lump or two? Or would you rather have sherry?" She tried to imagine working with the formidable Mrs. Murphy in the stainless-steel kitchen and instructing the gardener to prune the roses.

Would there be any space in this house that would be just for her, any corner that would feel like home to her? Elaine searched for it.

She ascended the curving staircase, her hand trailing on the satiny-smooth wood of the banister where the hands of three generations of Marilyn Stewart's family had trailed. She could almost sense the pride Marilyn Stewart must have taken in being the mistress of such a house. Elaine's own life had been lived in a succession of rented houses and apartments. It was hard for her to imagine the permanence and feeling of belonging such a house must have provided its occupants.

There were many generations represented among the family portraits lining the hallway. Oil portraits of men and women of wealth and breeding stared down at her from brocaded walls.

One area of the hallway had been set aside for framed awards and citations—some honoring Marilyn and some Nathan—from civic clubs, their respective alma maters, churches, museums, hospitals, various charities, the state government, the federal government. And there were photographs of dignitaries, many shaking hands with one of the Stewarts. Elaine recognized state political figures, congressional representatives, entertainers. She stared for a long time at a picture of Nathan and Marilyn with the governor and his wife. It was taken in the garden room of this very house.

Across the hall were childhood pictures of Rebecca and Robert and many photographs of a younger Nathan with his lovely wife and family. Elaine recognized the picture of Marilyn that had been in the bedside table drawer.

Nathan had removed it from his bedroom and hung it out here with the other pictures. Elaine pondered what that might mean.

Finally, she entered Nathan's bedroom, looking first at the bare bedside table. Would she ever feel right putting something that belonged to her on a table that once served as a shrine to Marilyn?

Elaine went into the dressing room and opened the closets. Nathan's clothes occupied one of the closets. The other larger one was empty. So many clothes it would take to fill all that space. Elaine counted cubbyholes for forty pairs of shoes and two dozen handbags.

Then she went to the bed and pulled back the covers. Slipping off only her shoes, she lay down on the smooth percale sheets and pulled the comforter up to her chin. Nathan had bought the bed just for them, she should feel okay in it. No ghosts here. So why was she unable to hold back the tears threatening to spill down her face?

That was how Nathan found her—crying in his bed. He took her in his arms and rocked her back and forth like a baby. He kissed her salty cheeks. He stroked her hair and whispered soothing words until her tense body relaxed.

"Make love to me," she whispered.

With Nathan loving her, she could forget for a time where she was. Making love with Nathan was like going to another place—a high lofty place far above the real world. Their journey there took them beyond fear and pain and worry. They flew together like two eagles, swooping and diving, intermittently floating on gentle breezes and soaring with hurricane winds.

Nathan held back time and again, dedicating himself to pleasuring her, finding that his greatest joy came from making her cry out in ecstasy. He would like to spend the rest of his life loving her, discovering new nuances to their lovemaking, new ways to bring her release and joy.

At last, he could hold back no longer, and he gave himself over to the total soul-jarring passion that awaited. His body and spirit merged with the woman he loved.

Spent, Elaine curled herself in his arms and slept. Nathan held her for a long time before he gently lowered her head to the pillow.

"I love you, Elaine," he said to the sleeping woman as he smoothed the hair from her forehead and kissed the smooth skin there.

Chapter Ten

Nathan turned in his wet towel and gathered his sweaty clothing into his satchel. His jogging and weight-lifting session at the Fitness Center had become a daily ritual. Always before, his bouts of working out had come in bursts. He would remain quite faithful to an exercise regimen for a period of time but then be interrupted by a trip or by heavy social and business schedules. He was becoming more and more like Elaine, however, with some sort of physical exercise a daily requirement, just like eating or bathing.

He left the locker room and headed down the hall, anxious to see Elaine after a whole day away from her. Nathan realized he had come to regard all the tasks associated with his law practice, his judgeship and his political campaign as ones he had to get through so he could spend the evening with Elaine. The time he spent with her was the sustaining, vital part of his days. When he was away from her, it was as if he were only half alive. He hated the evenings when he had a political banquet or dinner meeting or one of the increasing number of prenuptial parties held for Rebecca and her fiancé. On those evenings, his time with Elaine was too short. He always tried to see her if it was for only an hour or so, but even when they spent the entire evening together, it was never long enough. Never.

He was obsessed with the idea of living with Elaine. Only then would there be the remotest possibility of seeing her enough, of being able to touch her and hear her and make love to her enough.

But after his conversation yesterday with Jonathan, Nathan wondered whether he should put on hold his plan to convince Elaine to move in with him. Nathan supposed his brother-in-law was right about the need to be more private about his relationship with Elaine, but he resented the hell out of it. If he had his way, he'd take out a billboard on the highway and announce to the world that he was absolutely crazy about and totally smitten by a certain Elaine Farrell. He adored her. He wanted to spend every waking and sleeping moment with her. However, his life didn't seem to be his own these days, what with that damned political campaign and Rebecca's wedding festivities.

But soon Rebecca would be married, and he either would or would not be his party's nominee for the state senate in the fall election. Either way, maybe then he could relax and devote himself more to Elaine.

The door to Elaine's office was standing open. Nathan tapped lightly on the door frame. "Hey, beautiful lady, ready to eat?"

Elaine didn't look up as he entered the room. She was staring at the front page of a newspaper resting in front of her on the desk. Even upside-down Nathan recognized his rotund brother-in-law's picture. Jonathan was with two other men. He was handing something to one of them.

A sinking feeling hit the pit of Nathan's stomach. *That son of a bitch,* Nathan thought furiously. He hadn't said anything about making the award for that park design so soon. Jonathan had just told him about the committee's decision yesterday. Why couldn't Jonathan have waited long enough for him to let Elaine know about it before it appeared in the newspaper, Nathan wondered. He resisted the urge to pick up the phone and curse the banker soundly. But that would have to wait for later. Right now he needed to deal with Elaine.

Nathan rounded the desk, put his hands on Elaine's shoulders and stared down at the picture. Under it was a lengthy caption:

Mayor Samuel Taylor looks on as Jonathan Miles, president and chairman of the board of First Federal Bank and chairman of the city park commission, awards a plaque and check for $2,500 to landscape architect Brenton Brooks for his winning design of a physical-fitness trail to be built in the Marilyn Miles Stewart Memorial Park, which is scheduled to be completed this fall. Money for the fitness-trail competition and for construction of the trail itself was donated by the Stewart family.

"Oh, Elaine, I'm so sorry," Nathan said. "I had no idea that was going to be announced so soon. I was going to tell you about it before you read it in the paper."

"I saw Brenton Brook's presentation that night when we all appeared before the park commission," Elaine said in a hollow voice. "It was not nearly so innovative or appropriate for the terrain as mine was."

"I know, my darling," Nathan said, hating himself for not figuring out a way for Elaine to have received the award. He should have insisted and damned the consequences. "Yours was the best by far, Elaine, but the committee was afraid everyone would think you got the award because of your relationship with me. They didn't think that would do your career or mine any good. I'm so sorry. I know how you need the money, and it's so damned unfair!"

"Nothing ever is," she said. Nathan didn't like the flatness in her voice.

"Ever is what?" he asked.

"Fair."

"If you want to protest the decision, I'll support you," Nathan offered, surprised to realize how much he meant those words. In fact, he would welcome filing a lawsuit against the entire park commission over this even though the publicity would be terrible for both of them.

"No, that would only link our name publicly, which is what the committee was trying to avoid in the first place. They are probably right," she said with a resigned sigh, her shoulders slumping. "Everyone *would* think I had gotten a special favor and that I'd earned the money in ways other than designing park trails. This hurts," she said, indicating the picture in the paper, "but that sort of scandal would hurt even more, I suppose. Oh, Nathan, do you get the feeling that we were never supposed to be together? I feel like the cards are really stacked against us."

Nathan knelt beside Elaine's chair and put his arms around her. "You are so very precious to me, and I hate to see you hurt. And I know things seem mixed up right now, but bear with me, Elaine. I'm beginning to understand that somehow I've got to simplify my life, to take away some of those obstacles to our being together. I'm not sure how, but more and more I'm starting to feel different about things. Like right now when I look at that picture of my brother-in-law, a man I've always thought was my best friend, I feel a distance that wasn't there before."

"Oh, Nathan, I don't want to come between you and your friends. That's the last thing I'd ever want to do. And I don't want you to mess up your future because of me, either. Let's just put it behind us for now and get something to eat. Shall we go out?"

Nathan thought guiltily of Jonathan's admonishment not to see Elaine in public places. How he hated the whole mess! "I'll take you wherever you want to go," Nathan told her firmly. "Just name the place!"

"Actually, I'm awfully tired," Elaine admitted. "Why don't we just pick up something and eat at my apartment?"

"You sure?" Nathan said, wondering if he should insist she go home and change clothes and then take her to the fanciest restaurant in town.

"Positive. I'll pick up the food and meet you at the apartment," Elaine said. "Why don't you stop and get some wine."

But her car would not start. Just great, she thought sarcastically as she ground the motor again. A fitting ending to a terrible day. She probably needed a new battery, she thought, wondering how much it would cost and what she would do if she was facing more expensive repairs.

Fortunately, she was able to flag Nathan down before he left the parking lot.

"No problem," he said. "Get in and we'll both go pick up dinner and the wine. I'll see that you get to work in the morning."

Maybe there'd be no problem in getting to work in the morning, Elaine thought, but what about the problem of paying to get the car fixed? And her transportation while it was in the shop? But she didn't say anything. She was afraid it would sound as if she were asking for financial help, and that she would never do. She rubbed the back of her neck and tried to relax. In the past, she always managed somehow to figure a way out of her dilemmas—financial and otherwise. But her spirit was sagging these days.

They stopped for Chinese food, and Nathan prodded her into taking an interest in helping him select their dinner. "I've heard cashew nuts are aphrodisiacs," he whispered when she placed an order for cashew chicken.

"And I heard that only oversexed people eat water chestnuts," she told him when he ordered extra for the chop suey.

Soon they had a half-dozen little white cartons and a small sack of fortune cookies to take to Elaine's apartment.

Already her spirits were better. Being with Nathan was the best elixir in the world. She put her arm through his and squeezed it. "I rather like you, Mr. Stewart," she told him, giving his arm an affectionate squeeze. Even riding in the car with him on the way to her apartment was such pleasure. She repeated a joke someone had told her and did an imitation of Mark's starry-eyed girlfriend. By the time they reached her apartment, she felt good enough to sing along with the radio.

The phone was ringing when Elaine unlocked the door. Clyde welcomed them in his inimitable way as Elaine raced to get the phone.

It was her mother.

"We've checked your father into the hospital," Martha Farrell said. "It's his liver again. He's really sick, honey."

"I'll be right there," Elaine said.

Nathan insisted on taking her. "Which hospital?" he asked as he opened the car door for her.

"There's only one hospital in this town where you take down-and-out alcoholics with no money," Elaine said harshly, the realities of her world robbing her of her good spirits. "He's at County." She got into the car without looking at him.

Nathan rounded the Mercedes and slid behind the steering wheel. "I didn't know about your father's problem," Nathan said, taking her in his arms and drawing her close. "I'm so sorry. You've really had a rough time of it, haven't you?"

"Of course you didn't know," Elaine said wryly, her body stiff and unresponding to his embrace. "I hadn't told you. It's just another of the many reasons why I'm unsuitable for you, Nathan. I'm hardly a young woman of breeding."

"I've known bank presidents who were alcoholics," Nathan said. "And it makes no difference to me who or what your father is. I don't care if he's an ax murderer. It's his daughter who enchants me, not him."

"Well, my father hasn't enchanted anyone for a long time," Elaine said with a sigh, "but he used to be quite a guy. He owned an auto-repair shop and did rather well. But then he started drinking, and he lost the business.

Things went from bad to worse, as they say. At least I can remember him when he was still himself. My brother has never known him any other way.''

NATHAN HAD DRIVEN by the grim-looking gray building many times in the past. County Hospital had been a landmark of east-side Heritage since before he was born. But he had never set foot inside its doors. He had been in the city's other hospitals on many occasions, but he had never even known anyone who was hospitalized at County.

They stopped at the information desk, and an over-cheerful woman in a pink volunteer's smock told them where Vince Farrell was located in the hospital. As they walked across the poorly lit lobby area, Elaine insisted that Nathan did not need to accompany her up to the fourth-floor ward.

"Would it bother you if I did?" Nathan asked.

Elaine pressed the elevator up button, then turned to look at him. "I thought we agreed no families in our relationship for the time being. And my family is hardly at its best right now. This isn't the time to meet them."

"Then I'll wait for you down here."

Elaine touched his face. "Look, Nathan, my mother can take me home when the time comes. I don't have any idea how long we will stay here—maybe all night. I appreciate your concern. Really I do. But this isn't your problem."

The elevator door opened. Nathan blocked the door with his foot to hold it. "I'll wait down here for a while. If there's anything you can think of I can do for you or your family, will you come back down and tell me?"

Elaine nodded.

"And if you don't want him hospitalized here, I'd be glad to—"

She put a finger to his lips to stop his words and shook her head no. "I know you would. But some of us poor folks have a lot of pride. It helps make up for the lack of money."

Nathan watched the elevator swallow her. He wanted to be of some use to her, but there was nothing he could do. He felt helpless. It was a feeling he didn't care for at all.

A canteen just off the lobby offered an array of vending machines. Nathan fished around in his pocket but came up with only two nickels. A change machine had an out-of-order sign on it. A white-coated man was feeding coins to a coffee machine.

"Excuse me," Nathan asked the man. "Would you have change for a dollar?"

The black man turned and stared openly for a minute. "No, but allow me," he said, offering Nathan two quarters. The sleeve of his immaculately clean white coat was frayed around the edges, as was the starched white shirt cuff that protruded from the sleeve.

"Oh, no, I couldn't," Nathan said, somewhat embarrassed. He looked around at the eight or ten silent people sitting on the mismatched assortment of shabby chairs that populated the lobby, thinking maybe he could ask one of them to change his dollar.

"What'd you want—coffee?" the tired-looking young man asked in a rather insistent tone.

Nathan nodded. "That's awfully nice of you."

"No problem. I find it amusing to be buying a cup of coffee for someone wearing a pair of shoes that cost more than a resident's salary at this hospital for an entire month. It'll make a good story to tell in surgery tomorrow.''

Nathan looked down at his shoes. Gucci. He supposed they had cost a great deal. He had charged them and really hadn't noticed how much. Of course, Nathan considered good shoes a wise investment, since he usually wore such shoes for years. His belt was Gucci, too. And his casual shirt was a silk-and-linen knit by Perry Ellis. Suddenly he had more than an inkling what Elaine must have felt like at the country-club party he had taken her to. Nathan mentally stood back and looked at himself the way the young impoverished resident must be regarding him. For the first time in his life, Nathan's clothes embarrassed him. He didn't fit in at County Hospital.

The doctor gestured to a wooden chair by a white metal table that looked as if it belonged in a kitchen. ''Won't you join me?''

''Sure,'' Nathan said. ''Thanks.''

The young physician put two Styrofoam cups of muddy-looking coffee on the table. Before they sat down, he offered Nathan his hand. ''Judge Stewart, right? I'm Todd Henderson. Third-year surgery resident at this noble institution.''

Nathan was startled. ''How did you know my name?''

''Well, I do occasionally find time to read a newspaper or watch the news on television, and you've been featured lately. Running for the state senate against old Billingsly, aren't you?''

''Yes, it seems I am.''

''Corrupt old coot,'' Dr. Henderson said between sips. ''We've got some of his buddies occupying the few carpeted offices we have around here. I never have figured out just what their jobs are, however. But Billingsly has promised to try to save some of the low-rent housing that seems to be slated for destruction. That'll get him lots of votes on this side of town.''

"I wasn't aware that any of the low-rent housing was threatened," Nathan said.

"Well, some of it went when they started building that park named for your wife," Henderson explained. "And I understand a lot of the land adjoining is slated for an industrial park. The buildings there will probably be torn down, too."

"Are you sure houses were torn down to build that park?" Nathan asked, distractedly emptying an extra packet of sugar into his cup. The coffee was terrible.

"Forty units," Henderson said with a shrug. "They weren't much to look at, but they were home to forty families."

"I had no idea," Nathan admitted. "By the time I saw the area, it had been cleared, and the dirt work was under way. I was so pleased to have a nice park for that end of town that I guess I never thought about what that land was used for before. We've needed a park over there for years."

"Well, it would be a nice place for all the children from the tenements to play—except there apparently aren't going to be any more tenements there," the doctor said in a low, even voice as he raised his cup to his lips.

"I don't know where you get your information, Dr. Henderson," Nathan said, "but an industrial park for this city is strictly in the planning stage. No one has a location in mind yet. The legislation enabling such a project hasn't even been enacted yet."

"That so?" Henderson said, toying with a plastic spoon, his tone lacking conviction. "Probably all those new landlords are too strapped for funds to make improvements on their buildings and have just been making up the stories they have their people tell the tenants about no money being spent on repairs since the whole project is scheduled for razing some time next year. The representatives of those anonymous landlords are probably just using that as an excuse to get folks off their backs about fixing furnaces and plumbing and stuff like that. Of course, you have to admit that area would make a right handsome industrial park with that spacious, beautiful park adjoining it. Lovely place for the executives to take their morning jog or schedule employee picnics. And it will serve as a greenbelt to enhance the view for all those executive offices. It will certainly be a whole lot more attractive than tenements. Yes, sir, that park will mean the folks who own all the adjoining property could really clean up—provided, of course, it is purchased for an industrial park. Trouble is, this city has such a shortage of low-rent housing now, I just don't know where all those displaced families will move. Seems to me, the industrial park could be built some place that won't displace so many hundreds of people."

Nathan felt a strange tingling in his scalp. Could this obscure young physician be correct? And if so, how strange Jonathan had not mentioned that dwellings were razed to build that park. Nathan had certainly been led to believe that a location for the industrial park had not been decided, that it was just a wonderful vague dream for the city's future.

"How about a tour of our facility?" Dr. Henderson asked as he crumpled his cup and put it in the trash. "If

you win that election, I'd like you to remember old
County Hospital when the state money comes up for
grabs.''

Nathan toured. Dr. Henderson spared him nothing.

THE MAN IN THE BED next to Vince Farrell was a chronic
lung patient. Every breath was a great rasping struggle.
Elaine could hear him all the way down the hall when she
went to the ladies' room. There seemed to be no escap-
ing the horrible rattles emitting from the man's chest. The
two elderly men on the other side of the four-bed room
were sleeping.

Vince himself drifted in and out of awareness. He was
jaundiced and thin and in need of a shave. He looked
scared. It was the first time Elaine had seen fear in his
eyes. He kept telling his family how sorry he was, that he
was going to ''dry out.''

''Just you wait and see, Laine,'' he said, patting her
hand. ''Your old pop isn't over the hill yet—not by a long
shot.'' For some reason, Elaine sensed a new conviction
in his voice. It was as though he were truly weary of being
this way, of being a burden to those who loved him.

But she knew her father was too old and weak and ill
to fight this battle without professional help. And the sort
of help he needed was only available to those who could
afford it.

The Hispanic physician who tended Vince explained to
Elaine and her mother that drying out was no longer a
choice.

''He has very little liver function left,'' the brusque
young woman told them. ''I think we can pull him
through this time, but if he goes on another binge, I can't
promise anything.''

Elaine left her mother in the hospital room and went to call her brother. Then she went downstairs to find Nathan.

She walked with him to his car. "There's something you can do for me," she told him.

"Anything," Nathan said, wanting desperately to touch her but put off by the distracted look on her face.

"Here's an extra key to my apartment. Would you go by and feed Clyde and make sure he has water? I'm going to stay up here with mother."

"How's your father?" Nathan asked.

"Not good," Elaine said. "The doctor says she thinks he'll pull through this time, but his liver won't stand anymore."

"What about your brother? Do you need anyone to look after him?"

"He's at the neighbors. I talked to him on the telephone. He said to tell Dad that he loved him and wanted him to get well and come to one of his baseball games." Elaine's voice broke a bit. Nathan dared to reach out for her. She hesitated, then came readily to his arms.

Nathan fervently wished he could smooth away her problems. Her pain was his pain. He could almost feel her taking comfort and strength from his embrace. He wished he could hold her like that forever.

"SORRY I'M LATE," Nathan said curtly as he entered his brother-in-law's study. "I've been touring County Hospital." He ignored the inquisitive look his remark brought to Jonathan's face and quickly shook hands with the three other men in attendance.

"We've been discussing fund-raising," Jonathan began as soon as Nathan was seated.

"Which means we've been making a list of everyone we can hit on for a contribution," said the silver-haired president of Heritages's chamber of commerce. "You have an impressive list of friends, Nathan. And Billingsly has an impressive list of enemies. The two lists together should serve us nicely."

"Here," Jonathan said, "look these lists over and see what you think. We still need to work on that list of women who worked with Marilyn on her projects and did club work with her. It never hurts to have a little gentle pressure exerted by the fairer sex on their husbands."

Nathan took the pages and laid them down on the desk beside him without looking at them.

"And we need to go over your statement for the League of Women Voters' forum tomorrow night. Billingsly and the other two candidates will all be there. It will be a wonderful chance for you to shine. There'll be full media coverage. Did you bring along a copy of your opening statement?"

"There's something we need to talk about, gentlemen," Nathan said, ignoring Jonathan's question. "Who owns the property adjoining the park that's being built in Marilyn's honor?"

Jonathan leaned back in his chair and regarded Nathan through narrowed eyes. Then, with an overwide smile, he said, "I think Nathan and I need to have a little talk. If you gentlemen don't mind, we'll finish our fund-raising discussion later in the week. I'll have my secretary get in touch."

Nathan watched the three men leave the room. He could hear Jonathan's wife scurrying down the hall to see them off. "You gentlemen rushing off so soon?" He got up and closed the study door.

"Well?" he questioned, standing in front of the desk and looking down at the overweight man sitting behind it. "What about that land?"

"Now, why would I know about that?" Jonathan asked. "Who have you been listening to, Nathan, and just what are you implying?"

"I'll just go to the courthouse tomorrow and look this up, so you might as well tell me," Nathan challenged. "And don't think you're protected if it's listed under some dummy corporation. There are ways to check on such things, you know."

"Now just get off your high horse, my friend. Sit down and tell me, why is this suddenly so important?" Jonathan asked, leaning back in his huge leather desk chair.

Nathan ignored the request that he sit down. Instead, he put his hands on the desk and leaned forward. "The people who live down there apparently have been told by their *new* landlords that repairs won't be made on those dwellings," he continued, "because they're scheduled to be torn down to make way for an industrial park."

"Well, that certainly is premature. Several tracts of land are being considered. You know that, Nathan."

"No, I know no such thing," Nathan said, his tone deliberately icy. "I'm just wondering how much else I don't know. I didn't know homes were torn down to build that park, either. Boy, have I ever spent the past year in a daze."

"Now you calm down," Jonathan said sternly. "The low-rent project located on that land was an eyesore. The city was more than willing to condemn the property and dedicate the land to a park. You know that a park over there was Marilyn's idea. She had already started the ball rolling on that project before she died."

"That's true," Nathan agreed. "She thought the children over there needed a safe place to play. I've been so caught up with my personal life here lately that it never occurred to me that your plans for that park didn't include any playground area." Nathan swung away from the desk and paced the room twice before turning back to face his brother-in-law. "Where are the swings, Jonathan, and the slides and the sandboxes? That's not a kids' park, and you know it. That park has been designed to serve as a recreational facility and greenbelt for your industrial park."

"*My* industrial park. Come off it, Nathan. That industrial park, if it's ever built, would be for the whole city. It could spell the difference between economic growth and stagnation for this community."

"And it could spell a nice profit for whoever happens to own the land that is ultimately purchased with funding from a state industrial trust—provided that legislation you're so hot for is passed. I think you have used the whole Marilyn Miles Stewart Memorial Park scheme to ensure the desirability of that tract of land. And I want to know why. Who is going to profit? Who owns that land now? I demand to know."

"Several investors have incorporated and purchased those tracts of land that might be considered for such a development," Jonathan said cautiously. "But it's all speculation. Investors have been speculating since day one. It's part of the American system."

"And if those investors happen to be in a position to influence the outcome of such land purchases—is that also part of the American system?"

"Oh, Nathan, grow up and spare me your idealism. If what is best for this city also benefits the men who are

willing to shoulder certain financial risks to make sure
suitable land is available when the time comes, what's the
harm? Just tell me that. What's the harm?''

Nathan spun around from his pacing, stopping directly in front of Jonathan. ''For starters, there're the
people who live down there. Where do you suggest they
move when they are forced out of their homes?

Chapter Eleven

As Nathan drove to Elaine's apartment, his thoughts were a strange mixture of Elaine herself and of a young black physician who showed him a side of the world he had never seen before.

Well, Nathan thought ruefully, the uptown lawyer who was running for a state senate seat from this district had quite a night. He felt as though he had lived his entire life cloistered away in some make-believe world and for the first time tonight had strayed over into the real one.

How providential that he was with Elaine when she got the call about her father and took her to that hospital. If he hadn't been with her tonight, he might never have met Dr. Todd Henderson. Could he have gone through this entire political campaign without discovering the true motivations of Jonathan and the other men who had convinced him to make the race? Nathan wanted to believe otherwise, but he suspected they picked him because he had been so damned naive when it came to politics. But no more. Had he ever wised up!

And to think he so righteously had considered himself above vested interests! What a joke that was, Nathan thought. If he hadn't had that brief conversation with

Henderson, no telling how long he would have been the dupe of his so-called political backers in their pursuit of personal wealth and power.

And no telling how long he would have gone on thinking he really understood the needs of his community. Why, he only knew about the needs of the people who lived in his own neighborhood—the country-club set, the power brokers of this town. Before tonight, he hardly had been aware of the majority of the people who inhabited Heritage. And there were far more people who lived in low-rent housing than lived in stately mansions on Weatherford Drive.

Nathan pulled up in front of Elaine's somewhat run-down apartment house, acutely aware for the first time since he had started coming here of the contrast between his expensive vehicle and the modest compacts and elderly sedans parked along this street. Suddenly his Mercedes seemed uncomfortably ostentatious.

Clyde greeted him with a raucous "What the hell!" the instant he opened the door.

"You tell me, old man," Nathan said, fumbling for the light switch. As soon as the light came on, Clyde screeched, "Damn! Damn! Damn!"

"What's the matter? The light hurt your eyes?" Nathan asked solicitously. "Well, pal, I have instructions to feed and water you. Looks like you could use a little of both. Right?"

Clyde cocked his head to one side and regarded Nathan quizzically. He warbled a funny little sound deep in his throat as though agreeing with Nathan's assessment of the situation, then busied himself preening his feathers.

Nathan washed the bird's water dish and filled it. He poured out a fresh supply of bird seed and changed the newspaper in the bottom of the cage. Clyde allowed Nathan to scratch the back of his head.

Soon he couldn't think of anything else to do for the bird, yet Nathan found he didn't want to leave Elaine's apartment. He swept up the bird-seed hulls from under Clyde's cage, then walked around aimlessly, switching on lamps, straightening pictures, arranging magazines, throwing away newspapers, picking up the pair of loafers Elaine had kicked off under the dining table and the pair of athletic shoes parked by the sofa. When he put the shoes in her closet, he saw the red pair lined up with assorted other shoes. He picked one of the red shoes up and polished its toe against his sleeve. He closed his eyes, conjuring up an image of the first time he had seen Elaine marching up to the bench in his courtroom wearing those shoes. He had realized even then that she was special.

He emptied the dishwasher and sprinkled a bit of food in the goldfish bowl. He opened the refrigerator and peered in, realizing he hadn't eaten since lunch. But the refrigerator offered only milk, several bottles of assorted fruit juices, cottage cheese, lettuce, a wedge of some unidentifiable cheese, some leftover beans and a very dried-out pork chop. Then he remembered the Chinese food that was supposed to have been their quiet, romantic dinner.

Nathan retrieved the sack of small white cartons from the living-room table, going through the same greeting ritual with Clyde when he reentered the room. "How about a fortune cookie?" Nathan asked the bird. He broke open a cookie, removed the fortune and put the pieces of cookie in the bird's dish.

"It says here, Clyde, that your talents heretofore have gone unrecognized but will soon be appreciated by others," Nathan said as he read the fortune he had taken from Clyde's cookie.

"Let's see about one for me," Nathan said, breaking open another cookie.

Nathan read, then reread the line on the small strip of paper. "You stand at the crossroads of life. Follow the turning marked Love."

Love. A rather simple looking word. It had a pleasing round, open sound when said aloud. But Nathan had not used the word much lately. He had said it to Elaine only once while she was sleeping, at a time when the word would not be heard. Why, he wondered. Was he holding back out of the loyalty he still felt toward Marilyn? He told Marilyn almost daily that he loved her—and he had meant it. Yet he had never experienced such intense feeling for her as he felt for the woman who lived in this apartment. His relationship with his wife had been a calmer, more dignified one. With Elaine, he always felt that he was alternately soaring and falling out of control. He had loved Marilyn with his mind; what he felt for Elaine seemed to reside in his chest.

As he stood in her small, inexpensive apartment, he forced himself to face the reason he had never told Elaine that he loved her. It had something to do with the intensity of his feelings for her. They were too strong to be believed. Surely such feelings did not represent a permanent condition but some stage he was passing through.

Nathan realized he mistrusted so much intense emotional involvement. What he felt for Elaine was so different from anything he had ever experienced before that he had no faith in it—and wondered if it was the product of passion rather than enduring love. He was absolutely certain he had loved his wife. So if that was love, he assumed what he felt for Elaine must be something else. He had made the mistake of assuming it was something less, but now he understood that it was more. Marilyn had been a vital and loving part of his life. Elaine was his life.

But Elaine was pulling away from him. Nathan had felt this other times but dismissed the feeling as unfounded. But tonight, after the call came about her father, he sensed Elaine retreating from him—going back to her own world with her own people.

Nathan refused to believe before that the span between his life and hers was unbridgeable. It would be ridiculous to allow class considerations to interfere. That was as outdated as the horse and buggy. In modern-day America it simply didn't matter that her blue-collar background didn't match his privileged one. In her very special way, Elaine had more charm and sensitivity than any woman he had ever known. Nathan felt more at ease, more like himself, with her than at any other time.

Yet he was acutely aware of Elaine's discomfort when she came to his home, and he wondered if he could ever inflict another evening with his friends on her after the fiasco at the country club. Even if he bought her the most expensive gown in the world, she wouldn't feel comfortable.

And would Rebecca ever be accepting of his relationship with Elaine? It seemed as though he should be taking Elaine to his daughter's wedding. It bothered Nathan that he was not. After all, she was the woman in his life. But it would offend his daughter and his dead wife's friends and family if he did.

Nathan looked again at the strip of paper in his hand. "Follow the turning marked Love." Advice from a fortune cookie! Hardly the sort of thing one took seriously. Yet he smoothed the small piece of paper between his fingers, then carefully stored it away in his billfold.

He picked up the sack of food and carried it to the kitchen. He opened up five small cartons and placed a serving of each of the Oriental delights on a plate, then slipped the plate in the microwave. "See, I don't need to be waited on," he told Clyde through the open door. "In fact, I rather like doing for myself."

Clyde made his warbling sound again. This time it carried a note of dismissal. Nathan decided it must be Clyde's bedtime and turned out the light in the small dining alcove.

He returned to the kitchen and poured himself a glass of Elaine's corkless wine, placed it on the tray with his dinner and carried it into the living room. "I don't do this at home," he told Clyde as he passed the bird's cage. "I always eat my dinner in the dining room."

Clyde stared at him glassy-eyed but offered no response.

Nathan switched on the stereo, kicked off his shoes and settled down in the overstuffed easy chair. Nathan ate his dinner and absorbed the feel of the wonderfully whimsical room with its plants and parrot and refinished garage-sale "finds." He loved Elaine's apartment.

Yet he had wanted to take the woman who had created this charming, comfortable home for herself and install her in the stiff formality of Weatherford Drive.

After Nathan finished his meal, he put the leftovers in the refrigerator and straightened up the small kitchen.

There was no reason for him to stay any longer, but he couldn't bring himself to leave.

He spent the night in Elaine's bed. Her scent was on the pillow, the smooth sheets reminded him of her skin. His mind was filled with her. He yearned for her so.

Nathan's body cruelly responded to his thoughts. With his mind and his aroused body, he wanted Elaine more than he ever had before. Mental images of making love to her tortured him and he could almost sense how it would feel to sink into a timeless yet frenzied celebration of her beautiful body. He would kiss her forever and touch her endlessly. He would leave no part of her untouched, unkissed, unloved.

And she would touch him. Elaine held nothing back. She took such delight in satisfying him. She knew his body better than he knew it himself.

"Oh, Elaine," his muffled voice said into the pillow. "Darling, Elaine. I do love you."

THERE WAS NO QUESTION about her need for more money, Elaine thought as she reread the letter from Mr. Dunn. With her father's release from the hospital, her mother had been forced, at least temporarily, to leave her job at a local day-care center to stay at home and care for her convalescing husband. Elaine's contribution to her family's support would have to be increased.

And Mr. Dunn of American Fitness was again offering her an opportunity to make a promotional tour over the next few months as a consultant and spokesperson for their national chain of fitness studios, this time with a very attractive money figure affixed to the offer and with no contingency to sell the Fitness Center.

However, the letter went on to say that their local attorney would soon be in touch with her concerning their forthcoming offer to buy her facility, and Dunn certainly hoped she would give the offer her full consideration.

The letter ended with an invitation to come to their head office in St. Louis to discuss both matters.

When Elaine first read the letter this morning, her immediate reaction to the prospect of taking a job that would put her on the road for the next few months was— *no way.* Her father was sick, she had a business to run— a business that finally seemed slowly to be turning itself around and showing some signs of success—and how could she possibly leave Nathan? She had tossed the letter on her desk and gone to lead a women's weight-lifting class.

But she thought about it as she was introducing the women to the equipment and explaining the principle behind each weight-lifting device. When she returned to her office an hour later, there it was, still on her desk.

On second reading, her practical side forced her at least to consider it. After all, she had no money, and she did have a family to support. Although the Fitness Center was gaining each month, she realized it would be at least a year before the business was profitable.

By evening, she was ready to try to negotiate a limited tour with American Fitness that would allow her to come home frequently. Mark could run the business while she was gone. And perhaps it would be best for her to get away from Nathan for a time. Maybe distance would put their relationship in perspective, and she could take a more objective look at it. Maybe if she left town for a while, she could come home and start afresh on a new life—one in which she was not a television exercise girl.

But even while Elaine tried to convince herself that leaving Nathan for a time would be for the best, she realized that if it weren't for the money, she wouldn't be considering a separation. Actually, she couldn't stand the thought of being apart from him. She felt as though she couldn't survive even a day without him.

Intellectually, however, Elaine knew she could and would survive and that her family was desperate for the money she would be paid. At this time, she really had no choice.

Elaine also sensed that the time for other decisions was at hand. Either she sold the Fitness Center and attempted to clean up her act in hopes of her and Nathan forming a permanent relationship, or she came to terms with the temporary nature of their current arrangement.

But was anything permanent possible? She remembered how Nathan looked there in the lobby of County Hospital. Even in his casual clothes, he stood out as someone who didn't belong. Anyone would know just by looking at him that he was from the other side of town. She had even found herself resenting his expensive clothes, his luxury automobile, his high-dollar education, his secure life. She had sent him away.

Elaine fully realized that unless she somehow molded a more sophisticated image for herself in this community, it was only a matter of time before Nathan found a more appropriate woman to install in his elegant house and replace his beloved Marilyn. He would find a woman his daughter and his friends could accept. It was inevitable. Elaine had too much pride to continue seeing him when that happened.

But oh, how it would hurt. How it hurt now just thinking about it. She felt as if bands of steel were being pulled around her chest, making breathing difficult. Elaine hugged herself and rocked back and forth in her chair to try to relieve the pain.

Oh, my darling Nathan, I love you too much, she thought in her agony. *I'll always love you too much. What is to happen to me if I lose you?*

But Nathan had never spoken to her of love. No man had ever been more attentive, more adoring, more loving to her, than Nathan. He had never said words of love, however. He had never speculated about what the two of them would be doing next month or next year or five years from now. Would he include her in his future if she changed into a different sort of woman? Could she change enough?

Elaine felt as if she were crumbling into a million pieces, as if she were losing herself. She didn't care for the feeling at all. She was a take-charge person who was just sitting there losing control of her life.

Picking up Mr. Dunn's letter again, she read it once more. It seemed to offer her only hope—short-term and long-term. Short-term for the money she needed right now; long-term for changing the direction of her life.

She inhaled deeply and tried to rub away the painful tightness in her neck. Absently, she stared at the stack of unopened mail still piled on her desk from this morning. There were equipment catalogs, several envelopes and a cardboard mailing tube. She thumbed through the envelopes without opening any. Mostly bills, she decided with a sigh.

She picked up the mailing tube and idly pulled the rolled contents from the tube, only mildly curious. It was probably another of the many posters sent with great regularity from one of the manufacturers of athletic equipment. But the poster she unrolled wasn't advertising athletic equipment. It was advertising her own television show. She stared down in horror at her own glossy image.

"Elaine Farrell exercising for health and beauty" the caption read, followed by the times her show appeared on television and the logo of the television station. But the words were not the problem. It was the picture!

This was not at all like the cardboard placard the station manager had indicated he planned to have made. This was a full-sized wall poster done in full color on glossy paper! *Oh, my God,* Elaine thought in panic. *Are they going to put these things all over town?*

She stared at the professional-looking poster, trying to see it as others might. The woman was pretty enough, Elaine supposed, and she seemed trim and physically fit as she bent forward halfway through a toe touch. The picture was taken from a side angle, her face and upper torso turned toward the camera. One arm was extended over her back, the other on its way to the floor. Her smiling face, surrounded by a lustrous mane of shiny, rich brown hair, was turned toward the camera. But bending over like that exposed too much of her bust beneath the V-neck of the hot-pink leotards and her fanny was thrust out behind her in what looked like a provocative stance. Why had they chosen that pose, Elaine wondered, when she had performed jumping jacks, high kicks, sit-ups, body twists, push-ups, all sorts of maneuvers, for the photographer?

The provocative pose had been selected, however. She should have known better, Elaine thought with growing anguish. She should have insisted on the right of approval, but she hadn't thought of it until now. She hadn't realized how a picture might be used.

The poster made her look like a sex kitten.

A feeling of panic swept over Elaine. She couldn't have that thing circulated around the community!

Maybe she could stop distribution. After all, Clark had misled her. A small cardboard placard this was not. She dialed the number of the television station. Clark wasn't in, but his secretary informed her that the posters had all been mailed out yesterday.

Elaine grabbed the poster from her desk, crumpled it and stuffed it in the wastebasket, then wiped her hands on her sweatpants as though she just had touched something foul.

She slumped back in her chair and stared at the wastebasket in horror, the full ramifications of what that poster meant to her life beginning to sink in. Women who appeared on posters were not married by men running for the state senate.

NATHAN KNEW SOMETHING was wrong as soon as he unlocked the door to her apartment. He had been trying to reach her all weekend. At the Fitness Center, they didn't seem to know where she was—just that she wouldn't be in this weekend and would call in either Sunday evening or Monday morning. And there was no answer at her apartment when he called.

Finally, in desperation, he drove over. He still had the key she have given him the night her father was hospitalized, and he used it to open the door.

He was greeted by absolute silence.

Where was Clyde? Nathan had expected his raucous greeting. He switched on the light but the cage and Clyde were no longer in the small dining alcove. The apartment seemed surprisingly vacant without the bird.

Trying to decide what the bird's absence meant, Nathan walked through the apartment. Everything seemed in order. The television and stereo were still in place. No drawers were standing open. It didn't look as though the apartment had been broken into. Nathan wondered if someone would steal just a parrot. He supposed the bird was valuable.

Almost as an afterthought, he looked in the large, old-fashioned bathroom. Elaine's cosmetics were missing from the shelf under the mirror. It took Nathan a minute to digest the implication of that. Had she taken a trip without telling him, he wondered. Or perhaps she was staying over at her parents' house. Maybe her father had taken a turn for the worse.

He picked up the telephone book and searched through the Farrells. What was her father's name? He ran his finger down the list until he came to the end. Vince. That rang a bell.

Nathan dialed the number. It was no longer a working number.

Picking up the phone book again, he checked the address—4155 Front Street. He left.

The street was lined with tired old dwellings that had been modest the day they were built, and many were now on the verge of shabby. Number 4155 had reached the latter state. The covered front porch sloped forward to sunken concrete steps. The house had not been painted in years.

Nathan rang the bell but heard no sound. He tried knocking. A bright-eyed youngster of about eight or nine answered the door. Clyde was screaming his profanities from the back of the house. Nathan was relieved. Elaine must be staying here, too, if Clyde was in the house.

"Is your mother or sister here?" Nathan asked.

"My mother is," the boy said. "I'll get her." He turned and shot down a center hallway that probably led to the kitchen. Shortly, a woman appeared, drying her hands on her apron. "Yes?" she asked through the screen door.

She had gray hair and could easily have passed for the boy's grandmother. But there was a dignity about her features that impressed Nathan, and he realized, on second look, that she wasn't old so much as she was worn-looking. With her hair professionally styled and dressed in other clothing, she might have been attractive.

"I'm Nathan Stewart."

"I thought maybe you were," she said in a carefully neutral tone. "I'm Martha Farrell, Elaine's mother."

"Is Elaine here?"

"No, she went to St. Louis for a few days."

"St. Louis. Why?" Nathan asked, shocked. He had no idea Elaine was planning a trip.

"Something about a job. I'm sure she'll tell you all about it when she gets back. She brought the parrot over for Tim to take care of." The woman hesitated a minute, then asked, "Would you like to come in?"

"Oh, no. I don't want to put you out."

"No problem. Maybe it's time you see where Lainie's family lives," Martha Farrell said in a somewhat commanding tone as she pushed at the screen door. She held it open for Nathan to enter.

Nathan reluctantly stepped inside and, feeling very ill at ease, followed the woman into a small living room to the right of the center hallway. Martha indicated he was to sit on the sofa.

"I'll get coffee," she announced, leaving him to study the room.

The room was dominated by an upright piano on which sat pictures of an adolescent Elaine and the youngster who had come to the door, holding a baseball and dressed in a baseball shirt and hat. A clean but somewhat threadbare rug almost covered the linoleum floor. Fringed furniture throws almost covered the outdated pieces. A sturdy but scarred oak table stood in front of the room's one window, and on it was an inexpensive imitation of a Tiffany lamp.

The room's plainness had been softened by a pair of Audubon bird prints that hung over the sofa and several healthy ferns and other greenery in clay pots. The most impressive thing about the room was its cleanliness. The piano's finish was scarred but still polished to a high gloss, the window glass sparkled, and the furniture throws looked freshly laundered, as did the starched white sheer curtains that crisscrossed over the window. Elaine's remark at the hospital about "poor but proud" came to Nathan's mind. That's what this room said about the woman who lived here. She didn't have much money, but she had standards. Like the woman herself, the room had a dignity that Nathan found himself admiring.

From the rear of the small house, Nathan could hear a man coughing. Elaine's father, he supposed. The coughing apparently disturbed Clyde, and the parrot let out with his now-familiar string of "Damns." A boyish voice responded to the bird, but Nathan couldn't hear what he said. Martha's footsteps came purposefully down the bare wooden floor of the hallway.

When she returned with two cups of coffee along with cream and sugar on a small tray, Martha had removed her apron and added a touch of color to her face. Nathan could see a little of Elaine in her face—around the eyes especially.

Martha handed him coffee in a china cup. Her own was in an earthenware mug.

Silence hung over the room for a minute while both sipped at their cups. The coffee was good—strong, and brewed rather than instant. The unseen man in the back of the house coughed again. Clyde did not respond this time. The back door slammed, and Nathan could hear the sound of the gravel in the drive crunching under running feet, followed by childish voices greeting one another.

"When is Elaine supposed to return?" Nathan asked, wondering why she hadn't called him before she left.

"She wasn't sure when she'd get back," Martha said as she regarded Nathan with open curiosity. "The whole notion of the trip came up rather suddenly. I recall her saying she left a message with your housekeeper about leaving town. I guess you didn't get it."

"I haven't been at home much lately. I guess she hasn't had a chance to tell me yet," Nathan said, wondering if Mrs. Murphy had conveniently forgotten to leave the message on the notepad on his desk, where she usually left his phone messages. "Whom did Elaine go to see?" he wanted to know.

"Why don't you let Elaine tell you about that when she gets back," Martha said rather curtly.

"I'd rather give her a call today," Nathan insisted. "Do you know where she's staying?"

"I think what my daughter needs right now is to be left alone," Martha said, her tone inviting no argument. "She was upset about something when she left here and seemed to feel that getting away for a time would be good for her. In fact, Elaine hasn't been herself lately—not since she started seeing you."

"You don't approve of Elaine's going with me, do you, Mrs. Farrell?" Nathan asked, sensing the woman's disapproval.

Martha took her time answering him, first sipping at her coffee, flicking an imaginary piece of dust from her navy skirt.

"No, I guess I don't," she said at last. "Seems to me it's a dead-end arrangement between you and my daughter that can't be doing either one of you any good. You won't be wanting to marry her. Elaine's just put her life on hold so she can chase around making herself unhappy over you. I'd like to see her find someone closer to her own age and with some of the same interests and then get married. Maybe it's partly that I'm just being selfish, but most women my age have a grandchild or two. And here my daughter is going with a man who is not much younger than I am and has grown-up children. He probably isn't interested in starting another family, but even if he were, marriage to my daughter is probably out of the question. But more than wanting grandchildren, I want what is best for my daughter, Mr. Stewart."

"I'm sure you do, Mrs. Farrell," Nathan interjected. But before he had a chance to explain that he, too, wanted what was best for her daughter, Martha continued.

"That wife of yours that you lost—she was a fine lady," Martha said matter-of-factly. "My Laine had never been to a fancy college. She's worked hard and never had much to show for it until now—not until she built that business of hers. Can you imagine what an achievement that was for her? How many years she spent getting established so she could get financing for that sort of project? And that television show has made her famous in this town. Not in a way your sort can appreciate, but for someone with Elaine's background to get that much attention is a small miracle. And now you know what I see? I see her being ashamed of all that. I see her being ashamed to be on television, ashamed to be who she is. And that's because she keeps measuring herself against a woman who was born and grew up with every advantage under the sun. Well, she can't be another Marilyn Stewart. No one's going to name a park after Elaine when she dies."

Chapter Twelve

Nathan didn't want to be in his house tonight. During dinner, he decided it was foolish to eat his solitary meals in the huge formal dining room with its table large enough to seat twelve. And Mrs. Murphy's constant hovering irritated him. "No, damn it, I do not want more green beans!" he said the third time she had run the vegetable bowl by him. "And quit putting more ice in my tea. It's just fine the way it is."

As soon as the words were out of his mouth, Nathan was sorry. Mrs. Murphy always hovered. She regarded that as a function of her "position." And if he wanted her to change, he should tell her in a more diplomatic way.

Nathan pushed back his chair and followed the housekeeper out into the kitchen to apologize. She accepted his apology with a stiff, disapproving nod, saying that she understood. He'd been under a lot of strain with the campaign and Miss Rebecca's wedding.

"You will be wanting dessert?" Her question sounded more like a command.

Nathan looked at the wedge of lemon chiffon pie she had already cut. Somehow Mrs. Murphy had decided years ago that lemon chiffon was his favorite dessert and had made him one without fail every week for the past twenty years. But he really didn't care for it and had never had the heart to tell her. So for twenty years he had dutifully eaten that yellow fluff masquerading as a pie and told her how wonderful it tasted and how good she was to prepare one especially for him.

The whole pie situation reminded him of those stuffy chamber-music recitals. Nathan had never really liked going to the Chamber Music Society performances that Marilyn had been so enthusiastic about. But he had made the mistake of trying to please his wife once years ago by telling her it was a delightful way to spend an evening. So six times a year, he had put on a dinner jacket and desperately tried to avoid nodding off while Marilyn's cultured friends performed their way through the meticulously deadly measured strains of Haydn and Beethoven.

"Mrs. Murphy, you make the best lemon chiffon pie I have ever tasted," Nathan said enthusiastically, "but I think I'm ready to change allegiance. Starting right now, I'm going to adopt a new favorite pie. You and I both are in a rut, and I think it's time we got out. Have you ever made just plain old garden-variety apple? I think I'd like that one day real soon. Yes, homemade apple pie, warm, with a scoop of vanilla ice cream on top. I had a piece just like that with Robby out at some truck stop on the highway and discovered I had forgotten just how good a piece of pie could be. And could we have chicken-fried steak every so often—with mashed potatoes and gravy?"

Mrs. Murphy's shoulders squared. Her chin went up. "Whatever you say, sir," she said icily.

Nathan knew exactly what the housekeeper was implying with her tone and inflection. "The missus" would never have made such a request of her—that chicken-fried steak and gravy were not the sort of fare one was supposed to cook in *this* kitchen.

"Oh, come on, Mrs. Murphy," he said with a conciliatory pat on the woman's plump arm. "Before your husband died, I bet you fixed chicken-fried steak at home for him all the time—and apple pie, too. You don't have to put on airs to cook for me."

At this, the woman sputtered. "Well, I never—" But she apparently decided it was best not to finish her sentence. Instead, she marched to the counter and slid the piece of chiffon pie from its china plate back into the pie plate.

Nathan returned to his meal, wondering why one person living alone even needed someone to cook for him. He could learn to cook, or at least manage to microwave frozen dinners. Maybe it was time he found a new position for Mrs. Murphy. It would save him money, and he was sure a lot of Marilyn's friends would be happy to have her. Mrs. Murphy had the reputation around the neighborhood of being "an absolute jewel." But then, Nathan reasoned, the woman did keep this enormous house in order. She was efficient; he'd hand her that. He supposed that as long as he maintained such an establishment as this, he would need a housekeeper.

After dinner, he retired to his study to read his paper and enjoy his coffee. But he didn't enjoy it. Mrs. Murphy always placed a small sterling coffee server filled with fresh coffee on the table beside his favorite chair. However, Nathan liked his coffee very hot. Coffee served from the silver pot was never as hot as it was straight from the percolator. What warmth there was at the time it was poured disappeared shortly after it hit a china cup. Before, he had always just accepted tepid coffee after dinner. Tonight, however, having to drink tepid coffee struck him as totally unnecessary. Maybe he should start stopping by the kitchen on his way to the study and fetch his coffee in a nice heavy mug. But, Nathan decided, he'd deal with that problem tomorrow. The pie bit was quite enough to throw at Mrs. Murphy tonight.

He took a couple of sips of the lukewarm brew, then opened his newspaper, but even reading his newspaper didn't feel right. He squirmed around a bit, trying to decide what was bothering him now. Then he remembered the big ottoman in front of Elaine's overstuffed chair. He could prop his feet up on it whether he was sitting in the chair or on her sofa. It was grand. But this room had no ottoman.

Nathan looked around the study a minute, then got up and fetched the desk chair from behind his desk and placed it in front of the wingback chair. He sat down, kicked off his shoes and propped up his stocking feet. At first he thought the arrangement would be satisfactory, but soon he realized the chair was too high to serve as a truly comfortable footstool. He defiantly left his feet there, however. Tomorrow he was going to buy the biggest ottoman he could find. He didn't care if it wasn't in keeping with the decor of the room. He wished Elaine were in town. She could help him pick one out. Of course, if she were in town, maybe he wouldn't need one. Maybe he would be sitting in her apartment with his stocking feet right beside hers on the ottoman.

His thoughts were interrupted by the inevitable tapping at the study door.

"Yes, Mrs. Murphy," he said without looking.

Nathan mouthed the words to himself as Mrs. Murphy offered her usual prim "Will that be all, sir?"

"Yes, thank you. Good night."

"Is there something the matter with your feet, sir?" Mrs. Murphy inquired, her curiosity apparently getting the best of her need to remain aloof.

"They were suffering from acute discomfort caused by the lack of a footstool in this room. Good night, Mrs. Murphy."

He read for a while, trying not to notice the silence, but soon it got to him. He slid aside a panel in the bookshelf and turned on the television that was hidden away behind it. Flipping the dial, he finally decided on a baseball game as background noise for his newspaper reading. Maybe he'd even watch some of the game later.

Settling himself in his chair for the third time, he picked up the editorial page. The newspaper had come out with a strong endorsement of the incumbent in the state senate primary. Billingsly had, according to the newspaper, "served his constituents with honor and fairness without succumbing to the pressure of special-interest groups."

Except for serving the special interest of his own pocketbook, Nathan thought with irritation as he turned the page. But after all the trouble to get comfortable so he could enjoy his newspaper, Nathan found himself totally out of the mood to finish reading it.

What he wouldn't give just to hear Elaine's voice, Nathan admitted to himself as he tossed the newspaper on the end table. If only he knew where she was staying in St. Louis, he'd call her. But Mrs. Farrell had refused to give him that information, pointing out that if Elaine wanted to talk to him, she could call him herself.

The phone hadn't rung all evening. Nathan hadn't talked to Elaine for three days.

She was pulling away from him, and the thought made Nathan's blood run cold. He closed his eyes and leaned his head against the high back of the chair. The prospect of life without Elaine seemed so stark, so dull, so loveless, that it was more than he could bear. Night after night in this stiff room either alone or with some woman he brought here because he was too weak to stand the loneliness he deserved.

Yes, *deserved*. For what had he thus far offered Elaine? An indefinite live-in arrangement in another woman's house. For this house—even now, over a year after her death—was still Marilyn's house. It would always be Marilyn's house. Nathan had asked Elaine to live here with him in a house that stifled her, a house that robbed her of the very things about her he adored. Here, in Marilyn's house, Elaine could never be herself. Nathan realized that even if his home wasn't an obstacle, Elaine never would jeopardize his upcoming political race by becoming his live-in woman. And she recognized what a political liability she already was to him even without live-in status. God, how unfair it all was, Nathan thought angrily. Why did life have to be so damned complicated?

Suddenly restless, Nathan made a tour of his house—the house that had become such an obstacle in his and Elaine's relationship. While a part of him had come to resent the splendid house with its expensive upkeep and ostentatious ambience, it was filled with so many memories—some bad but most good. He and Marilyn had been newlyweds in this house. Their children had been raised here. He thought of all the family celebrations—christenings, birthday parties, anniversaries, Christmases, prom nights, graduations. He remembered silly little things such as the time Marilyn had dressed up as Glenda the Good Witch to hand out Halloween candy to trick-or-treaters or the games of hide-and-seek they played when the children were small. He remembered bicycles and new puppies under Christmas trees and Thanksgiving dinners with both sets of grandparents in attendance.

As he climbed the gracious curving staircase, Nathan thought of the times he had carried sleeping children up these stairs to put them to bed. He remembered going up those stairs so many evenings with his arm around Marilyn on the way to their room. It might be Marilyn's house, but it was a part of him. Could he ever let it go? Doing so would almost seem as if he were letting Marilyn go.

Nathan lingered in the hallway in front of the family pictures. The history of his family was displayed here, lovingly arranged by a proud Marilyn. But she was dead, the children were grown, and he was alone.

Elaine's mother wanted her daughter to have children. She assumed Nathan would not be interested in fathering a second family. And frankly, he hadn't given it a whole lot of thought until Elaine came into his life. Now, however, the thought of having a baby with her absolutely enchanted him. He could even feel a great swelling of love for such an infant. But where would the pictures of such a baby be hung? They wouldn't belong here in this hallway alongside all these other pictures.

Finally, Nathan gave a sad sigh and shuffled on down the hall to his bedroom, feeling very old and tired and lonely. If only he could call Elaine. Just hearing her voice would help so much. And he would try to tell her how he felt, try to explain to her why he was still tied to the past, still living the life that he had always expected to live. He would tell her that change was building in his soul like thunderheads on the horizon, that he didn't have everything worked out yet but he would—somehow he would. He would ask her for her continued patience, for her to stay with him, that someday he'd like to have a baby with her. And he would tell her that he loved her. Yes, he would definitely tell her that. Was it too late for him finally to say words of love? *Oh, please, don't let it be too late,* Nathan thought fervently. *Please.*

He switched on the bedroom television as a buffer against the intolerable silence. The ball game was still on—top of the eighth; the Rangers were ahead. He sank onto the sofa and half watched the game as a means of purging his mind of troubled thoughts.

After the Texas team had put the game away, beating the Yankees twelve to nine in an error-filled fiasco, Nathan took a shower. He stood for a long time under the strong, hot spray, as though trying to wash away some of his growing depression. But as he was drying, he found himself staring into Marilyn's empty closet—the closet that had once been filled with her most personal possessions. Somehow the closet's bareness affected him tonight more than it ever had before. He felt more lonely at that moment than he ever had in his life.

He called the Sheraton and the Hilton in St. Louis. And he tried the Daniele, the Marriott, the Mayfair, both Holiday Inns, all three Howard Johnsons and all five Ramada Inns. There was no Elaine Farrell registered at any of the motels or hotels, and he couldn't think of any more places to call. He rummaged around unsuccessfully searching for a *Mobile Travel Guide* so he could find out the names of the rest of the hotels and motels in St. Louis.

Then he put his clothes on and went to Elaine's apartment. It, too, seemed empty without Clyde.

Nathan sat in the big chair for a long time before he finally lay down in her unusual bed with its park-bench headboard. Sleep did not come for a long, long time.

"Mr. Jonathan Miles to see you, sir," said Mrs. Hopkins's voice over Nathan's intercom.

Jonathan here? That was a shock. Nathan could not remember the last time his brother-in-law had descended from his lofty office in the high-rise First Federal Bank Building to come to someone else's office.

As soon as the overweight man, his face an angry red, came puffing through the door, Nathan could see that the nature of the banker's visit was not social.

Nathan stood and extended his hand. "Jonathan," Nathan said, "what a surprise."

Jonathan did not shake hands. He offered no greeting. He simply unrolled the large piece of paper he had carried into the office.

It was a poster. An exercising Elaine in vivid-color looked up at him, her mouth smiling, her eyes wide and sparkling, her fanny jutting out enticingly behind her, the posturing of her body offering a bird's-eye view of her cleavage.

Nathan stared down at the picture, not quite knowing what to make of it. The poster was designed to advertise Elaine's exercise show on the local television station, but it seemed totally out of character for her to appear on such a blatantly provocative promotional piece. There she was, however.

Nathan felt an overwhelming stab of disappointment—even anger. This was beneath Elaine. And surely she must have realized how dreadfully this would complicate their already shaky relationship. Was this her way of bowing out, Nathan wondered.

The still-silent Jonathan tossed a newspaper on top of the poster. And there on the front page was a picture of the poster.

The caption under the picture read:

Move over Bo Derrick and Farrah Fawcett. Heritage has its own sexy lady decorating our town. Elaine Farrell, who works at a local exercise studio and bares her talents on a fitness show on Channel Six, appears on this promotional poster that is being prominently displayed about town and will surely become a sought-after work of "art" to decorate the closet doors of adolescent boys. When Ms Farrell is not posing for photographers, the nubile young lady keeps company with municipal judge Nathan Stewart, 45, who is somehow finding time to campaign for this district's state senate seat now held by incumbent Frank Billingsly. Judge Stewart's wife, the late Marilyn Miles Stewart, prominent Heritage club woman and civic worker, is credited with being the moving force behind the Civic Center Auditorium project.

Nathan felt his blood pressure soaring as he read the flagrantly slanted caption. Elaine didn't work at an exercise studio; she owned one. The wording made it sound as if she were half his age when in reality fifteen years separated their ages. The part about his "somehow finding time to campaign" certainly implied that Nathan's mind was not on politics these days. And their references to Marilyn only made the whole story seem all the more sordid.

"Well, what do you think of your little paramour now?" Jonathan demanded, leaning over Nathan's desk and repeatedly stabbing at the newspaper with his forefinger. "Nathan, I told you to keep that broad under wraps. What the hell is she doing posing for pictures? I'll bet she's working for Billingsly. I'll bet he planned the whole thing, and she went along with it. Damn it, Nathan, I can't believe this," Jonathan said, throwing up his hands in a disgusted gesture. "Probably the only untainted man of prominence left in this community and you blow it like this!"

"Are you saying you think I should drop out of the race?" Nathan asked his brother-in-law.

"Drop out? Let Billingsly have the nomination virtually unopposed? Hell, no. We've got too damned much invested in you. But this means there isn't a prayer of winning the primary without a runoff. Not a prayer! A runoff's going to up the ante, Nathan. It means this senate seat is going to cost more than we bargained for. You'd damn sure better not disappoint me when you get up to Jefferson City!"

"And just what do you mean by that?" Nathan demanded, his voice rising. "If you think I'm planning to go sit up there in the statehouse and let you pull my strings, you've got another think coming, Jonathan Miles. If I win this damn race, I sure as hell plan to be my own man!"

"Grow up, Nathan," Jonathan said in disgust as he sank heavily into a nearby chair. "There is no such thing as being one's own man in the political arena. Don't start believing your own campaign rhetoric about no vested interests and not being beholden to any special-interest group. You can tell that bull to the voters all you want, but the truth of the matter is you've got special interests just like the rest of us."

"Well, I'm sorry to disappoint you, but that's just not so," Nathan said angrily, "so why don't you just go back down to your bank and forget about my candidacy and campaign. I'll handle things myself from now on. And believe me, I plan to get to the bottom of this industrial-park business. From where I'm sitting, that whole thing looks corrupt as hell. And if you think I'm going to introduce a bill that's especially designed so people like you can rip off this state and this community, then you're terribly mistaken."

"People like me?" Jonathan asked, his eyebrow cocked cynically. "What you mean is people like *you* and me. It's graduation day, my boy. It's time you learn just what Heritage politics are all about. Tell me, brother-in-law, what percentage of your investments are First Federal stock?"

"The majority of it," Nathan admitted. "Why?"

"Because, dear boy," Jonathan said sarcastically, leaning his bulky torso forward in the chair and shaking a thick finger at Nathan, "the bank's never recovered from all those bad loans to independent oil companies back during the oil boom. This land deal can bail us out. There have been a great deal of insider loans given through our family bank to purchase that land for the industrial park, and it took a hell of a lot of money. If that park isn't built on that site, the bank will be in big trouble. Of course, when Heritage gets that wonderful low-interest money from the state to purchase the land, at our prices, then the loans will be repaid, and no one will be the wiser. The city will have a rebirth of industrial growth, the bank will be solvent, and a lot of us, including you and your children, will be a hell of a lot richer. Without the park, we're holding a bunch of worthless east-side land and housing projects with no prospect of repaying those illegal loans. Just think of it, Nathan. You'd be poor."

Jonathan paused to relight his cigar. Like bellows, his pudgy cheeks puffed new life in the oversized cigar. Acrid smoke rose in a cloud around him.

Stunned by the banker's foreboding words, Nathan realized there were more. How bad was it, he wondered.

"Your children's inheritance from their mother would be wiped out," Jonathan continued between puffs. "Your family name and Marilyn's family name would be tainted. So I suggest you come down out of your ivory tower and enter the real world. Get rid of the girl. Start going out with some respectable widowed matron with connections. And hit the campaign trail hard. Practice your Kennedy smile, get out there and kiss babies and ladies, and shake hands until your palm is raw. And we're going to get you elected, Nathan, no matter how much it costs. You're going to march your charismatic self up to Jefferson City, and you're going to reintroduce that industrial-trust legislation that that jackass Billingsly managed to kill last session. And you are going to wheel and deal like it's never been done before. You will do whatever is necessary to garner support. Bribe. Threaten. Trade votes. You will sell your soul if necessary to get that bill through. 'Cause if you don't, the Miles and the Stewarts are finished in this state! Finished!''

NATHAN STOPPED on his way home and bought a *Mobile Travel Guide.* He started down the list of St. Louis hotels and motels. After ten phone calls, he found her. Elaine was staying at the Forest Park, but she was out. Nathan left a message. "Please call."

He called her again in an hour and left another identical message. Then he called every fifteen minutes. At ten-thirty, Elaine's voice said, "Hello." She sounded tired.

"Elaine, I've been trying to get hold of you for hours. Are you okay?"

Now that he had her on the line, Nathan wasn't sure what he wanted to say to her. Last night he was desperate to tell her he loved her and assure her that there was a future for them. But today he had seen that poster. Today he was unsure what she wanted out of their relationship, if she even wanted his love.

"I suppose you're calling about the poster," she said wearily.

"Well, maybe I am," he said. He rubbed at his temple with his free hand. What a mess this was. "It was a real shock to me," he admitted. "I'd like to understand how it came to be. Do you know that it made the front page of the Heritage newspaper and that you were identified as 'keeping company' with me? I understand the posters are all over town, and the television station has ordered a second printing. It certainly complicates things for us, Elaine.''

"Yeah, not the sort of thing a man running for office likes to have his lady friend do," she said. Her voice was so soft he could hardly hear her.

"I'm sure you just didn't realize how people would react," Nathan offered.

"Well, maybe it's just as well, Nathan. I don't think there's anyplace for you and me to go. Hanging on to things is just prolonging the agony."

"Is that what it's meant to you?" he asked. "Agony?"

"It's been glorious, my darling. But yes, it's been agony, because I knew it couldn't last. I'm sorry about any trouble that poster caused. I won't cause you any more trouble. Be happy."

The line went dead.

He dialed the number of the hotel again.

"I'm sorry, sir. Miss Farrell seems to be out," the hotel operator reported after a number of rings. "Would you care to leave a message?"

ELAINE STARED NUMBLY at the telephone for a long time after she had hung up. She jumped when it started ringing again.

"Oh, Nathan," she cried out, "don't do this to me!"

She put her hands over her ears to shut out the ringing, but she could still hear it. She went into the bathroom and shut the door, but she could still hear the incessant ringing. She tunred on the water in the bathtub. Still she could hear it.

Then, as abruptly as it started, the ringing ended. The silence had an overwhelming note of finality to it. Elaine couldn't stand it. She opened the door to the bathroom and stumbled over to the bed. She could call him. She could tell him the poster wasn't planned, and she would do anything to make amends. But Nathan said the poster had been on the front page of the newspaper. Such embarrassment she had caused him! Inadvertently or not, she was a liability in his life.

Elaine picked up the folder of papers from the bedside table and once again stared at the contracts inside. One was a contract spelling out her responsibilities should she go to work for American Fitness on a more permanent basis—a job that would headquarter her in St. Louis and involve a great deal of traveling, doing promotional work for the national chain and also serving as a consultant for individual franchises.

The second contract was one to sell the Fitness Center. Strange how when she was first approached to sell her business, Elaine thought perhaps doing so would make her more acceptable as the future wife of Nathan Stewart. Now she was going to sell her business to separate herself completely from him. She had proved once and for all that there was no way for her and Nathan to stay together. They lived and always would live in two different worlds.

It was dark, so she didn't dare go out and jog along the parkway that surrounded the hotel. She slipped on her bathing suit and went out to the darkened pool. A sign prohibited swimming after ten o'clock, but she ignored it.

Elaine eased her body into the dark, cold water and began to swim. She swam as though she were being chased by some horrible aquatic demon. Lap after lap she swam until her body was at last overtaken by exhaustion.

She dragged her body and sat heaving on the side. *I won't think about him,* she instructed herself. *Don't think at all. Just don't think about anything.*

Her legs trembled with fatigue when she tried to walk. When she got back to the room, she called room service. It was closed for the night. With a sigh, she pulled on a pair of jeans and a shirt and slipped her feet into a pair of sandals. Without bothering to dry her hair, she went down to the bar.

A bored bartender took her order. While she waited, Elaine watched the only two other patrons of the bar slowly dance around the tiny dance floor to the soft sound of the music. The couple was a million miles away. Watching them made her feel sad.

She quickly downed three bourbon and waters, then went back to her room and promptly threw up. *Damn,* she said out loud. *I can't even get drunk right.*

Finally, there was nothing to do but go to bed. And when she got in bed, there was nothing to do but cry. Her exhaustion only made it worse. In the darkness, she cried for the dream that was never to be.

Chapter Thirteen

"I'm sorry, sir," the desk clerk said. "Ms Farrell checked out this morning."

"Do you know where she was going?" Nathan asked, a feeling of urgency pushing against his chest. He had to find her. He had to see her.

He finally had slept a few hours the night before—there in her bed—but was awake by four. By four-thirty, he had decided to drive to St. Louis. The decision made, he was able to doze another hour or so, lingering in a half sleep, his mind sliding from unconscious, spontaneous dreams into those he consciously choreographed—both varieties starring Elaine. The Elaine of his unconscious dreams was elusive and shrouded in mist. He never could get close enough to touch her. The Elaine of his conscious dreaming was in his arms, moaning soft sounds of pure ecstasy in response to his lovemaking.

By eight-thirty, Nathan was dressed and ready to go, but he delayed his departure long enough to put a call into the public relations director at Channel Six. There were some questions he wanted answered about the development of a certain poster promoting a Channel Six exercise show.

It was straight-on noon when Nathan walked into the Forest Park Hotel and tried to contact Elaine on the house phone. Nathan realized that Elaine might be out for the day, but he was prepared to wait in the lobby until she returned. What he was not prepared for was the possibility that she had checked out. Elaine had not only left for the day, the desk clerk had gone on to inform him, but Ms Farrell had left altogether.

"No, sir. I have no idea where Ms Farrell went," the uniformed clerk said, and pointedly turned his attention back to the computer.

Nathan pulled a ten-dollar bill from his billfold. "I'd appreciate it if you could find out how she left here and if anyone knows where she was going."

The man eyed the bill tentatively. Nathan put another beside it. "Very well, sir. If you'll have a seat in the lobby, I'll see what I can find out."

Nathan didn't feel like sitting and paced instead. When the desk clerk returned, he was apologetic. "She left in an airport limousine. There is just no way to know where she was going."

Nathan felt deflated. He turned and headed for the door. All he could think of to do was call Elaine's mother again and see if he could get anything out of her. But somehow he felt that would be a dead end. If only he knew with whom Elaine had business here in the city. There was nothing to do but return to Heritage and prepare for all the family festivities. The park dedication was the day after tomorrow. Rebecca was getting married in four days. The relatives would start arriving this afternoon. The thought of being the cordial host to a houseful of people was almost more than Nathan could bear.

But somehow he knew he would manage. He owed it to Rebecca—and to Marilyn.

Feeling totally frustrated by his inability to contact Elaine, Nathan began the sixty-mile trip back to Heritage. He was distracted by his thoughts and had a hard time keeping his mind on driving. Just west of Eureka, he was picked up for speeding. The highway patrolman reported clocking Nathan at seventy-two miles per hour.

"You're a judge over in Heritage, aren't you?" the patrolman said as he studied Nathan's driver's license.

"Yes, but not above breaking the law myself, it seems," Nathan said wryly, "even after all the fines and lectures I've given to speeders in my courtroom. I don't know what got into me. Sorry."

"Well, those things happen. You slow down, hear," the man said, handing Nathan back his license.

"Why aren't you ticketing me?" Nathan demanded. "I thought over seventy was considered reckless driving."

The patrolman actually winked. "Well, it is for some folks. But not for certain special people. There's no need for you to be concerned about it, judge. Good luck in the election."

"I think you should write that ticket, officer," Nathan said sternly. "I'm no better than any other speeder and don't like special privileges for politicians."

On his way again, the ticket tucked in his billfold, Nathan wondered what his brother-in-law would have thought of the little scenario that had just taken place. Jonathan could have given his "Come down out of your ivory tower" lecture again. Jonathan believed in special privileges for the few. He believed that he and other First Federal stockholders were above the federal banking laws, that they could use bank funds illegally for unsecured, insider loans to further their own fortunes, that it was all right as long as they didn't get caught. Jonathan saw no problem with tearing down the homes of a hundred families in order to make a killing on a land deal. He saw no problem with making millions of dollars from the taxpayers of Heritage when he resold the land to the community for an industrial park at an infinitely greater price than he and his partners had paid for it—and after he had pulled the strings behind the scene to make sure that a particular tract of land was the one to be purchased. Jonathan saw no problem with using whatever means possible to make sure the bank's property was purchased rather than a site that might be better or cost less or not roust all those people out of their homes. He even saw no problem in enhancing the tract's appeal for an industrial park by convincing the city to donate the adjoining parcel of land for a park honoring his dead sister.

Making that patrolman give him a speeding ticket seemed like a futile protest against political graft and corruption, but it did offer Nathan a small degree of satisfaction.

THE WEATHER WAS GLORIOUS—a perfect day for the park dedication. Jonathan hosted a luncheon for all the aunts, uncles, cousins and other assorted relatives and friends in the bank's dining room.

Robby had watched his father throughout the meal—a thinner father than he was used to seeing, and tired looking. *There's no spark there,* Robby thought. *I'm looking at an unhappy man.*

"What's with Dad?" Robby asked his sister over their veal cordon bleu. Rebecca was seated on his left, her fiancé to her left, looking very proper in a pin-striped three-piece suit.

"What do you mean?" Rebecca asked.

"He looks like hell. What's going on with him and Elaine Farrell these days?"

"Robert! How can you talk about *her* at a luncheon honoring our mother?" Rebecca asked in a horrified whisper while looking around to see if anyone else had heard.

"Oh, grow up, Rebecca. Dad's not required to take up vows of celibacy just because he's a widower. Good grief, he's been going with a wonderful woman, and now he looks like hell. Chances are either he's having romantic problems or he's sick. I'd like to know which."

"Wonderful woman!" Rebecca said in an outraged whisper. "You've got to be kidding. Surely you've seen that disgraceful poster that's plastered all over this town! Did it ever occur to you that with all the disgusting publicity over that sexpot exercise queen, he might be worried about the election. Which reminds me—I haven't seen you out nailing any campaign posters to trees. And did it ever occur to you that he might still be grieving for our mother?"

"Yeah, it'd suit you just fine if he grieved away his years in that mausoleum of a house, keeping it as a shrine for our mother and proving to the world that no one could possibly follow in her footsteps. And you, the dutiful daughter, could take care of him, and everyone would say what a fine woman you are—'just like her wonderful mother.' And then someday, when you die, they'll name something for you."

Through clenched teeth, Rebecca said, "Robert Stewart, you are not only irreverent; you are disgusting and crude."

"I've been called worse," he said with what he hoped was an irritating smile. "And as for Dad being worried about the election, I wish he'd worry himself into dropping out of the race."

"Drop out? You can't be serious!" Rebecca said incredulously. "Why in the world would he do a thing like that?"

"Because he'd realize he's not cut out to be a politician," Robby said, knowing he was wasting his breath but feeling compelled to try to explain his feelings to his sister. "You either have to be corrupt or a cynical realist like me to survive in politics—with a touch of the barracuda either way. Dad is neither. He's an idealist. He doesn't have a corrupt bone in his body, and he's not realistic enough to decide which things he can do something about and be able to look the other way on the rest. He'll get up there to Jefferson City and try to right all the wrongs. It'll kill him, Rebecca."

"Oh, don't be ridiculous," Rebecca said with an airy wave of her hand. "It isn't like that at all. Uncle Jonathan wouldn't be behind Daddy if he wasn't the right man for the job. Mother always said he had the makings of a statesman. This election is just the beginning of a brilliant political career. I am so proud to be his daughter, and I just can't believe you're not in favor of your own father's political career. Why, you sound like you think you're better suited for politics than Daddy is."

"Well, Sis, as a matter of fact, I do. In a few years, I'll be running for political office myself—probably city council, followed by the state legislature. I figure three years for law school, three working for Legal Aid experience to get myself old enough, and I'll launch my political career. Then you can nail posters to trees with my face on them,'' he said, playfully punching his sister's arm.

"That'll be the day. More likely I'll be bailing you out of jail—you know, loitering, no visible means of support. And don't call me 'Sis,'" she said through clenched teeth. "My name is Rebecca!"

Robby gave up on his sister and dug into his chocolate mousse. He asked for a second helping, then, out of boredom, proceeded to outrage the female cousin who sat on his right. She was home for the summer from Wellesley, and Robby found her boring and snobbish. He couldn't resist telling her a slightly off-color joke about the sexual appetites of young women who attended girls' schools. Then he warned her that she shouldn't eat her avocado. "It'll make you horny," he said with a wink. She turned her back to him and pointedly gave all her attention to an elderly aunt sitting on her right.

Then Rebecca surprised him by leaning close and asking, "You don't really think Daddy's sick, do you? I hadn't noticed before, but I guess he has lost some weight. And he hasn't smiled too much lately."

"No, I don't think he's physically sick—yet," Robby said. "But lovesick—yes."

"But I don't want him to be in love with that woman. I want him to be in love with our mother," Rebecca said, her eyes misting. "Oh, Robby, what if he got real crazy and married her? I can't stand the thought of any woman in Mother's house, but especially one of the wrong sort. If he married her, she'd be our *stepmother*. I wouldn't be able to stand that, Robert. Please tell me that's not ever going to happen."

"Let me see, Rebecca. *You* can't stand the thought of someone living in Mother's house. *You* can't stand the thought of Elaine Farrell being our stepmother. Did you ever stop to think what Dad might not be able to stand? Maybe *he* can't stand being without her."

Rebecca stared at him for a long moment, then abruptly excused herself and headed for the powder room.

Following the meal, Jonathan got up and gave a rather poignant tribute to his sister, recalling several incidents from their childhood when their parents were still alive. Jonathan was followed by his and Marilyn's two sisters and several others who wished to take the opportunity to share their special remembrances of Marilyn Stewart.

Rebecca was radiant but teary eyed as she held the hand of her soon-to-be bridegroom while she listened to these personal tributes to her mother.

Finally, Rebecca herself rose to her feet. "I know I can't talk without crying," she said, "but if you will bear with me, I want to add my words of praise. I hope I always can follow my mother's example. No woman was ever a better mother or wife or citizen of her community. I loved her very much and will miss her every day of my life."

Robby straightened his tie, then self-consciously rose to take his turn. "I, too, loved and admired my mother very much. I didn't always please her, and I didn't always agree with her. But in spite of our differences, I always knew she loved me. And we were starting to be good friends. I'm really sorry we never got to finish the process. I think we could have taught each other a lot."

Robby took his seat, then reached for his handkerchief and blew his nose rather loudly. When he realized everyone was still watching him, he grinned sheepishly and said, "Well, one of the things my mother taught me was always have a clean handkerchief in my pocket." He acknowledged a thumbs-up gesture from his father with a grateful nod.

Nathan was last. "You'll hear my speech out at the park, so I won't say much here except that this day would have pleased Marilyn very much. She believed in family. She would have been proud of hers. And like my children, I miss Marilyn. But Marilyn herself survived many tragedies during her lifetime—the death of her parents, the death of a brother in Vietnam, the death of an infant daughter who lived only one week and the deaths of others whom she loved. I believe she understood that life is for the living, that one grieves fully, then puts grief aside and sorts out the rest of one's life. Marilyn's last words in this life were 'Tell everyone I love them.' So I tell you that today. Marilyn loved you."

Following the luncheon, limousines taxied everyone to the park, where chairs had been set up under a canvas pavilion. Members of the media were setting up their cameras, and many local dignitaries were already seated. A smattering of residents—mostly children—from the nearby housing projects were watching the proceedings but keeping their distance.

The mayor presided at the brief ceremony, formally declaring the park to be named the Marilyn Miles Stewart Memorial Park and reading a lengthy list of the various ways Marilyn served her community. He recognized the Stewart family's contribution to the building of the fitness trail, then spoke of the park as fulfilling a campaign promise he had made to the residents of the city's east side.

One park, Nathan thought, and they all pat themselves on the back when the other side of town is dotted with parks and greenbelts and golf courses and tennis courts. Over here, but for this lonely park, there were only black-topped school playgrounds that were locked after hours—and the streets. If a certain group of behind-the-scenes investors headed by Jonathan Miles had their way, this token park would soon be surrounded by various light-industrial facilities. Jonathan intended for the executives from those industries to do their daily jog around the trail Nathan himself had financed. And those children keeping their distance from the pavilion would no longer live here. Their families would be forced to seek even less adequate housing from the shrinking number of low-rent units this city had to offer.

As the mayor spoke, Nathan studied the assembled gathering, noting the contrast of those inside and those outside the pavilion. The ladies and gentlemen seated under the canvas roof were expensively attired and coiffured. One look and you knew they certainly didn't live around here, that they had crossed town only briefly to ease their consciences and prove that their city did indeed build parks on the east side. The children and adults gathered outside the tent were attired in the nondescript clothing of the poor. The scene in the park provided a contrast between silk and faded denim, between clothes purchased at boutiques and those purchased at thrift shops.

Nathan was the family spokesperson at the event. He thanked the city for the land and the honor they had paid his wife. He told how distressed she had been over the lack of park facilities in this quadrant of Heritage, which made this park an especially fitting tribute to her.

"I hope this park will always be a place where children and families come to play, to enjoy nature, to find a bit of shade on a hot summer day. And if those of you from this neighborhood," Nathan said, raising his voice slightly to better direct his remarks to those outside the pavilion, "are wondering about the lack of playground equipment for the children, let me assure you, it is to come. I would like to announce that First Federal Bank under its president Jonathan Miles has graciously offered to donate the swings, slides, monkey bars, wading pool, sandboxes, teeter-totters and whatever else is needed to provide a playground area in this park."

Jonathan looked stunned. He struggled to correct his expression as a woman with a shoulder-held television camera moved in close.

"All right!" a young voice said enthusiastically from under a tree. He was joined by the cheers of those around him, and soon a round of applause erupted among the seated guests.

Nathan indicated Jonathan should join him at the podium and say a few words. Jonathan, wearing a reluctant smile, covered the microphone with his hand and said through clenched teeth, "You son of a bitch! What the hell are you up to?"

By way of response, Nathan took his brother-in-law's free hand and shook it heartily. "Ladies and gentlemen," he called out without benefit of the microphone, "may I present the brother of Marilyn Miles Stewart, my generous brother-in-law, Jonathan Miles of First Federal Bank."

Nathan returned to his seat behind the podium. Robby, who was seated in the front row, caught his father's eye. It was his turn to offer the thumbs-up gesture. Nathan could tell by the grin on his son's face that Robby realized his father had just pulled a fast one on his pompous uncle. Nathan grinned back. Robby was okay.

ELAINE WAS ON THE ROAD two weeks, making stops in St. Joseph, Omaha, Wichita, Oklahoma City, Dallas, Houston and El Paso and spending her thirty-first birthday alone in Shreveport. There were television appearances, demonstrations at shopping malls, conferences with spa managers and a gala ribbon cutting and public opening for the new American Fitness facility in St. Joseph. The days were busy; the nights were dreadful. Elaine felt like an empty shell of a human being. Outwardly, she seemed normal, but inside she was hollow, with no hope, no joy, no expectations. In that succession of lonely hotel rooms, she wept until she wearied of weeping. Finally, a new resolve started to grow within her. She would live for her family—for her parents and Tim. She would support them, put her father in some sort of rehabilitation program, save for her brother's college education. Maybe she could even buy them a little house with a decent yard and a front porch to sit on in the evenings.

Perhaps someday there would be another man in her life. Maybe she could find someone like herself who had been scarred emotionally and did not expect too much out of life. They could be kind to each other, care about each other, but understand that they had spent true love on someone else. Maybe they would have a family to ward off some of the loneliness.

For Elaine had no illusions. She knew her love for Nathan would haunt her for the rest of her life. She would look for his face in crowds for years to come. She would search newspapers from her hometown for mention of him. She would not be able to resist driving by his Weatherford Drive home whenever she was in Heritage. But Nathan was lost to her.

In a poignant way, Elaine was glad that the poster had been published. It forced her to face what she had known in her heart all along—that Nathan was only hers temporarily. Their lives could never have meshed. The poster brought things to an abrupt end and prevented a dragging out of their relationship, and it came at a time when she had a job offer that would take her away from Heritage and provide a buyer for her business. She should feel fortunate, but she didn't. All she felt was miserable.

Often at night, Elaine would try to convince herself that she could maintain some sort of sexual liaison with Nathan over the years to come. Other people did. With a clandestine affair, she would at least occupy a part of his life. In daylight, however, she put such notions aside, partly out of respect for whomever they each might eventually marry but also because of the knowledge of how painful it would feel always to be saying goodbye. Elaine knew she must store away her treasured memories and not taint them with a lifetime of stolen moments.

Then she went through a nightly phase of wishing constantly for one last night with Nathan. She became obsessed with the notion, planning out elaborate fantasies for such a night. But again, in the light of day, Elaine knew she would not go through with that plan, either. A last night together would have to end, and the inevitable moment of parting would bring more pain than she could bear. Elaine understood that their final goodbye was best left unsaid.

She passed back through St. Louis and rented a small apartment. She had to have a place to get her mail and keep her belongings, and St. Louis would now be home base to her. After a day of conferences with the American Fitness home staff, Elaine headed back to Heritage to see her family and move out of her apartment. The sooner she left Heritage behind, the sooner she could start trying to come to terms with the end of the most important relationship of her life. Strange how falling in love with Nathan had been the easiest thing she had ever done in her life. It was as though a trap door had opened and she simply had fallen in. But falling out of love with him would be impossible.

It was almost seven in the evening when she drove up in front of her parents' house to check in with her family and to pick up Clyde. Tim was watching television in the front room. He hugged his sister exuberantly and was wide-eyed over the Reggie Jackson baseball mitt she brought him. "Gee, this is as good as they use in the majors," he said in awe. "I've never seen a glove this nice before."

"Well, you deserve it," Elaine said, thinking how much she was going to miss being involved in her brother's life on a day-to-day basis. In just the two weeks she had been away, it seemed he had grown. And she had missed several of his baseball games. Never once had she gotten to take Nathan to one of Tim's games. She wished she could have done that.

"When you come to see me in St. Louis, we can go to a Cardinals game," Elaine promised.

"No kidding! A real professional game?"

"You bet. Where're Mom and Dad?"

"Mom's keeping the nursery at the PTA meeting at school. Dad isn't feeling well and went to bed early. You want me to wake him up?"

"No, I'll just take Clyde off your hands and be on my way. Tell them I'll be back in the morning."

After Elaine had left, Tim resumed his television watching. It was a rerun of his favorite, the "Beverly Hillbillies." The phone rang just as Granny started chasing Jethro around the kitchen with a skillet. Reluctantly, Tim went to answer it.

"Elaine? No, she's not here. She just got back from St. Louis and picked up Clyde. That's her parrot. He's real neat."

ELAINE'S HEAD was already throbbing before Clyde screeched all the way home. "I don't know why I thought I had to get you tonight," she said to the agitated bird. Except she did know why. Even a parrot with a very limited vocabulary would help buffer the emptiness of an apartment in which she had spent so many wonderful evenings with Nathan.

By the time she unlocked the door to her apartment, her headache felt as if it were going to take off the top of her head. She'd better get some aspirin, coffee and food quickly and in that order. Then she wanted to get out of her dress and pantyhose and into a bathrobe.

She hung Clyde's cage from his perch and turned to survey her apartment. *Good old Mom,* she thought. The place was clean—really clean. The rug was freshly vacuumed, the plants looked healthy and watered, and the furniture glowed with a coat of fresh polish.

She took the aspirin tin from her purse and went into the kitchen to get a drink of water. Then she put a cup of water in the microwave to heat for instant coffee and turned to check the refrigerator, hoping there would at least be some stale bread to put with some peanut butter.

But the refrigerator was full—fuller than it had ever been since she had been living here. There was ham and fried chicken and cheeses and fruit and wine. How could her mother have afforded all that food? And the wine looked expensive. Elaine wondered just what was going on.

She cut herself a generous wedge of cheese, then returned to her car and brought her suitcases upstairs. She put the big one in the bedroom and took her cosmetics bag to the bathroom. Everything was so tidy that it took her a minute for the shaving mug on the shelf beneath the mirror to register. What was a shaving mug doing in her bathroom? But her puzzled thoughts were interrupted by the doorbell.

No one could possibly know she was back, Elaine thought as she crossed the living room. Leaving the chain guard on the door, she peeked through the opening and was greeted by a grinning Robby Stewart. What in the world was Nathan's son doing here, Elaine wondered as she unfastened the chain.

"Howdy, ma'am," Robby said, taking off his western hat and bowing to her. "I'm searching for a school-marm to rescue. Seen any around?"

"Did anyone ever tell you that you look just like your father?" Elaine said, standing to one side so he could step in.

"What? Me?" he said as he frantically felt his face, checking his jaw, his nose, his mouth and his chin, as though to verify her words. "Just like my father? You're kidding."

In spite of her headache, Elaine had to laugh. "You're such a clown. But I know you didn't come here to make me laugh. What can I do for you?"

"Actually, I just happened to be in the neighborhood and saw your light on and had an overwhelming urge for apple pie. Do you have any?"

"I'm afraid not," Elaine said, wondering just what he was up to.

"What? No apple pie for a starving college student? Then you're just going to have to take me out to Fred's Truck Stop and Cafe and buy me some."

"Oh, Robby, you're sweet, but I just got home from a long, hard trip. I'm hungry and tired and would really rather grab a bite here and go to bed."

"Sleep?" he said incredulously. "You can sleep when you're dead. And one of these days I'll grow up and be a serious lawyer and quit asking beautiful ladies to go with me to Fred's Truck Stop and Cafe, and then you'll be sorry you didn't go with me when you had the chance. In the rocking chair at the rest home, you'll be rocking back and forth, saying, 'If only I had gone to eat apple pie at Fred's Truck Stop and Cafe with that nice young man, my life might have turned out differently.'"

"You think so?" Elaine asked, feeling herself weakening. He was an outrageous young man but utterly charming and hard to resist.

"There is no question in my mind," he said, placing his hat at a rakish angle on the back of his head. "And besides, I checked both of our horoscopes for today, and they said it was absolutely imperative that we go on this mission. The sun is in your Jupiter, the moon is in my Neptune, and the stars are out to lunch.''

"Did my horoscope tell you that I'm no longer going with your father and that I wouldn't understand why in the world you'd want to bother with me?"

"Oh, yes," he said knowingly. "I read all about your love life. But believe it or not, I have other friends who don't go out with my father, so I think it's okay."

Robby picked up her purse from the coffee table and handed it to her. "Say goodbye to Clyde," he directed.

"You've never been here before. How did you know my parrot's name?" Elaine asked suspiciously as she hung her purse from her shoulder.

"Why, it was right there in that horoscope," he said innocently, and gently shoved her out the door as though afraid she might change her mind.

"Just one more thing, Mr. Stewart," Elaine said while they navigated the narrow stairway. "When's my birthday?"

"Your birthday?" he asked as he opened the screen door for her.

"Yes. Isn't it hard to check my horoscope when you don't know my birthday?"

"Oh, that. I have a special horoscope book that uses eye color and addresses rather than birthdays," Robby said. He opened the door to his truck. "Your carriage awaits, milady."

"I see your truck is still muddy," Elaine commented after they were under way.

"Fresh mud. Been four-wheeling. But I want you to know what a good brother I am—I kept it parked in the garage all week."

"For the wedding?" Elaine asked.

"Yes, relatives were all over the place for it and the park dedication."

"How was the wedding?" Elaine asked.

"A real snooty affair," Robby complained. "When I get married, I want to do it out in a meadow someplace with wildflowers and lutes."

"But you wore the tux like your sister wanted?

"Yeah—but with cowboy boots. She didn't notice the boots until I got to the church, but she handled it very well, I must say. Took all the fun out of it."

"And your father?" Elaine couldn't stop herself from asking. "How is he?"

"Lonesome," Robby said simply.

After that, they drove in silence until Elaine realized Robby had driven past the interstate exit. When she commented on it, he said, "I need to run by the public library real fast. Won't take long."

When Robby drove into the parking lot, Nathan's Mercedes was parked in the first row of cars.

"What are you up to, Robby?" Elaine said, fighting a feeling of panic that was rising in her breast.

"Please, Elaine," he said. "Dad's giving a speech. I want you to go with me."

"Why didn't you tell me?" Elaine asked, her anger rising. "I don't appreciate having tricks played on me!"

"Because if I told you, I was afraid you wouldn't come."

"Look, Robby, your father told me about the newspaper coverage of that poster. I am a political liability with a capital L. I don't want to go in there."

"No one will notice. There'll be hundreds of people in there. Come on, Elaine. We're already late."

"You go on. I'll call a cab from the service station on the corner."

Robby grabbed her arm as she started to open the door. "He wants you to be there, Elaine. Dad asked me to bring you."

Chapter Fourteen

The library's large public meeting room was full. Robby explained that the gathering was one in a series of public forums held by the local chapter of the League of Women Voters in order to present candidates in the upcoming elections. Tonight's forum was the second one held during this campaign for the four men and one woman running for their party's nomination in the state senate from this district. The only candidate not appearing was the lone candidate from the opposition party, who had declined the league's invitation.

In addition to the incumbent, Frank Billingsly, the panel of candidates consisted of Nathan; Jason Washington, a young black attorney who had served a term on the city council and was currently serving as assistant district attorney; Martha Blaylock, a political newcomer who had done little campaigning; and Willy Kirk, a perennial candidate who filed for some office in every election and had never won anything. The current president of the league was presiding.

The forum was already under way when Robby and Elaine entered a side door. The front of the room was brilliantly lit by a bank of lights, and the proceedings were being televised by crews from both the commercial and the cable television stations. Elaine recognized the Channel Six reporter and camera operator. The woman candidate, Blaylock, was speaking.

Robby stood by the door for a minute, scanning the crowd. "There she is," he said, grabbing Elaine's arm, and steering her toward two empty seats.

Elaine hesitated when she realized the two seats for which they were heading were being saved by a purse and sweater belonging to Rebecca. There must be some mistake. Robby surely didn't expect her to take a seat next to his sister. Didn't he know how Rebecca felt about her?

"It's okay," Robby whispered as Rebecca gathered up her possessions and offered Elaine a tentative smile.

Elaine sat down. There seemed to be nothing else to do. She couldn't believe she was sitting here at a public political forum between Nathan's two children. What if that Channel Six reporter had recognized her? Elaine sat low in her chair, half expecting a television camera to swing in her direction and someone to point an accusing finger. "There she is—the hussy from the poster."

She buried her face in her hands. This was too much. She shouldn't be here. It was going to be like that country-club fiasco. She'd end up disgracing Nathan. Had he seen her come in? She prayed he hadn't. Robby must be mistaken about his father wanting her here.

Rebecca touched Elaine's shoulder. "It's all right," she said. "I've retracted my claws." And to her brother, Rebecca whispered, "Kirk and Washington have already given their opening statements. Kirk's an idiot. But Washington—well, he's really sharp. Why haven't I been aware of him before?"

"No money," Robby whispered back. "Brilliant guy, but he has no financial backing. All he's been able to do is door-to-door stuff. Even so, he'll probably carry the east side."

When candidate Blaylock took her seat, the panel moderator introduced Nathan, who was greeted by generous applause.

"Before I begin," Nathan said, "I'd like to introduce four people in the audience. First, I'd like you to meet Dr. Todd Henderson."

Nathan paused while the young doctor stood. "Dr. Henderson is a resident at County Hospital and is here as my guest tonight. The doctor played a very important part in my political education—something for which I am very grateful."

After Dr. Henderson was seated, Nathan said, "Now I'd like to introduce the three most special people in my life—my daughter, Rebecca, who is a living tribute to her lovely mother; my son, Robert, who I suspect has taught me a whole lot more than I ever taught him; and the woman I love, Elaine Farrell, who is the healthiest person in Heritage and who does her best to get the rest of us in shape."

Whispers erupted all over the room. People turned in their seats. Where was she? The poster girl—the one they wrote about in the newspaper.

Elaine's head was swimming. She didn't understand what was happening. A flush rushed to her face as Robby grabbed her arm and firmly pulled her to her feet to acknowledge the smattering of polite applause. The whispers, however, were considerably louder than the applause. In the back of the room people were standing to see her better. Elaine sat down almost instantly and covered her mouth with her hands in an effort to regain her composure. Her heart threatened to beat its way right out of her chest.

As though oblivious of the commotion he had caused, Nathan continued. "It seems like I've been spending far too much time standing at podiums lately," Nathan said as he grasped both sides of the one in front of him. The room began to quiet. "And I can't honestly say it's my favorite way to communicate with people. Back when I first graduated from law school, I was a trial lawyer. I liked being able to walk around and to look each juror in the eye when I talked to them. But there's too many of you here tonight to look each one of you in the eye.

"If I could, however, I'd do that and shake your hand and tell you I was grateful for your interest—and for your support if you supported me—but that I was not the best man to represent this district in the state senate."

A stunned silence overtook the room for a half-dozen heartbeats before a loud murmur erupted and spread over the room.

People turned to each other. "Did he say what I thought he said?"

Just to the right of the podium, Frank Billingsly sat straighter in his chair and looked as if he'd just been named first-team all-America.

"Sometimes we map out a plan for our lives in our youth and really never rethink that plan," Nathan continued. "I had always assumed I eventually would serve in some political capacity, and two years ago I ran for municipal judge—which is really only quasipolitical but which I saw as a stepping-stone to the state senate race.

"But this race was a mistake. Politics is for a special breed of people. I don't belong to that breed. I have my son, Robby, and Dr. Henderson and, in a way, my brother-in-law, Jonathan Miles, to thank for helping to lead me to that realization. But most of all, I have a certain beautiful young woman to thank. Through her, I was able to take off the blinders I have worn all my life and see what life and love are all about. Through an association with her, I began to see that I really only understand the problems of a select segment of the population of this community. I had always considered myself above vested interests, but I began to see as long as I wore those blinders and didn't look around me, I could not help but represent only a small portion of the citizens of this district. So don't vote for me. It's too late for me to get my name off the ballot, but just ignore it. I've decided to serve out my term on the bench and go back to lawyering—on my own time. No law firm. Just a plain old general lawyer. I hope I have the opportunity to serve some of you in that capacity in the future."

Nathan paused here. He scanned the room as though trying to look each of those hundreds of people in the eye. "When I go to the poll on election day, I'm going to vote for Jason Washington, who grew up on the east side of our town and is a product of our city's public schools. He has gone on to distinguish himself at our state university, graduating magna cum laude from his law class seven years ago. He served with sensitivity and fairness on our city council and has had a brilliant record as an assistant district attorney since that time. In his young life, by virtue of his roots, his educational background and his present position, Washington has been exposed far more to the real problems of this district than I have. And after visiting at some length with Mr. Washington and after listening to his speech here tonight, I have satisfied myself that he never owned a pair of blinders. I hope you give him your full consideration. I know of no other man better qualified to serve the people of this district in the senate of the Missouri state assembly.''

He turned to the woman on his left. ''So, Madame Chairperson, I relinquish any further time I may have coming to me for the question-and-answer portion of this panel and ask to be excused from further participation. I need to get on with the rest of my life.''

Elaine's eyes were so full of tears she could hardly see Nathan leaving the podium and walking around to the side aisle where they sat. It was a dream. It wasn't happening. It was too good to be true.

She was acutely aware of the lack of sound in the crowded room. She almost dropped her purse while groping around for a tissue as Robby stood and shook his father's hand. Rebecca rose and moved in front of Elaine to embrace her father.

Nathan was standing beside her. ''Elaine,'' he said, reaching out his hand. Her purse fell from her lap as she stood, hitting the floor of the silent room with a resounding thud. She could hear coins and lipstick tubes and God knows what else rolling across the floor as she fell into his arms.

''This is where I came in,'' Nathan whispered before he kissed her, and as he kissed her, the applause began— simultaneously, all across the room. Everywhere people rose to their feet. The television crews came rushing over. Nathan and Elaine were bathed in white light.

It was true, Elaine's mind kept telling her over and over again. Believe.

She was in his arms again. Mingled joy and relief washed through her veins. After all the pain, there was to be joy. Such joy! Oh, could it really be?

Elaine closed her eyes to shut out the television lights, to shut out the world. The feel of his body against hers was so solid, so reassuring. Love radiated from him to her and back again. Love engulfed them.

The applause grew and grew, rising to a deafening roar. The people had come for politics, but this was better. The rich guy and the exercise girl. In love! This was one for the books—and for the late-night news. And they were there to see it happen.

When at last Nathan drew away from her, he turned and waved to a roomful of cheering people. Lipstick smudges covered Jonathan's mouth. They loved it.

Elaine couldn't take her eyes from his face. That sheepish grin, that beautiful smudged mouth, those wonderful eyes. Could all this really be happening? It was still like something she had wished for, not something that was real.

Someone yelled for him to kiss her again. Nathan obliged. Elaine surrendered to his mouth. She didn't care if hundreds of people were watching. It didn't matter. Nothing mattered except that he never leave her.

The kiss was long. The applause was deafening.

Elaine was vaguely aware of Robby crawling around on the floor, retrieving her possessions. When he stood, the four of them left the room. Nathan turned at the door and waved again. The applause continued as they hurried down the hall.

Were her feet really touching the ground, Elaine wondered. It felt as though she were floating. She was living in a dream—a dream come true.

THE LIGHTS HAD BEEN TURNED ON in the parking lot, attracting dozens of invading summer bugs. Robby took charge. "I'll take Rebecca. It's time she rode in a truck, anyway. Dad and Elaine can go in the Benz, since I rather imagine they might possibly want to be alone. We'll see you two tomorrow, okay?"

Rebecca hugged her father again and turned to Elaine. At first, she started to offer her hand, then changed her mind and clumsily embraced Elaine, purse and all. "I'm glad he has someone to make him happy," she whispered.

Robby opened the door of his truck for his sister. "Good grief, Robert Stewart, don't you ever wash this vehicle?" Rebecca said as she crawled in. "I can't believe you drive around in a truck when you have a perfectly good car. If you didn't look so much like Daddy, I'd swear you were a foundling."

"Spare me, Sis. I've heard it all before!"

"Don't call me 'Sis.' My name is Rebecca!"

Robby waved before he got in. "I wouldn't have missed tonight for the world," he told them merrily. "It's enough to make a cynic believe in 'happily ever after.' Hell, maybe there's even a Tooth Fairy and a Santa Claus."

As they watched the truck drive away, Elaine leaned against Nathan, her knees needing all the help they could get. He kissed her before opening the car door for her. He kissed her again when he got in the car. And again. She touched his arms, his chest, his thighs. He was really here with her. It wasn't a dream.

She was so full of happiness, it hurt. Her chest felt as though it was bursting with happiness, but the pain was glorious.

"You said in there that I was the woman you loved," Elaine said, her voice sounding quite strange to her.

"And you are. I want to spend the rest of my life loving you. I want you to marry me. But before I ask you that, I need to let you know that I no longer own the house on Weatherford Drive."

"Oh, Nathan, I didn't want you to give up your beautiful home."

"The children and I talked about it at some length," he said, stroking her cheek and neck with his fingertips. "First, I had to explain to them that most of the family holdings are tied up in First Federal stock, and I wouldn't be surprised if the bank goes under sometime next year. I showed them how much it cost to maintain the house and just what a financial burden it has been over the years. I simply don't want to be strapped with it anymore. I don't want to work at a job I don't care for in order to support a house. I'd like to simplify my life and work at the job I want rather than the one that makes the most money. I offered to give the house to Rebecca, but she realizes she and her new husband will never be able to afford such a place—especially if her inheritance from her mother does turn out to be mainly worthless stock in a failed bank. It makes her sad, but she's beginning to understand that very few people in this day and age can live in mansions. The house is a dinosaur—a holdover of another era that really doesn't fit in today's world. So the kids and I decided to give it to the county historical society to be used as their museum and headquarters."

"Oh, Nathan, are you sure? I know how much that house meant to you."

"Very sure. And in the end, I didn't really do it for you. I did it for me. It was what I needed to do—the end of a chapter, the beginning of a new one."

"But where will you live?"

"For the time being, where I've been living for the past two weeks—at your apartment, that is if you and Clyde will have me. Then, eventually, maybe we should move someplace else. Your mother thinks we'll need a bigger place to house her grandchildren—and my grandchildren—when they come to visit us. Martha already has it planned so that you can continue to run your business while she baby-sits for our babies."

"But I sold my business, Nathan," Elaine said. "I thought I was going to have to leave—"

"Do you wish you hadn't sold it?"

"Well, sure, now that I don't have to move away. The Fitness Center means a lot to me after all those years of working so hard to achieve it. But it's done. I already sold it," she told him.

"Well, you haven't exactly. One of the lawyers in my firm handles American Fitness's legal work, so I got wind of the sale and managed to throw a kink or two to put things on hold. A good attorney can get the sale stopped—and I am a good attorney. I want you to keep that business, Elaine. You're so good at what you do, and the business is really starting to take off. We're going to need lots of money to get Tim through college, your dad cured of his alcoholism, our own children raised, your mother a new house, a new cage for Clyde—"

Elaine had heard enough. "Take us home," she commanded.

Clyde used his "damn" greeting when they opened the door to the apartment. Elaine ignored the bird and embraced Nathan. "Now, was there something you wanted to ask me?"

He held her away from him so he could look into her face. "Will you marry me? Will you share your life with me?"

"If I don't die of happiness first," Elaine said, laughing and crying at the same time. "I love you so much."

"Oh, and I love you, Elaine," he said, touching her face tenderly, so very tenderly. "I think I fell in love with you that day you dropped all those marbles in my courtroom, but I just had to work through a lot of loose ends in my life before I was ready to admit it myself."

"Have you really been staying here for two weeks?" Elaine asked, looking around her very clean apartment.

"Uh-huh," he said, touching her hair now.

"And you slept in my bed?"

Nathan nodded.

"Did you think about me at night?"

"I thought of you incessantly, but especially when I went to bed," he said as he nuzzled her neck.

"Did you think of what would happen if I were there with you?" Elaine asked, tipping her head to one side to give him better access.

"Oh, yes. I'm a very creative thinker," he said, slipping his arm around her waist and directing her toward the bedroom door.

"Excuse us, Clyde," Elaine said over her shoulder. "Nathan and I have some unfinished business we need to take care of."

"What the hell!" Clyde responded.

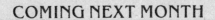

Harlequin American Romance

COMING NEXT MONTH

#137 CONVICTIONS by Beverly Sommers

Madelyn never expected to find Eddie on her doorstep. They had been pen pals for three years, but he had never told her, in his letters, that he was being released from prison. Nor, she realized, what crime he had committed. Now that he was out, what did he want from her?

#138 THE EDGE OF FOREVER by Barbara Bretton

Meg Lindstrom feared success. Years ago she put down her camera after her sister's heroic death. Now at the bequest of her mentor, Meg has one last job to do. Only Meg never planned on working with novelist Joe Alessio—a man who will challenge both her talent and her heart.

#139 JACKPOT by Judith Arnold

Money. A river of it poured from the slot machine and pooled at Lucia's feet. Cameras clicked, a crowd gathered and Lucia felt ill. She didn't want the money; it brought out people's greed. Like the stranger beside her. Was he taking charge of her and her newfound wealth—or was he taking *advantage* of them?

#140 EVER SINCE EVE by Pamela Browning

Blacklisted by the mill owners, Eve had exhausted all conventional options. What Derek and Kelly Lang offered was not precisely a job but more a service they needed rendered. All Eve had to do was sign the papers that would bind her to the Langs for at least nine months—the time it would take to carry their child to term.

WORLDWIDE LIBRARY IS YOUR TICKET TO ROMANCE, ADVENTURE AND EXCITEMENT

Experience it all in these big, bold Bestsellers— Yours exclusively from WORLDWIDE LIBRARY WHILE QUANTITIES LAST

To receive these Bestsellers, complete the order form, detach and send together with your check or money order (include 75¢ postage and handling), payable to WORLDWIDE LIBRARY, to:

In the U.S.
WORLDWIDE LIBRARY
P.O. Box 1397
Buffalo, NY
14240-1397

In Canada
WORLDWIDE LIBRARY
P.O. Box 2800, 5170 Yonge Street
Postal Station A, Willowdale, Ontario
M2N 6J3

Quant.	Title	Price
_____	**WILD CONCERTO**, Anne Mather	$2.95
_____	**A VIOLATION**, Charlotte Lamb	$3.50
_____	**SECRETS**, Sheila Holland	$3.50
_____	**SWEET MEMORIES**, LaVyrle Spencer	$3.50
_____	**FLORA**, Anne Weale	$3.50
_____	**SUMMER'S AWAKENING**, Anne Weale	$3.50
_____	**FINGER PRINTS**, Barbara Delinsky	$3.50
_____	**DREAMWEAVER**, Felicia Gallant/Rebecca Flanders	$3.50
_____	**EYE OF THE STORM**, Maura Seger	$3.50
_____	**HIDDEN IN THE FLAME**, Anne Mather	$3.50
_____	**ECHO OF THUNDER**, Maura Seger	$3.95
_____	**DREAM OF DARKNESS**, Jocelyn Haley	$3.95

	YOUR ORDER TOTAL	$_____
	New York residents add appropriate sales tax	$_____
	Postage and Handling	$___.75
	I enclose	$_____

NAME _____

ADDRESS _____ APT.# _____

CITY _____

STATE/PROV. _____ ZIP/POSTAL CODE _____

WW3R

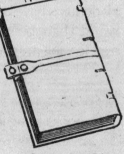

What readers say about Harlequin romance fiction...

"I absolutely adore Harlequin romances! They are fun and relaxing to read, and each book provides a wonderful escape."
—N.E.,* Pacific Palisades, California

"Harlequin is the best in romantic reading."
—K.G.,* Philadelphia, Pennsylvania

"Harlequins have been my passport to the world. I have been many places without ever leaving my doorstep."
—P.Z.,* Belvedere, Illinois

"My praise for the warmth and adventure your books bring into my life."
—D.F.,* Hicksville, New York

"A pleasant way to relax after a busy day."
—P.W.,* Rector, Arkansas

*Names available on request.